AROUND THE WORLD
IN EIGHTY DAYS

While visiting his social club one evening, Victorian gentleman Phileas Fogg is drawn into a wager that it is impossible to travel around the world in eighty days. He is determined to prove his colleagues wrong and collect his £20,000. Accompanied by his faithful and resourceful manservant, Passepartout, Fogg leaves London that night and embarks upon an extraordinary adventure that includes saving a young Indian woman from being sacrificed on a funeral pyre and escaping an attack by Sioux warriors, all the while being dogged by a detective who mistakes Fogg for a bank robber. Will the travellers make it back to London in time to win the bet?

Books by Jules Verne
Published by The House of Ulverscroft:

FIVE WEEKS IN A BALLOON

JULES VERNE

AROUND THE WORLD IN EIGHTY DAYS

Complete and Unabridged

ULVERSCROFT
Leicester

First published in Great Britain in 1873

This Large Print Edition
published 2014

A catalogue record for this book is available
from the British Library.

ISBN 978–1–4448–2112–3

Published by
F. A. Thorpe (Publishing)
Anstey, Leicestershire

Set by Words & Graphics Ltd.
Anstey, Leicestershire
Printed and bound in Great Britain by
T. J. International Ltd., Padstow, Cornwall

This book is printed on acid-free paper

Contents

AROUND THE WORLD IN EIGHTY DAYS

1

*In which Phileas Fogg and Passepartout
accept each other as master and man*

In the year 1872, No. 7 Savile Row,
Burlington Gardens, the house in which
Sheridan died in 1816, was occupied by
Phileas Fogg, Esq. Of the members of the
Reform Club in London few, if any, were
more peculiar or more specially noticed than
Phileas Fogg, although he seemed to make a
point of doing nothing that could draw
attention.

So one of the greatest orators who honour
England had for a successor this man, Phileas
Fogg, a sphinx-like person, of whom nothing
was known except that he was a thorough
gentleman and one of the handsomest men in
English high society.

He was said to be like Byron — his head, at
least, was supposed to be like Byron's, for his
feet were faultless — a Byron with moustache
and whiskers, a phlegmatic Byron, who would
have lived a thousand years without getting
any older.

English Phileas Fogg certainly was, though

perhaps not a Londoner. No one had ever seen him at the Stock Exchange or the Bank, or at any of the offices in the City.

No ship owned by Phileas Fogg had ever been berthed in the basins or docks of London. He was not to be found on any board of directors. His name had never been heard among the barristers of the Temple, Lincoln's Inn or Gray's Inn. He was never known to plead in the Court of Chancery or of Queen's Bench, in the Court of Exchequer or in an Ecclesiastical Court. He was neither manufacturer nor merchant, tradesman nor farmer. The Royal Society of Great Britain, the London Society, the Workmen's Society, the Russell Society, the Western Literary Society, the Law Society, the Society of United Arts and Sciences, which is under the patronage of Her Gracious Majesty — he belonged to none of these. In a word, he was not a member of a single one of the many associations that swarm in the English capital, from the Armonica Society to the Entomological Society, founded chiefly for the object of destroying noxious insects.

Phileas Fogg was a member of the Reform Club, he was nothing else.

That such a mysterious person should have been numbered among this honourable company might cause astonishment; let me

2

say, then, that he was admitted on the recommendation of Messrs Baring Brothers, on whom he was at liberty to draw to an extent unlimited. From this fact he derived a certain standing, as his cheques were regularly cashed at sight out of the balance of his current account, always in credit.

Phileas Fogg was undeniably a wealthy man, but how he had made his fortune was more than the best-informed could say, and Mr Fogg was the last person to whom it would have been wise to apply for information on the subject. At all events, while in no way extravagant, he was not mean, for wherever a sum of money was wanted to make up the amount required for some noble, useful or generous object, he gave it quietly and even anonymously. Well, nothing could be more uncommunicative than this gentleman. He spoke as little as possible, and this silence made him appear all the more mysterious. And yet he lived quite openly, but there was ever such a mathematical regularity about everything he did, that imagination was disappointed and went beyond the facts. Had he travelled? Probably, for nobody had a more intimate knowledge of the map of the world. There was not a spot, however remote, with which he did not appear to be specially acquainted. Sometimes, in a few words succinct and clear, he would correct the statements innumerable current in the Club about those travellers who had been lost or had gone astray; he would point out what had in all probability happened, and his words often turned out to have been as though inspired by a gift of second-sight, so completely justified were they always in the event.

The man must have travelled everywhere — mentally, if in no other way.

One thing was certain, however: Phileas Fogg had not left London for years. Those who had the honour of knowing him a little better than the rest asserted that no one could say he had ever seen him elsewhere than at the Club, or on his way to the Club, whither he went straight from his house day after day.

His one pastime consisted in reading the papers and playing whist. At this silent game, so congenial to his nature, he often won, but the money he won never went into his purse; it represented an important sum in the budget of his charity. Moreover, be it noted that Mr Fogg obviously played for the sake of playing, not of winning. For him the game was a fight, a struggle against a difficulty, but a struggle free from motion, change of place or fatigue. This just suited his temperament.

As far as anyone knew, Phileas Fogg had neither wife nor child, which may happen to the most respectable people; he had no relations, no friends, which verily is more exceptional.

Phileas Fogg lived by himself in his house in Savile Row, which nobody ever entered.

Of his home life never a word.

One servant ministered to all his wants. He lunched and dined at the Club at absolutely regular hours, in the same room, at the same table; he never treated his fellow-members, never invited a stranger. He never availed himself of those comfortable bedrooms that the Reform Club places at the disposal of its members, but went home at midnight punctually, just to go to bed. Out of twenty-four hours he spent ten at home, either sleeping or attending to his toilet. If he took walking exercise, he invariably did so with measured step on the inlaid floor of the front hall, or in the circular gallery under a dome of blue glass supported by twenty Ionic pillars of red porphyry. Whether he dined or lunched, it was the Club's kitchens, the Club's larder, pantry, fish-stores, and dairy that supplied his table with their savoury provisions; it was the Club's waiters, solemn-faced men in dress-coats, with molleton under the soles of their shoes, who served his food on special china, upon admirable Saxony napery; it was out of the Club's matchless glasses that he drank his sherry, his port, or his claret flavoured with cinnamon and capillaire; and it was the ice of the Club, imported at great expense from the American lakes, that kept his beverages in a satisfactory state of coolness.

If such a mode of life denotes eccentricity, there is no denying that eccentricity has points. Though not palatial, the house in Savile Row was commendable for extreme comfort. And the habits of its tenant being what they were, the service was very light; but Phileas Fogg required quite exceptional punctuality and regularity of his one servant.

That very day, the second of October, Phileas Fogg had dismissed James Foster, because the fellow had committed the offence of bringing him shaving-water at eighty-four Fahrenheit instead of eighty-six, and he was expecting the new servant, who was to report himself between eleven and half-past.

Phileas Fogg, sitting in his armchair, squarely and bolt upright, with head erect, his feet close together like those of a soldier on parade, his hands resting on his knees, was watching the progress of the hand of the clock, a complicated piece of mechanism, which marked the hours, the minutes, the seconds, the days of the month with their names, and the year. On the stroke of half-past eleven Mr Fogg, as was his wont day after day, would be leaving home to go to the Reform Club.

At this moment there was a knock at the door of the morning-room in which Mr Phileas Fogg was sitting. James Foster, the dismissed servant, appeared and said:

'The new servant.'

A man some thirty years of age presented himself and bowed.

'You are a Frenchman, and your name is John?' queried Phileas Fogg.

'Jean, if you please, sir,' replied the newcomer, 'Jean Passepartout. The surname has stuck to me, justified as it was by my natural gumption for getting out of scrapes. I believe I am an honest fellow, sir, but, to tell you the truth, I have done more things than one to earn a living. Street singing, vaulting like Léotard, tight-rope walking like Blondin; I did all this and then, to make better use of my attainments, I became a teacher of gymnastics, and last I was a sergeant of firemen in Paris. My service record actually contains mention of noteworthy fires. But it is now five years since I left France and became a valet in England, having a mind to see how I should like family life. Now, being out of a place, and hearing that Mr Phileas Fogg was the most particular and most sedentary gentleman in the United Kingdom, I have come to you, sir, in the hope of living here in peace and quietness, and forgetting the very name of Passepartout.'

'Passepartout suits me very well,' replied the gentleman; 'you have been recommended to me. Your references are good. You know my terms?'

'Yes, sir.'

'That is all right. What time do you make it?'

'Twenty-two minutes past eleven,' answered Passepartout, pulling out a huge silver watch from the depths of his pocket.

'You are slow,' said Mr Fogg.

'Pardon me, sir, but that's impossible.'

'You are four minutes slow. It is of no consequence; I wish to point out the error, nothing more. Well then, from this moment, eleven-twenty-nine a.m., Wednesday, October 2nd, 1872, you are in my service.'

Thereupon Phileas Fogg got up, took his hat with his left hand, put it on his head with the action of an automaton, and disappeared without saying another word.

Passepartout heard the street-door shut once; it was his new master going out; then he heard it shut a second time; that was his predecessor, James Foster, likewise making his exit.

Passepartout remained alone in the house in Savile Row.

2

*In which Passepartout is convinced that
he has at last found his ideal*

'My word,' said Passepartout to himself, a little dazed at first, 'I have known at Madame Tussaud's folks with just as much life in them as my new master!'

It should be said that Madame Tussaud's 'folks' are wax figures, very popular with sight-seers in London, and in which speech alone is lacking. Passepartout had just had a very hurried glimpse of Phileas Fogg, but he had quickly, yet carefully, looked over his new master.

His age might have been forty, his countenance was noble and handsome, his figure tall, and none the worse for a slight tendency to stoutness, his hair and whiskers were fair, his forehead was smooth and bore no signs of wrinkles at the temples; the face had little colour, the teeth were splendid. He appeared to possess in the highest degree what physiognomists call 'rest in action,' a virtue shared by all who are more efficient than noisy. Even-tempered, phlegmatic, with a clear and steady eye, he was the perfect type of those cool Englishmen who are fairly numerous in the United Kingdom, and whose somewhat academic pose has been wonderfully portrayed by the brush of Angelica Kaufmann. When you considered the various functions of this man's existence, you conceived the idea of a being well balanced and accurately harmonised throughout, as perfect as a chronometer by Leroy or Earnshaw.

The fact is Phileas Fogg was the personification of accuracy. This was clearly shown by the 'expression of his feet and hands,' for in man, as well as in animals, the limbs themselves are organs that express the passions.

Phileas Fogg was one of those mathematically precise people who, never hurried and always ready, waste no step or movement. He always went by the shortest way, so never took a stride more than was needed. He never gave the ceiling an unnecessary glance, and never indulged in a superfluous gesture. No one ever saw him moved or put out. Though no man ever hurried so little, he was always in time.

Howbeit, one can understand why he lived alone, and, so to speak, outside all social intercourse. He knew that there is always in

11

social life a certain amount of friction to be taken into account, and, as friction is a cause of delay, he avoided all human contact.

As for Jean, surnamed Passepartout, he was a real Parisian of Paris; for five years he had been living in England, acting as valet in London, and in vain looking for a master he could like. He was none of your swaggering comedy flunkeys, with a look of airy assurance and callous indifference — impudent rascals at best. Not a bit of it. Passepartout was a good fellow with a pleasant face, lips rather prominent, ever ready to taste and to kiss; he was a gentle, obliging creature, with one of those honest round heads that you like to see on the shoulders of a friend. His eyes were blue, his complexion warm, his face was chubby enough to allow him to see his cheek-bones. His chest was broad, his frame big and muscular, and he was endowed with Herculean strength which had been admirably developed by the exercises of his youth. His hair, which was brown, was somewhat ruffled. If the sculptors of antiquity knew eighteen ways of dressing Minerva's locks, Passepartout knew but one for the disposal of his: three strokes of a large toothcomb, and the operation was over.

Whether or not the man's open-hearted,

impulsive nature would harmonise with Phileas Fogg's, the most elementary prudence forbids us to say. Would Passepartout prove to be the thoroughly precise and punctual servant his master required? Experience alone could show. His youth, as we know, had been largely spent in wandering about, and he was now anxious to settle down. Having heard much good of English regularity of life and the proverbial reserve of English gentlemen, he came to try his luck in England. Hitherto, however, fate had been unkind. He had not been able to take root anywhere. He had been in ten places. In every one his employers were crotchety, capricious, fond of adventures or travelling, which no longer appealed to Passepartout. His last master, young Lord Longsferry, M.P., after spending his nights at the Haymarket Oyster Rooms, only too often returned home on the shoulders of the police. Passepartout, who more than anything wanted to be able to respect his master, ventured on a few words of humble remonstrance, which were not well received, so he left. He, thereupon, heard that Phileas Fogg, Esq., was looking out for a servant, and found out what he could about this gentleman. A man whose manner of life was so regular, who never slept out, never travelled, who was never away from home, even for a day, must be just what he wanted. He called and was accepted as we have seen.

Well, half-past eleven had struck, and Passepartout was alone in the house in Savile Row. He forthwith began to inspect this house. He went over it from cellar to attic. It was a clean house, orderly, austere, puritanical, well arranged for service; he liked it. It gave him the impression of a handsome snail-shell, but a shell lighted and heated by gas, for all the requirements of light and warmth were supplied through the agency of carburetted hydrogen. Passepartout had no difficulty in finding, on the third floor, the room intended for him. He liked it. Electric bells and speaking-tubes enabled him to communicate with the rooms on the first and second floors. On the mantelpiece stood an electric clock synchronising with the clock in Phileas Fogg's bedroom; the two time-keepers beat the same second at the very same instant. 'This is all right; this will suit me down to the ground,' said Passepartout to himself. He likewise noticed in his room a card of instructions stuck over the clock. This was the daily-service routine.

From eight o'clock in the morning, the regulation time at which Phileas Fogg got up, till half-past eleven, the hour at which he went out to lunch at the Reform Club, it specified every item of service: the tea and toast at twenty-three minutes past eight, the shaving-water at thirty-seven minutes past nine, the hair-dressing at twenty minutes to ten, etc. Then from half-past twelve in the morning to twelve at night, when the methodical gentleman went to bed, everything was noted down and settled in advance. To think over this programme and impress its various details on his mind was sheer delight to Passepartout. The gentleman's wardrobe was very well supplied and chosen with excellent judgement. Every pair of trousers, coat or waistcoat, bore a number; this number was reproduced on a register, which stated when the garments were put in or taken out, and showed the date at which they were to be worn in turn, according to the time of the year. Like regulations obtained for the boots and shoes.

This house in Savile Row, which must have been the temple of disorder in the days of the illustrious but dissipated Sheridan, was furnished with a comfort that told of ample means. There was no library, no books, which would have been of no use to Mr Fogg, as the Reform Club placed two libraries at his disposal, one for general literature, the other for law and politics. In his bedroom stood an average-sized safe, which was so constructed as to defy fire and theft alike. There were no weapons in the house, not a single utensil of the hunter or warrior. Everything pointed to the most pacific habits.

After a detailed examination of the house, Passepartout rubbed his hands, his broad face beamed, and he joyfully said over and over again: 'This will suit me! It's the very thing I wanted! We shall get on famously together, Mr Fogg and I! A man of stay-at-home and regular habits! A real machine! Well, I'm not sorry to serve a machine!'

3

*In which a conversation takes place
which may prove costly for Phileas Fogg*

Phileas Fogg left his house in Savile Row at half-past eleven and, when he had put down his right foot five hundred and seventy-five times before his left foot, and his left foot five hundred and seventy-six times before his right foot, he arrived at the Reform Club, a huge edifice, standing in Pall Mall, that cost quite a hundred and twenty thousand pounds to build.

Phileas Fogg went straight into the dining-room, whose nine windows looked out on a beautiful garden with trees already touched with the gilding of autumn. He sat down at the accustomed table, where his place was ready for him. His lunch consisted of a side-dish, boiled fish with tip-top Reading sauce, underdone roast beef flavoured with mushroom ketchup, rhubarb and gooseberry tart, and a piece of Cheshire cheese, washed down with a few cups of that excellent tea specially procured for the Reform Club's buttery.

At forty-seven minutes past twelve, he got up and made his way to the big drawing-room, a magnificent room adorned with paintings in splendid frames. There a servant handed him the uncut *Times*, which Phileas Fogg unfolded and cut with much care and a dexterity that denoted great familiarity with this difficult operation. The reading of this paper occupied Phileas Fogg till forty-five minutes past three, and that of the *Standard*, which followed, lasted till dinner. This meal was accomplished in the same conditions as lunch, with the addition of Royal British sauce.

At twenty minutes to six, he returned to the big drawing-room and gave his whole attention to the *Morning Chronicle*. Half an hour later, several members of the Reform Club came in and drew near to the hearth on which burnt a coal fire. They were Mr Phileas Fogg's habitual partners at whist, passionately fond of the game like himself: the engineer Andrew Stuart, the bankers John Sullivan and Samuel Fallentin, the brewer Thomas Flanagan, and Gauthier Ralph, one of the governors of the Bank of England.

They were wealthy and respected persons even in this Club, which numbers amongst its members the princes of industry and finance.

'How now, Ralph,' said Thomas Flanagan,

'what about this theft business?' 'Well,' replied Andrew Stuart, 'the Bank will lose the money.' 'I think not,' said Gauthier Ralph. 'I hope we shall lay hands on the thief. Police-inspectors, very smart fellows, have been sent to America and the Continent, to all the principal ports, and the gentleman will have a job to escape them.' 'Have they his description, then?' asked Andrew Stuart. 'In the first place, the man is not a thief,' replied Gauthier Ralph seriously. 'Not a thief, what? the fellow who purloined fifty-five thousand pounds in banknotes!' 'No,' answered Gauthier Ralph. 'What then, is he a manufacturer?' said John Sullivan.

'The *Morning Chronicle* says he's a gentleman.' The man who gave this reply was none other than Phileas Fogg, whose head was at that moment emerging from the sea of paper about him.

So saying, Phileas Fogg bowed to his fellow-members, who returned his salutation.

The case in question, which was being keenly discussed in all the newspapers of the United Kingdom, had happened three days before, on the 29th of September. A bundle of banknotes, amounting to the enormous sum of fifty-five thousand pounds, had been taken from the table of the chief cashier of the Bank of England.

When someone expressed astonishment that such a theft could have been carried out so easily, the sub-manager, Gauthier Ralph, replied simply that at that very moment the cashier was busy entering the receipt of three shillings and sixpence, and that a man could not attend to everything.

But there is one thing to be said which makes the matter more explicable: that admirable establishment, the Bank of England, appears to have the utmost regard for the dignity of the public. There are no guards, no old soldiers, no gratings! The gold, silver and banknotes are freely exposed and, so to speak, at the mercy of anyone. It would not do to cast the slur of suspicion on the respectability of the man in the street, no matter who he may be. One of the best observers of English customs relates the following incident.

He happened one day to be in one of the rooms of the Bank and, feeling curious to see more closely an ingot of gold weighing seven or eight pounds, which lay on the cashier's table, he took it up, examined it, passed it on to his neighbour, who handed it to someone else, so that this ingot travelled from hand to hand to the very end of a dark passage, and it was half an hour before it returned to its former place, and the cashier never even looked up.

But, on September 29, things did not happen quite in this manner. The bundle of banknotes did not return, and when the magnificent clock, installed over the drawing-office, struck five, the closing hour, the Bank of England was reduced to passing fifty-five thousand pounds to the account of profit and loss.

When the theft had been duly verified, picked detectives were sent to the principal ports, to Liverpool, Glasgow, Havre, Suez, Brindisi, New York, etc., and, in case of success, there was a promise of a reward of two thousand pounds and five per cent, of the sum recovered.

Until the inquiry, which had been opened immediately, should furnish them with information, these police-officers were to watch closely all arriving or departing travellers.

Now, as was stated in the *Morning Chronicle*, there was reason to suppose that the man who had committed the theft was not a member of any English gang. On that day of September 29, a well-dressed gentleman of polished manners and refined appearance had been observed walking about the pay-room, where the theft had taken place. As a result of the inquiry, a fairly precise description of this gentleman was obtained and this description at once dispatched to all the detectives of the United Kingdom and the Continent. In consequence a few sensible people, one of whom was Gauthier Ralph, felt justified in hoping that the culprit would not escape. The event, as you can imagine, was the daily talk of London and the whole country. People argued excitedly for or against the probabilities of the Metropolitan Police being successful. A debate of the same question among the members of the Reform Club will, therefore, cause no astonishment, all the more that one of them was a sub-manager of the Bank.

The Honourable Gauthier Ralph refused to believe that this search would fail, as he considered that the proffered reward must make the detectives exceptionally keen and acute. But his colleague, Andrew Stuart, was far from sharing this confidence. The discussion continued even after they had sat down at a card-table, Stuart opposite Flanagan, and Fallentin opposite Phileas Fogg. When play started conversation ceased, but it was renewed between the rubbers, and became more and more heated.

'I maintain,' said Andrew Stuart, 'that the chances are in favour of the thief, who is sure to be no fool.' 'Nonsense!' replied Ralph, 'there is not a country left in which he can take refuge.' 'What an idea!' 'Where do you want him to go?' 'I can't say,' replied Andrew Stuart, 'but, after all, the world is large enough.' 'It was so . . . ' said Phileas Fogg in an undertone. Then, placing the cards before Thomas Flanagan, he added, 'Will you cut?'

The discussion was interrupted during the rubber. But Andrew Stuart soon took it up again, saying: 'What do you mean by *was*? Has the world got smaller, eh?' 'Of course it has,' rejoined Gauthier Ralph; 'I agree with Mr Fogg. The world has got smaller, since one can travel over it ten times more rapidly than a hundred years ago. And that is just the thing that will hasten the pursuit of the thief.' 'And will likewise facilitate his escape!' 'It is your turn to play, Mr Stuart,' said Phileas Fogg. But the incredulous Stuart was not convinced. 'You must confess,' he said, addressing Ralph, when the rubber was finished, 'that you have hit upon a funny way of showing that the world has got smaller. So, because one can now go round it in three months . . . '

'In as few as eighty days,' said Phileas Fogg.

'Yes, indeed,' added John Sullivan, 'in eighty days, now that the section of the Great Indian Peninsula Railway between Rothal and

Allahabad has been opened; and this is how the *Morning Chronicle* tabulates the journey:

From London to Suez via Mont-Cenis and Brindisi, by rail and boat	7 days
From Suez to Bombay, by boat	13 days
From Bombay to Calcutta, by rail	3 days
From Calcutta to Hong-Kong (China), by boat	13 days
From Hong-Kong to Yokohama (Japan), by boat	6 days
From Yokohama to San Francisco, by boat	22 days
From San Francisco to New York, by rail	7 days
From New York to London, by boat and rail	9 days
Total	80 days.'

'Yes, eighty days!' exclaimed Andrew Stuart, who inadvertently trumped a winning card; 'but that is making no allowance for rough weather, head winds, wrecks, etc.'

'Allowing for everything,' replied Phileas Fogg, who went on playing, for by now they were talking regardless of the game.

'What! Even if the Hindus or Indians removed the rails!' cried Andrew Stuart; 'if they stopped the trains, plundered the luggage-vans, and scalped the travellers!'

'Allowing for everything,' replied Phileas Fogg, and added, laying his cards on the table: 'Two winning trumps.'

Andrew Stuart, whose turn it was to shuffle, picked up the cards and said:

'In theory you are right, Mr Fogg, but practically . . . ' 'Practically too, Mr Stuart.' 'I should like to see you do it.' 'That lies with you. Let us go together.' 'Heaven forbid!' cried Stuart, 'but I would readily wager four thousand pounds that such a journey, made in such conditions, is impossible.' 'Nay, rather, quite possible,' replied Mr Fogg. 'Well, then, go and do it!' 'Around the world in eighty days?' 'Yes.' 'All right.' 'When?' 'This minute. Only I warn you that I shall do it at your expense.' 'This is madness!' exclaimed Andrew Stuart, who was getting annoyed at his partner's pertinacity. 'Look here, better play on.' 'Shuffle again, then,' said Phileas Fogg, 'it's a misdeal.' Andrew Stuart took up the cards with a shaky hand, then suddenly he put them down again and said:

'Well, Mr Fogg, I will bet four thousand pounds! . . . ' 'My dear Stuart,' said Fallentin, 'calm yourself. This is not serious.'

'When I make a bet,' replied Andrew Stuart, 'I always mean what I say.' 'Very well,' said Mr Fogg, turning to his fellow-members; 'I have twenty thousand pounds on deposit at Baring's Bank. I am quite prepared to venture this sum . . . ' 'Twenty thousand pounds!' exclaimed John Sullivan, 'twenty thousand pounds that you might lose through a single unforeseen delay!' 'There is no such thing as the unforeseen,' was Phileas Fogg's simple reply. 'But, Mr Fogg, this space of eighty days is calculated as a minimum of time!'

'A minimum, if properly used, is sufficient for anything.' 'But, if you are not to exceed it, you will have to jump mathematically from trains to boats and from boats to trains!' 'I shall jump mathematically.' 'You are joking!' 'A true Englishman never jokes, when it is a question of a thing so serious as a wager,' replied Phileas Fogg. 'I will bet twenty thousand pounds with anyone that I shall make the tour of the world in eighty days or less, that is in nineteen hundred and twenty hours or one hundred and fifteen thousand two hundred minutes. Do you accept?'

Messrs Stuart, Fallentin, Sullivan, Flanagan and Ralph consulted together and signified their acceptance.

'Very well,' said Mr Fogg. 'The Dover train leaves at eight-forty-five. I shall take it.' 'This very evening?' asked Stuart. 'This very evening,' replied Phileas Fogg. 'Therefore,' he added, consulting a pocket-calendar, 'since today is Wednesday, the 2nd of October, I shall have to be back in London, in this very drawing-room of the Reform Club, on Saturday, the 21st of December, at eight-forty-five in the evening, in default of which the twenty thousand pounds deposited in my name at Baring's will be yours *de facto* and *de jure*, gentlemen. Here is a cheque for the amount.'

A statement of the wager was written down and signed there and then by the six persons interested. Phileas Fogg remained quite cool. He had not made the bet to win, and had only staked these twenty thousand pounds, the half of his fortune, because he foresaw he might have to spend the other half in order to achieve this difficult, not to say impracticable project. His adversaries, for their part, appeared uncomfortable, not on account of the amount of the stake, but because they felt that the conditions of the wager made it one-sided and unfair.

At that moment seven o'clock was striking. Mr Fogg was asked if he would like to stop playing, that he might prepare for his departure. 'I am always ready!' answered the impassive gentleman, and, having dealt, he said, 'Diamonds are trumps; you begin, Mr Stuart.'

4

In which Phileas Fogg astounds his servant Passepartout

At twenty-five minutes past seven, Phileas Fogg, who had won some twenty guineas at whist, took leave of his respected associates and left the Reform Club. At fifty minutes past seven he opened his front door and entered his house.

Passepartout, who had made a minute study of his programme, was somewhat surprised on seeing Mr Fogg commit such an act of irregularity, by turning up at this unwonted hour. According to the memorandum, this inmate of Savile Row was not to come in before twelve at night exactly.

Phileas Fogg went straight to his bedroom, and then shouted, 'Passepartout.'

Passepartout made no reply. The call could not be meant for him. It was not the right time. 'Passepartout,' repeated Mr Fogg, in the same tone of voice. Passepartout made his appearance. 'I have called you twice,' said Mr Fogg. 'But it is not twelve o'clock,' replied Passepartout, watch in hand.

'I know it is not,' said Phileas Fogg, 'and I am not finding fault. We shall start for Dover and Calais in ten minutes.'

A faint grin peered on the Frenchman's round face. He could not have heard aright.

'Are you going away, sir?' he asked.

'Yes,' answered Phileas Fogg. 'We are going to travel round the world.'

Passepartout, with wide-staring eyes, hanging arms and limp body, then showed all the symptoms of astonishment bordering on stupor.

'Around the world,' he murmured. 'In eighty days,' replied Mr Fogg. 'So we must not lose a moment.'

'But the trunks?' said Passepartout, unconsciously swaying his head from side to side.

'No trunks. Just a travelling-bag. Put in two woollen shirts and three pairs of stockings, and the same for yourself. We shall buy what we require on the way. You will bring down my raincoat and travelling-rug. See that you have strong boots, though we shall do very little walking. Go ahead.'

Passepartout wished to say something in reply, but he simply could not. He went out of Mr Fogg's bedroom, went up to his own, collapsed on a chair and made use of a rather vulgar expression of his native land: 'Well, here's a go, and I thought I was going to have a quiet time.'

Then, mechanically, he made the required preparations for departure. Around the world in eighty days. Was his master a madman? No . . . it must be a joke? They were going to Dover, right; to Calais, right again. After all, the good fellow could not feel any great objection to this, as he had not trodden the soil of his native country for five years. It was just possible they might go as far as Paris, and there was no denying that it would give him pleasure to see the great capital again. But there could be no manner of doubt that a gentleman who was so economical of his footsteps would not go beyond Paris. — And yet the fact remained that this stay-at-home gentleman was now going away.

At eight o'clock, Passepartout had got ready the humble bag which contained his wardrobe and his master's; then, still very perturbed, he left his room, carefully closing the door, and went back to his master. Mr Fogg was ready. He had under his arm Bradshaw's *Continental Railway, Steam Transit and General Guide*, which was to provide him with all the information required for his journey. He took the bag from Passepartout's hands, opened it and slipped into it a large bundle of those beautiful banknotes which are current in all countries.

'You have forgotten nothing?' he asked.

'Nothing, sir.'

'Where are my raincoat and travelling-rug?' 'Here they are.' 'All right, take this bag.' Mr Fogg handed the bag to Passepartout. 'And take great care of it,' he added. 'It contains twenty thousand pounds.' Passepartout nearly dropped the bag, as though the twenty thousand pounds had been in gold and a considerable weight.

Master and man then came downstairs, and the street-door was double-locked. There was a cab-stand at the end of Savile Row, where Phileas Fogg and his servant jumped into a cab which conveyed them at a good pace to Charing Cross Station, the terminus of one of the branch lines of the South-Eastern Railway. At eight-twenty the cab stopped in front of the station railing and Passepartout jumped out. His master followed and paid the cab-driver.

At this moment, a poor beggar-woman, standing barefooted in the mud, wearing a crazy bonnet, from which drooped a miserable feather, and with a ragged shawl over her tatters, came up to Mr Fogg, holding a child by the hand, and begged of him. Mr Fogg took from his pocket the twenty guineas which he had just won at whist, and presented the beggar-woman with them, saying: 'Take this, my good woman, I am pleased to have met you.' Then he passed on. Passepartout felt his eyes grow moist. He began to love his master.

Mr Fogg and he at once went on to the main platform, and Passepartout was told to get two first-class tickets for Paris.

Turning round, Mr Fogg saw his five fellow-members of the Reform Club.

'Gentlemen,' he said, 'I am off; I am taking a passport with me, so that the various *visas* it will bear may enable you to check my itinerary when I return.' 'Oh, Mr Fogg, that is not necessary,' was Gauthier Ralph's polite reply. 'We will trust your word as a gentleman.' 'Better as it is,' said Mr Fogg. 'You remember the date when you are due here?' observed Andrew Stuart. 'In eighty days,' replied Mr Fogg, 'on Saturday, December 21st, 1872, at forty-five minutes past eight in the evening. Goodbye till we meet again, gentlemen.'

At eight-forty, Phileas Fogg and his servant took their seats in the same compartment. At eight-forty-five, a loud whistle was heard and the train started.

The night was dark and it was drizzling. Phileas Fogg settled down comfortably in his corner and remained silent. Passepartout, still bewildered, mechanically hugged the bag with the banknotes. But, before the train had passed Sydenham, he uttered a real cry of despair. 'What's the matter?' asked Mr Fogg. 'In my hurry and flurry . . . I forgot . . . ' 'What?' 'To put out the gas in my room!' 'Well, my boy,' replied Mr Fogg coldly, 'it will burn at your expense.'

5

In which a new kind of scrip makes its appearance on 'Change

Doubtless, as he left London, Phileas Fogg had no idea of the sensation his departure was about to produce. The report of the wager was first circulated among the members of the Reform Club, where it caused immense excitement. This excitement then passed from the Club to the papers through the reporters, and the papers communicated it to London and the whole of the United Kingdom. This 'question of a journey around the world' was commented, discussed, analysed, as keenly and passionately as if it had been a case of a new Alabama Claim. Some sided with Phileas Fogg, others, who were soon in a great majority, declared against him. Whatever it might be in theory and on paper, this journey around the world, to be made in this minimum of time, with the means of communication then available, was not only impossible but mad.

The Times, the *Standard*, the *Evening*

Star, the *Morning Chronicle*, and twenty other papers with a large circulation declared against Mr Fogg. The *Daily Telegraph* alone gave him a measure of support. The names of lunatic and madman were freely bestowed on Phileas Fogg, and his friends of the Reform Club were blamed for having taken this bet, which pointed to a decline in the mental faculties of the man who proposed it.

Highly impassioned but logical articles were published on the question. Everyone knows how keenly interested the English are in anything connected with geography. So every reader, no matter to what class he belonged, greedily pored over the columns devoted to the Phileas Fogg case.

In the early days, a few bold spirits, the women principally, backed him, especially after the *Illustrated London News* had published a likeness of him from a photograph left among the records of the Reform Club. There were men who ventured to say: 'Well, after all, why not? Things more extraordinary have been done.' Those who spoke thus were mostly readers of the *Daily Telegraph*. But it was soon felt that even this paper was growing lukewarm.

In fact, a long article appeared on October 7 in the Report of the Royal Geographical Society. The question was treated from every point of view, and the folly of the enterprise clearly demonstrated. According to this article, the traveller had everything against him — obstacles both human and natural. The success of the project presupposed a miraculous fitting-in of the departure and arrival of means of transport; this neither existed nor could exist. In Europe, where distances are comparatively moderate, one can just depend on the punctual arrival of trains; but with trains taking three days to cross India, and seven to cross the United States, could one possibly base the solution of such a problem on their punctuality? And then there were engine troubles, derailments, collisions, bad weather, snowdrifts; Phileas Fogg had everything to contend with. In winter, when travelling by boat, he would be at the mercy of storms and fogs. It was not such a rare occurrence for the fastest of ocean liners to be two or three days late. Now one single day's delay was enough to snap the chain of communications irretrievably. Should Phileas Fogg miss a boat, if only by a few hours, he would be compelled to wait for the next, and that one failure would fatally compromise his venture.

This article made a great sensation. It was reproduced in almost every paper, and Phileas Fogg shares went down badly. During the first days after the gentleman's departure, important transactions were started on the chances of his enterprise. Everybody knows the sort of people who go in for betting in England; they are a cleverer and better class than gamblers.

An Englishman is by nature inclined to bet; so not only did the members of the Reform Club wager considerable sums for or against Phileas Fogg, but the great majority of the public joined in.

Phileas Fogg was registered in a sort of stud-book, like a race-horse. He was also converted into stock, which was at once quoted on 'Change. 'Phileas Fogg' was asked for and offered at par or at a premium, and enormous business was done. But five days after his departure, after the publication of the article in the Royal Geographical Society's Report, offers of shares began to pour in. Phileas Fogg scrip declined. It was offered in bundles. At first people accepted five to one, then ten, and then not less than twenty, fifty, a hundred. One single supporter remained faithful to him: an old paralytic, Lord Albemarle. The noble lord, confined to his armchair, would have given his whole fortune to be able to travel around the world, in ten years even; and he bet four thousand pounds on Phileas Fogg. Whenever one showed him both the folly and the uselessness of the project, he simply replied: 'If the thing can be done, it is well that an Englishman should be the first to do it.'

This was the state of things, and the number of Phileas Fogg's backers was getting smaller and smaller; everyone was turning against him, not without reason; people would not take a bet on him at less than a hundred and fifty or two hundred to one; and seven days after his departure something absolutely unexpected happened, which put an end to all speculation on his success.

During that day, at nine o'clock in the evening, the Chief of the Metropolitan Police received a telegram which ran thus:

'Suez.

'Rowan, Chief of Police, Scotland Yard, London.

'Am shadowing bank thief, Phileas Fogg. Send without delay warrant for arrest Bombay.

Detective Fix.'

The effect of this telegram was immediate. The honourable gentleman vanished and was replaced by the bank thief.

His photograph, left at the Reform Club with those of all the other members, was examined, and reproduced feature for feature the man whose description had been obtained at the inquiry. The mysterious peculiarities of Phileas Fogg's mode of life were then recalled; his lonely existence, his sudden departure; and it appeared evident that the fellow had invented a journey around the world and propped it up by an insane wager to the sole end of putting the English detectives off the scent.

6

*In which Detective Fix shows very
justifiable impatience*

The telegram concerning Mr Phileas Fogg
was dispatched in the following circumstances. On Wednesday, October 9, the P. &
O. liner *Mongolia* was expected at eleven
a.m. at Suez. She was a screw-propelled steel
boat with spar-deck, of two thousand eight
hundred tons burden, and five hundred
horse-power. The *Mongolia* plied regularly
between Brindisi and Bombay through the
Suez Canal. She was one of the fastest boats
of the company, and had always beaten the
regulation speed of ten miles an hour
between Brindisi and Suez, and nine miles
and fifty-three-hundredths between Suez and
Bombay.

Awaiting the arrival of the *Mongolia* were
two men, walking about the quay amid the
crowd of natives and foreigners who flock to
this town, which was but lately a mere village,
and is now assured of considerable importance in the future by M. de Lesseps's great
work. Of these two men, one was the British

consul, resident at Suez, who, in spite of the unfavourable prognostications of the British Government and sinister predictions of the engineer, Stephenson, daily saw English ships pass through the canal, thus shortening by half the old route from England to India via the Cape of Good Hope. The other was a thin little man, fairly intelligent-looking and wiry, who kept on knitting his eyebrows with remarkable persistency. Through his long eyelashes shone a pair of very bright eyes, which he could make dull at will. At this particular moment he was showing certain signs of impatience, walking to and fro, and unable to stand still. This man's name was Fix. He was one of the English detectives who were sent to the different ports after the theft committed at the Bank of England. Fix was to keep the sharpest look-out on all travellers going through Suez, and should one of them seem suspicious, he was to shadow him until he received a warrant for his arrest. And two days before, Fix had received the description of the supposed culprit from the Chief of the Metropolitan Police. It was that of the well-dressed, gentlemanly person who had been noticed in the pay-room of the Bank.

The detective, obviously much attracted by the substantial reward held out in case of success, was therefore awaiting the arrival of the *Mongolia* with an impatience that needs no further explanation.

'I think you said she could not be long, sir?' asked Fix for the tenth time. 'No, Mr Fix, she won't be long,' replied the consul. 'She was signalled yesterday off Port Said, and the length of the canal, some ninety miles, does not count for such a fast boat. Let me tell you once more that the *Mongolia* has never failed to earn the bounty of twenty-five pounds granted by the Government for every twenty-four hours' gain over scheduled time.' 'This boat comes direct from Brindisi, does she not?' asked Fix.

'Yes, from Brindisi, where she took the Indian mail; she left Brindisi on Saturday at five p.m., so you can wait patiently; she cannot be long now. But I really fail to see how you will spot your man from the description you have received, even if he is on board the *Mongolia*.'

'Sir,' said Fix in reply, 'with these fellows it is more a case of scenting them out. It is *flair* that is required, and *flair* is a special sense in which ear, eye and nose all play a part. I have arrested more than one gentleman of the sort in my life, and, if only my thief is on board, I promise you he won't give me the slip.' 'I hope so, Mr Fix, for the robbery is a big one.' 'A glorious one,' replied the detective, with growing excitement, 'fifty-five thousand pounds! Such windfalls don't often come our way. Robbers are getting quite contemptible. The Jack Sheppards of today have no grit: they will go and get hanged for a few shillings.'

'Mr Fix,' rejoined the consul, 'I cannot hear you without heartily wishing you all success; but I say it again, with the means at your disposal, I fear you will find it no easy task. Do you realise that, according to the description you have received, the thief looks exactly like an honest man?' 'Sir,' answered the detective dogmatically, 'high-class thieves always look like honest people. You quite see that people with rascally faces have but one course open to them: they must keep straight, or they would be arrested. It is your honest-looking rogues that it is our special business to see through. This, I own, is a tough job. It ceases to be humdrum routine; it is art.'

Friend Fix had obviously a fair amount of conceit in his composition.

Meanwhile the wharf was gradually showing more signs of animation. There was a growing crowd of sailor-men of divers nationalities, of traders, brokers and porters. The arrival of the boat was evidently not far off. The weather was fair, but the air cold, the wind being easterly. A few minarets stood out above the town in the pale light of the sun. Towards the south a pier over two thousand yards in length stretched like an arm along the Suez roadstead. On the surface of the Red Sea rocked several fishing boats and coasting craft, some of which still preserve the graceful mould of the ancient galley. As he moved about this motley crowd, Fix, through professional habit, gave each of the passers-by a quick but searching glance. It was then half-past ten.

'Heaven knows when this boat will get here!' he cried, when he heard the port clock strike. 'She can't be far off,' replied the consul. 'How long will she put in for at Suez?' asked Fix. 'Four hours, just long enough to coal. From Suez to Aden, at the other end of the Red Sea, it is thirteen hundred and ten miles, so they have to take in a supply of fuel.'

'And does she go direct from Suez to Bombay?' asked Fix. 'Yes, direct, without breaking bulk.' 'Well, then,' continued Fix, 'if the culprit has taken this route and this boat, he must intend to land at Suez, so as to get to the Dutch or French colonies in Asia by some other route. He cannot but know that he would not be safe in India, which is British territory.' 'Unless,' replied the consul, 'the man is a particularly cunning customer. As

44

you know, an English criminal is always harder to find in London than he would be abroad.'

Having made this observation, which gave the detective considerable matter for reflection, the consul returned to his office close by. The police-officer, a prey to nervous impatience, remained alone with this somewhat strange feeling that the thief must be on board the *Mongolia*.

And, as a matter of fact, if the rascal had left England, intending to make for the New World, he would naturally choose the route through India, which was less watched and more difficult to watch than that of the Atlantic.

Fix was soon roused from his thoughts by the shrill signal announcing the arrival of the boat. The whole mob of porters and fellahs made a rush for the wharf, and the resulting scramble was somewhat alarming for the limbs and garments of the passengers. Some ten boats or so put out from the shore to go and meet the *Mongolia*.

Soon her huge hull was seen gliding along between the banks of the canal, and eleven o'clock struck as she cast anchor in the road, and her waste steam roared out of her escape-pipes. She had a considerable number of passengers on board, some of whom remained on the spardeck, gazing at the picturesque panorama of the town; while the majority were landed by means of the boats which had come alongside the steamer. Fix scrutinised with the utmost care every one of the passengers as he stepped ashore.

Thereupon one of them, vigorously forcing his way through the fellahs who assailed him with their offers of service, came up to him and asked with the utmost politeness if he could tell him where to find the British consulate. At the same time the traveller held out a passport for which, apparently, he wished to procure the British official's *visa*. Fix, instinctively, took the passport and glanced rapidly through the description it contained. An involuntary sign of emotion nearly escaped him. The paper shook in his hand. The description in the passport was identical with that which he had received from Scotland Yard.

'This passport is not yours, is it?' he asked. 'No,' replied the passenger, 'it is my master's.' 'Where is your master?' 'He has remained on board.' 'He will have to go to the consulate in person,' rejoined the detective, 'in order to prove his identity.' 'Oh, is that necessary?' 'Absolutely necessary.' 'Where is this office?' 'There, at the corner of the square,' replied Fix, pointing to a house two hundred yards away. 'All right then, I will fetch my master, but he won't be best pleased to have the bother of coming.'

Having said this, the passenger bowed and returned to the liner.

7

Which once more shows the futility of passports for police purposes

The detective made his way briskly down the quay to the consulate, where his urgent request to be admitted to the consul's presence was granted.

'Sir,' said he, going straight to the point, 'I have strong reasons for presuming that the man I am after is a passenger on board the *Mongolia*.' He then related the incident of the passport.

'Well, Mr Fix,' replied the consul, 'I should rather like to see the rascal's face. But I dare say he won't show himself in my office, if he is the sort of man you think him. A thief does not care to leave traces of his itinerary behind him; moreover, passports are no longer obligatory.'

'Sir,' replied the detective, 'if he is the clever fellow I take him for, he will come.'

'To have his passport *visaed*?' 'Yes, passports have but one use; to be a nuisance to honest people and assist the flight of rogues. I can assure you this passport will be in order, but I hope you will not *visa* it.' 'Why not?' answered the consul. 'If the passport is all right, I have no right to refuse my *visa*.' 'Still, sir, I am bound to keep the man here until I get a warrant from London.' 'Ah, that is your business, Mr Fix; but I cannot . . . '

The consul's sentence was not finished; there was a knock at the door and the office-boy introduced two strangers, one of whom was no other than the servant who had spoken to the detective on the quay. With him was his master, who produced his passport, and, in a few words, requested the favour of the consul's *visa*. The latter took the passport and read it attentively, while Fix observed or rather greedily eyed the stranger from a corner of the room.

'You are Mr Phileas Fogg?' queried the consul, when he had finished reading the passport. 'Yes.' 'And this man is your servant?' 'Yes. A Frenchman called Passepartout.' 'Do you come from London?' 'Yes.' 'And you are going to . . . ?' 'Bombay.' 'Very good, sir. You know that a *visa* is a formality of no value, and that travellers are no longer required to show passports?' 'I am aware of this, sir,' replied Phileas Fogg, 'but I want to prove by your *visa* that I passed through Suez.'

'All right, sir.'

The consul then signed and dated the passport, and stamped it with his official seal.

Mr Fogg paid the required fee, bowed stiffly, and went out, followed by his servant.

'Well?' said the detective. 'Well,' said the consul, 'he looks a perfectly honest man.' 'May be,' replied Fix, 'but that is not the point. In your opinion, is this phlegmatic gentleman in every feature the exact picture of the thief whose description I hold?' 'I agree, but, as you know, all descriptions . . .' 'I am going to make quite sure,' broke in Fix. 'The servant, I should say, is less inscrutable than the master. He is a Frenchman, too, so won't be able to keep his mouth shut. Goodbye for the present, consul.'

Meanwhile Mr Fogg, after leaving the consulate, made his way to the quay, gave some orders to his servant, took a boat and returned to the *Mongolia*. He then went to his cabin and took up his note-book, in which were jotted down the following memoranda:

'Left London, Wednesday, October 2nd, 8.45 p.m.

'Arrived Paris, Thursday, October 3rd, 7.20 a.m.

'Left Paris, Thursday, 8.40 a.m.

'Arrived Turin, by Mont-Cenis, Friday, October 4th, 6.35 a.m.

'Left Turin, Friday, 7.20 a.m.

'Arrived Brindisi, Saturday, October 5th, 4 p.m.

'Sailed on the *Mongolia*, Saturday, 5 p.m.

'Arrived Suez, Wednesday, October 9th, 11 a.m.

'Total hours spent, 158 or days, 6.'

Mr Fogg wrote down these dates in an itinerary divided into columns, showing, as from the 2nd of October to the 21st of December, the month, the day of the month, the scheduled and actual time of arrival at each principal place — Paris, Brindisi, Suez, Bombay, Calcutta, Singapore, Hong-Kong, Yokohama, San Francisco, New York, Liverpool, London — and enabling him to keep a record of his gain or loss on arrival at each stage of the journey. This methodical time-table contained every necessary information, so that Mr Fogg always knew whether he was gaining or losing time.

On this Wednesday, October 9, he noted down his arrival at Suez, by which, as it was in accordance with the scheduled time, he neither gained nor lost. Then he ordered lunch in his cabin. The thought of going ashore to see the town never occurred to him, for he was one of those Englishmen who, when travelling, leave their servants to do their sight-seeing for them.

8

In which Passepartout talks rather more freely, perhaps, than is advisable

Fix soon caught up Passepartout on the quay; he was strolling and looking about him, feeling under no obligation to deny himself the pleasure of seeing things just because his master took no interest in them.

'Well, my friend,' said Fix, going up to him, 'is your passport *visaed?*' 'Oh, it's you, is it, sir?' replied the Frenchman. 'Yes, everything is in order, thank you.' 'You are having a look round?' 'Yes, but we are travelling at such a pace that I seem to be going about in a dream. So this is Suez?' 'Yes.' 'In Egypt?' 'Yes, in Egypt, certainly.' 'And in Africa?' 'Of course.'

'In Africa!' repeated Passepartout. 'It's beyond me! Just think, sir, I looked upon Paris as the end of our journey, and absolutely all the time I had to renew acquaintance with the great capital was from twenty minutes past seven to forty minutes past eight in the morning, between the Northern and Lyons stations, through the windows of a cab and in pelting rain! I wanted to see Père Lachaise again and the circus in the Champs-Élysées.'

'Are you in such a desperate hurry, then?' asked the detective. 'I am not, but my master is. By the way, I must buy some socks and shirts. We came away without any trunks, with just a carpet-bag.' 'I will take you to a bazaar where you will find anything you want.' 'Really, sir, this is most kind of you.'

And they walked off together, Passepartout talking away all the time.

'There is one thing I must not do,' he said; 'that is, miss the boat.' 'There is plenty of time,' answered Fix, 'it is only twelve o'clock.' Passepartout took out his big watch. 'Twelve o'clock!' he exclaimed. 'Never! it is eight minutes to ten!' 'Your watch is slow,' replied Fix. 'My watch! A family watch which has been handed down from my great-grandfather! It doesn't vary five minutes in twelve months. It's a perfect chronometer.' 'I see what's the matter,' replied Fix. 'Your time is London time, which you have kept, and which is about two hours behind that of Suez. You must be careful to set your watch by the midday hour of each country.' 'I meddle with my watch! Never!' cried Passepartout. 'If you don't, it will never agree with the sun.' 'So much the worse for the sun, sir! The sun will be at fault, then, not my watch.' And the honest fellow replaced his watch in his pocket with a gesture of defiant pride.

A few moments later Fix was saying to him: 'So you left London in a great hurry?' 'I should say we did! Last Wednesday, Mr Fogg came home from his club at eight o'clock — a thing he never does — and three-quarters of an hour later we were off.' 'But where is your master going?' 'Right ahead all the time; he is going round the world.' 'Round the world?' cried Fix. 'Yes, in eighty days! He says it's for a bet. But, between us, I don't believe a word of it. The thing would be too absurd. There must be some other reason.'

'Your Mr Fogg is an odd sort of fellow, I see.' 'It seems so.' 'I suppose he is a wealthy man?' 'Oh, yes. He is taking with him a large sum of money in brand-new banknotes. And he spends freely on the way. Why, he has promised a handsome reward to the engineer of the *Mongolia* if we get to Bombay well in advance of time.'

'You have known your master for some time, I suppose?' 'No, I have not,' answered Passepartout; 'I entered his service on the very day of our departure.'

One can easily imagine what effect these replies were bound to produce on the detective's highly-excited mind.

The hurried departure from London a short time after the robbery, the large amount of money taken with him by Fogg, his anxiety to get to distant countries as fast as possible, this cover of a wild wager, all inevitably confirmed Fix in his theory. He continued to make the Frenchman talk and was soon convinced that his master was really a stranger to him, living to himself in London, where he was reputed to be rich, though no one knew whence this wealth came, and that he was a mysterious, inscrutable fellow and so on. At the same time, Fix acquired the certainty that Phileas Fogg would not escape at Suez, but was really going on to Bombay.

'Is Bombay a long way off?' asked Passepartout. 'It is some way off,' answered the detective. 'You will have to put in another ten days on the sea.' 'And where do you place Bombay?' 'In India.' 'In Asia?' 'Of course.'

'The deuce! — I must tell you, I have a great worry on my mind, my burner.'

'What burner?' 'My gas-burner. I forgot to turn it off, and the gas is burning at my expense. Now I reckon this costs me two shillings every twenty-fours hours, exactly sixpence more than I earn; and you can see that if the journey lasts any time . . . '

Whether Fix understood what Passepartout said about his gas trouble is very doubtful, as, by this time, he was not listening; he was making up his mind.

They now came to the bazaar, where he left the Frenchman to make his purchases, telling him to be sure not to miss the boat; he then hurried back to find the consul.

Feeling perfectly sure that he was right, Fix was now quite cool. 'Sir,' he said to the consul, 'it is an absolute certainty! I've got him. He wants to be taken for an eccentric bloke who has set his heart on going round the world in eighty days.' 'A cunning fellow, eh?' replied the consul. 'He expects to get back to London, after putting all the police agents of both continents off his track.' 'We shall see about that,' replied Fix. 'Are you not making a mistake?' the consul asked once more. 'I am making no mistake.' 'In that case, why did this thief insist on proving by means of a *visa* that he had been to Suez?'

'That I cannot say,' replied the detective, 'but listen to this.' And in a few words he made known to the consul the telling points of his conversation with Fogg's servant.

'Yes,' said the consul, 'to all appearances the man is guilty. What do you propose to do?'

'Send a telegram to London for the immediate dispatch of a warrant of arrest to Bombay, take a berth on the *Mongolia*, shadow my thief to India, and there, on British soil, speak to him politely, my warrant in one hand, and the other on his shoulder.'

Having uttered these words with cool decision, the detective took leave of the consul and went to the telegraph-office, whence he sent to the head of the Metropolitan Police the sensational message with which the reader is acquainted.

A quarter of an hour later, Fix stepped on board the *Mongolia*, holding a travelling-bag in his hand; he had no other luggage, but plenty of money; and ere long the powerful steamship was running at full speed over the waters of the Red Sea.

9

In which the Red Sea and the Indian Ocean prove favourable to the designs of Phileas Fogg

Between Suez and Aden the distance is exactly thirteen hundred and ten miles, and by the conditions of the company the boats are allowed one hundred and thirty-eight hours to cross it. The *Mongolia*, stoked as she was with exceptional zeal, was making such a quick passage that she would be in advance of her time.

The greater part of the passengers taken on board at Brindisi were bound for India.

Some were going to Bombay, others to Calcutta, via Bombay, for, now that a railway runs from one side to the other of the Indian Peninsula, it is no longer necessary to sail round past Ceylon.

Among these passengers of the *Mongolia* were a number of Civil Service men and officers of all grades; some of the latter were in the regular British forces, others commanded the native sepoy troops. They were all well paid, though now under the British

Government, which has assumed the rights and liabilities of the East India Company: second-lieutenants get £280 a-year, brigadiers £2400, and generals £4000. And the pay of Civil Servants is higher still.

Besides these men in Government employ, there were a certain number of young Englishmen well supplied with funds, on their way to found business establishments in distant parts. So the food on board the *Mongolia* was good and plentiful. The purser, the company's trusted servant, as important as the captain, did things lavishly. At breakfast, at two o'clock lunch, at half-past five dinner, at eight o'clock supper, the tables were loaded with dishes of fresh meat and entremets supplied from the boat's larder.

There were a few lady passengers. They changed their dresses twice daily; and there was music, and dancing even, when the sea allowed it.

But the Red Sea is liable to sudden and violent changes and very often rough, like all those long, narrow gulfs. When the wind blew from the Asiatic or the Arabian coast, the *Mongolia*, like a long screw-propelled spindle, being caught athwart, rolled horribly. At such times the ladies vanished; pianos were silent; songs and dances ceased at the same instant. Yet, despite squall and swell, the steamer,

59

impelled by its powerful engines, lost no time as she forged ahead to the Straits of Bab-el-Mandeb.

You wonder what Phileas Fogg was doing all this time. You probably think he was anxious and worrying over weather conditions that might impede the ship's progress, and the raging seas that might affect the engines; in short, over all possible damage that might compel the *Mongolia* to put into some port, thereby endangering the success of his journey.

But there was nothing of the sort, or at any rate, if he thought of these possibilities, he showed not the least sign of it.

He was ever the same impassive gentleman, the imperturbable member of the Reform Club, upon whom no incident or accident could come as a surprise. He appeared to be just as little affected as the ship's chronometers. He was seldom seen on deck, and seemed to feel but little curiosity to observe that Red Sea, so full of memories, the scene of the first historic happenings of mankind. He felt no interest in the curious towns scattered on its shores, and whose picturesque outlines occasionally stood out on the skyline. He did not even give a thought to the perils of this Arabic gulf of which the old historians, Strabo, Arrian, Arthemidorus and

Edrisi, always spoke with dread, and upon which, in the days of old, navigators never ventured without first commending their voyage to the protection of the gods with propitiatory sacrifices.

How was the whimsical fellow spending his time within the *Mongolia's* precincts? In the first place, as neither rolling nor pitching could put such a marvellously well-constituted machine out of order, he fed heartily four times a day; then he played whist, for he had found partners as infatuated with the game as himself: a collector of taxes on his way to his station at Goa, a clergyman, the Reverend Decimus Smith, returning to Bombay; and a brigadier-general of the English Army, who was rejoining his brigade at Benares. These three passengers were just as passionately fond of whist as Mr Fogg, and they played on for hours as silently absorbed as himself.

As for Passepartout, he was quite immune from sea-sickness; he had a cabin forward and, like his master, took his meals with scrupulous regularity. He was getting reconciled to the voyage in such conditions, and even began to enjoy it. He was well fed, had good quarters, saw new scenes, and, moreover, felt pretty confident this foolery would end at Bombay.

On October 10, the day after they left Suez, Passepartout was rather pleased to see on deck the obliging person to whom he had applied for information on landing in Egypt.

'If I am not mistaken,' he said, accosting him with his most genial smile, 'you are the gentleman who so kindly piloted me about in Suez?' 'Yes, of course,' replied the detective, 'I know you all right! You are the servant of that odd English fellow.' 'Quite right, Mr . . . ?'

'Fix; my name is Fix.' 'Mr Fix,' replied Passepartout, 'I am delighted to find you on board. Where are you going?' 'To Bombay, like yourself.' 'Is this your first trip to India?' 'No,' replied Fix. 'I have been there several times; I am in the service of the Peninsular and Oriental Company.' 'Then you know the country?' 'Yes, pretty well,' answered Fix, who was anxious not to commit himself.

'I suppose India is a curious sort of place?'

'Very; mosques, minarets, temples, fakirs, pagodas, tigers, snakes, Hindu dancing-girls! But it is to be hoped you will have time to see the country.' 'I hope so, Mr Fix. You see, no sane man can be expected to spend his life hopping from a steamer into a train, and from a train into a steamer again, just to go round the world in eighty days; there's no sense in it. All these antics will come to an end at Bombay, you may be sure.'

'And is Mr Fogg quite well?' asked Fix, in the most natural tone. 'Very well indeed, Mr Fix, and so am I. A ravenous ogre couldn't eat more than I do! It's the sea-air.' 'I never see your master on deck.' 'Never; he never wants to see anything.' 'You know, Mr Passepartout, this supposed tour in eighty days might be a blind concealing some secret mission — a diplomatic mission, possibly.' 'Honour bright, Mr Fix, I have not the least notion, I confess, and the fact is, I wouldn't give half-a-crown to know.'

This was the first of many similar conversations between Passepartout and Fix, as the detective was anxious to be on the best of terms with Fogg's servant. It might prove useful on occasion. Thus it was that he frequently treated him to a few glasses of whisky or pale ale, which the good fellow accepted unhesitatingly, even returning the compliment, so as not to lag in politeness, and thinking Fix a right-down good fellow.

Meanwhile the liner was making rapid progress. On the 13th, Mocha was sighted, peering out of its girdle of ruined walls, over which a few date-palms stood out in their greenery. In the distance, amid the mountains stretched wide fields of coffee trees. When he gazed upon this far-famed place, Passepartout was delighted; he even thought that its circular walls and a dismantled fort with the outline of a handle, gave it the look of an enormous coffee-cup.

During the following night, the *Mongolia* crossed the Straits of Bab-el-Mandeb, Arabic for 'gate of tears,' and on the morrow (14th), she put in at Steamer Point, north-west of Aden roadstead, in order to take in a fresh supply of coal.

This fuelling of steamers at such distances from the centres of production is a very serious matter. For the Peninsular Company alone it means an expense of eight hundred thousand pounds a-year. For coal depôts had to be established in several ports, and the coal comes to four pounds a ton. The *Mongolia* had another sixteen hundred and fifty miles to run before reaching Bombay, and it would take her four hours to fill her coal-bunkers at Steamer Point. But this delay could not have the slightest effect on Phileas Fogg's programme, for he had taken it into account. Moreover, the *Mongolia* arrived at Aden on the evening of the 14th, and she was not due before the morning of the 15th, a gain of fifteen hours.

Mr Fogg and his servant went ashore, as Mr Fogg wished to have his passport *visaed*. Fix followed him without being noticed. As soon as the passport was in order, Phileas

Fogg returned on board and continued his interrupted game of whist.

Passepartout went his way, and, as was his wont, sauntered about among the Somalis, Banyans, Parsees, Jews, Arabs, and Europeans who make up Aden's population of twenty-five thousand inhabitants. He admired the fortifications which make this town the Gibraltar of the Indian Ocean, and magnificent cisterns on which the English engineers were still at work, two thousand years after the engineers of King Solomon.

'Very curious, very curious,' said Passepartout to himself, returning on board. 'I can see that a man who wants to see something new loses nothing by travelling.'

At six o'clock in the evening the *Mongolia* was churning up the waters of the roadstead, and was soon running at full speed over the Indian Ocean. She was allowed a hundred and sixty-eight hours between Aden and Bombay. And the sea proved favourable, as the wind blew steadily from the north-west. She was able to put on all sail, which added considerably to her steam-power. Thus steadied, the ship had less roll on. The ladies, in fresh toilets, came up on deck, and singing and dancing went on again. The passage was quite pleasant, and Passepartout was delighted with the genial companion whom chance had put in his way.

On Sunday, October 20, about noon, the Indian coast was sighted, and two hours later the pilot came on board. On the horizon, a background of hills, showing up against the sky, made a fitting frame for the picture; and soon the rows of palms which spread their foliage over the town came clearly into view. The *Mongolia* made her way into this roadstead, formed by the islands of Salsette, Colaba, Elephanta and Butcher, and at half-past four she was brought alongside the quays of Bombay.

Phileas Fogg was at that moment finishing the thirty-third rubber of the day; and he and his partner, by a bold move, took all thirteen tricks, and ended a fine passage with a splendid slam.

The *Mongolia* was not due at Bombay before the 22nd. She arrived on the 20th. This constituted a gain of two days since Phileas Fogg's departure from London, and, methodically, he noted it down in his itinerary, in the column of gains.

10

In which Passepartout is only too fortunate in getting off with the loss of his shoes

Everybody knows that India, that great reversed triangle, with its base in the north and apex in the south, has an area of one million four hundred thousand square miles, over which is unequally distributed a population of one hundred and eighty millions of inhabitants.

The British Government exercises effective power over a certain portion of this huge country; there is a governor-general at Calcutta, a governor at Madras, another at Bombay and in Bengal, and a lieutenant-governor at Agra.

But British India, properly so-called, has an area of not more than seven hundred thousand square miles, with a population of from a hundred to a hundred and ten millions. No further proof is needed to show that there is still a considerable part of the country over which the Queen's Government has no authority. In fact, in the dominions of certain fierce and dreaded rajahs of the interior Hindu independence is still complete.

The first English settlement was founded in 1756, on the site now occupied by the city of Madras. From that time till the year of the great Mutiny of the sepoys the famous East India Company was all-powerful. It gradually annexed the various provinces obtained from the rajahs in return for annuities, of which little or nothing was paid them. It appointed its governor-general and all its servants, civil or military; but the East India Company is no more, and the British possessions in India are under the immediate control of the Crown. Thus it is that the general appearance, the manners and ethnographic divisions of the peninsula show day by day a tendency to change.

Formerly travellers in India used all the old means of locomotion; they went on foot, on horseback, in carts, wheel-barrows, palanquins, on men's backs, in coaches, and so on. But now fast steamboats ply on the Indus and the Ganges, and one can cross the peninsula from Bombay to Calcutta by rail in the short space of three days; and the main line is joined by numerous branch lines all along the route.

This railway does not cross India in a

straight line. The distance between Bombay and Calcutta as the crow flies is not more than one thousand to eleven hundred miles; trains of average speed would not take three days to cross it; but the distance is increased by a third, at least, by going round as far as Allahabad in the north.

Roughly the great Indian Peninsular Railway runs in the following way. Leaving the island of Bombay, it goes through Salsette, crosses over to the continent opposite Tannah, clears the range of the Western Ghauts, then runs in a north-east direction as far as Burhanpur, dashes through the almost independent territory of Bundelkhand, goes up to Allahabad, bends its course eastward, meets the Ganges at Benares, then leaves it at no great distance, and striking down again south-eastward through Burdwan and the French town of Chandernagore, has its terminus at Calcutta.

The passengers of the *Mongolia* landed at half-past four, and the train would leave Bombay for Calcutta at eight exactly.

So Mr Fogg, after saying goodbye to his whist partners, left the liner, sent his servant to make a few purchases, giving him strict injunctions to be at the station before eight, and with that regular step of his, that marked the seconds like the pendulum of an astronomic clock, made his way to the passport office.

The town hall, the magnificent library, the forts and docks, the cotton market, the bazaars, the mosques and synagogues, the Armenian churches, the splendid pagoda on Malabar Hill, with its two polygonal towers, to all these marvels of Bombay he gave not a thought. The masterpieces of Elephanta, the mysterious hypogea hidden away south-east of the harbour, those admirable remains of Buddhist architecture, the grottoes of Salsette Island, could all be treated with like indifference.

Phileas Fogg saw absolutely nothing.

On leaving the passport office, he quietly betook himself to the station and ordered dinner. Among the dishes there was a certain stew of 'native rabbit,' which the host thought fit to recommend to him in words of especial praise.

Phileas Fogg took some of this stew and tasted it with scrupulous care; but, in spite of the highly-spiced sauce, he found it abominable. He rang for the host, and, looking him in the face, he said to him, 'Is this rabbit, sir?' 'Yes, my lord,' the rascal replied without wincing, 'jungle rabbit.'

'Do you mean to say this rabbit didn't mew when it was killed?' 'Mew, my lord! a rabbit

70

mew! I swear to you . . . '

'Sir host,' returned Mr Fogg, frigidly, 'do not swear, and remember this: in India, cats were once held to be sacred animals. Those were happy days.'

'For the cat, my lord?'

'And possibly for travellers too!'

Having said this much, Mr Fogg quietly went on with his dinner.

Like Mr Fogg, and very soon after, Fix left the *Mongolia*, and hurried to the head-quarters of the Bombay police, where he made himself known as a detective. He then explained the nature of the business which had been entrusted to him, his position with respect to the supposed culprit, and inquired whether a warrant had been received from London. The answer was in the negative. Of course, the warrant having been dispatched after Fogg's departure, could not have arrived by then.

Fix was sorely put out. He tried to induce the chief of the Bombay police to give him a warrant for Fogg's arrest. This the chief of police would not do, as the case concerned the London police, which alone was empowered by law to issue a warrant. Such rigid principle and strict observance of legality are quite in accordance with English life, which will not tolerate arbitrary action where

71

individual liberty is concerned. Fix did not insist; he realised that he must resign himself to wait for the warrant, but determined not to lose sight of the inscrutable rascal for a moment while he stayed in Bombay. Like Passepartout, Fix felt convinced that Fogg would stay there some time, and meanwhile the warrant would arrive.

Nevertheless, after receiving his master's last orders on landing, Passepartout understood perfectly well that what had happened at Suez and Paris would happen at Bombay: that this was not the end of their journey, which would be pursued at least as far as Calcutta, possibly farther. And he began to wonder whether this wager of Mr Fogg's was not absolutely serious after all, and whether he who yearned for a life of repose was not really being compelled by fate to move round the world in eighty days.

Having purchased a few shirts and socks, he was strolling in the streets of Bombay, which were exceptionally crowded with the lower orders. In the midst of Europeans of all nationalities, there were Persians with pointed caps, Bunhyas with round turbans, Sindes with square bonnets, Armenians in flowing robes, Parsees with black mitres. It just happened that the Parsees or Guebres were observing a festival. These direct descendants of the followers of Zoroaster are the most industrious, most highly civilised, most intelligent and most austere of the Hindus, and at the present day the wealthiest native merchants of Bombay are Parsees. They were celebrating a sort of religious carnival, with processions, and entertainments at which dancing-girls clothed in pink gauze, embossed with gold and silver, danced to the sound of viols and the clang of tambourines with marvellous grace, and perfect decency withal.

Needless to say, Passepartout watched these ceremonies with wide-staring eyes and gaping mouth; he was so bent on losing nothing of it all, that his whole demeanour and expression portrayed the greenest booby one can imagine.

Unhappily for himself and for his master, whose venture he ran the risk of wrecking, his curiosity carried him to improper lengths.

When he had seen something of this Parsee carnival, Passepartout, on his way to the station, passed in front of the beautiful pagoda on Malabar Hill, and an unlucky thought moved him to see its interior. Now there are certain Indian pagodas which Christians are absolutely forbidden to enter, and into which even the faithful may not go without first leaving their shoes outside. Both these facts were quite unknown to Passepartout.

It should be mentioned in this connection that the British Government, from sound policy, not only respects the native religions, but enforces respect for the most trivial of native religious observances, and punishes severely anyone who offends against them.

Having entered the Malabar pagoda in all innocence, and like any simple tourist, Passepartout was gazing in admiration upon the dazzling tinsel of Brahmin ornamentation, when all of a sudden he was knocked down on the sacred flagging. Three furious-looking priests flung themselves upon him, wrenched off his shoes and socks, and proceeded to belabour him, uttering savage yells the while. The Frenchman, powerful and agile, was on his feet in a moment; with one blow of his fist he knocked down one of his adversaries, and with a kick he sent another sprawling, the long robes by which they were hampered making this the easier; then rushing out of the pagoda as fast as his legs would carry him, he soon left a long way behind him the third Hindu, who had hastened to give chase, hounding on the crowd as he went.

At five minutes to eight, a few minutes only

before the departure of the train, Passepartout reached the station, hatless and barefooted, and without the parcel containing his purchases, which had been lost in the scuffle.

Fix had followed Fogg to the station, and was there on the platform. He now perceived that the rogue was leaving Bombay, and at once made up his mind to accompany him as far as Calcutta, or farther, if necessary. Passepartout did not see Fix, who stood in a dark recess, but when he gave his master a hurried account of his adventures, Fix overheard him.

'I trust you will not do this sort of thing again,' was all Phileas Fogg said in reply, as he took his seat in the train.

The poor fellow, barefooted and utterly dejected, followed his master without saying a word.

Fix was on the point of stepping into another carriage, when a sudden idea made him there and then change his mind and stay.

'I don't go,' he said to himself. 'This is an offence committed on Indian soil. I've got him.'

At that moment the engine whistled loud, and the train vanished in the darkness of the night.

11

*In which Phileas Fogg buys a mount
at a fabulous price*

The train started at the scheduled time. There was a fair number of passengers, among whom were a few officers, some Indian Civil Servants, and opium and indigo merchants, whose presence was required by their business in the eastern part of the peninsula.

Passepartout was travelling in the same compartment as his master, and a third passenger faced them, seated in one of the opposite corners. This was Sir Francis Cromarty, one of the men who had played whist with Mr Fogg during the passage from Suez to Bombay, now on his way back to his men in cantonments near Benares.

Sir Francis Cromarty, a tall, fair man of some fifty years of age, had greatly distinguished himself in the last sepoy revolt.

He had gone to India in his youth, and had lived there ever since, with the exception of a few brief visits to his native country; so India was practically as much his home as if he had been a Hindu. Being a man of considerable learning, he would readily have supplied Phileas Fogg with information concerning the customs, history and organisation of India, if Phileas Fogg had been the sort of man to ask. But Phileas Fogg had no desire for information. He was not travelling, he was merely describing a circumference. He was a solid body moving through an orbit around the terrestrial globe, in obedience to the laws of rational mechanics. At this particular moment he was mentally reckoning up the hours spent since his departure from London, and, had not all useless manifestation been quite alien to his nature, he would have rubbed his hands for satisfaction.

The oddity of his fellow-traveller had not escaped Sir Francis Cromarty, although his sole opportunity for observing him had been during the game and between two rubbers. Well might he ask himself, then, whether a human heart actually beat under this cold exterior, and whether Phileas Fogg had a soul alive to the beauties of Nature and to moral aspirations. He was not sure. Of all the queer human specimens the brigadier-general had ever come across, none could be compared to this product of the exact sciences.

In talking to Sir Francis Cromarty, Phileas Fogg had made no secret of his projected tour around the world, and of the conditions of the enterprise. To the brigadier this wager seemed nothing but a silly whim, which could serve no useful purpose, and was therefore lacking in that *transire benefaciendo* which should guide every sensible man's judgement. Should this strange gentleman go on as he was doing, he would obviously pass through life without having done any good to himself or anybody else. An hour after leaving Bombay, the train had passed over the viaducts, crossed Salsette Island, and was speeding on its way over the continent. At Callyan it left on the right the branch line which descends through Kandallah and Poona towards south-eastern India, and came to Pauwell station. There it entered the far-spreading mountain system of the Western Ghauts, whose base is of trap rock and basalt, and whose highest peaks are densely wooded. From time to time, Sir Francis Cromarty and Phileas Fogg exchanged a few words, and now, renewing the conversation which constantly flagged, the brigadier said, 'A few years ago, Mr Fogg, you would have been so delayed here that your journey would probably not have ended at the appointed time.'

'Why, Sir Francis?' 'Because the railway did not go beyond the foot of these mountains, which had to be crossed in palanquins or on the backs of ponies to Kandallah station on the other side.' 'Such a delay would not have upset my plans in the least,' replied Mr Fogg. 'I have carefully anticipated the possibility of certain obstacles.'

'All the same, Mr Fogg,' returned the brigadier-general, 'you are in danger of having very serious unpleasantness to face in connection with this fellow's adventure.'

Passepartout, his feet wrapped up in his travelling-rug, was sound asleep and never dreamt that he was the subject of conversation. 'The British Government is extremely severe, and rightly so, on this kind of offence,' resumed Sir Francis. 'It makes a very special point of compelling respect for the religious customs of the Hindus, and if your servant had been caught . . . ' 'Well, Sir Francis,' replied Mr Fogg, 'if he had been caught, he would have been condemned and punished, and then would have returned to Europe without more ado. I fail to see in what way this matter could have delayed his master.' Here the conversation dropped again.

During the night the train crossed the Ghauts, passed through Nassik, and on the morrow, October 21, it ran at high speed through the comparatively flat country of the Khandeish. The land was well cultivated and dotted with villages, above which the minarets of the pagodas stood out like the church steeples of Europe. This fertile region was watered by a number of small streams, most of them direct or indirect tributaries of the Godavari.

Passepartout, now awake, was looking out, and could not believe he was crossing the land of the Hindus in a train of the great Peninsular Railway. The thing seemed fantastic. And yet it was a fact! The engine, driven by an Englishman and fuelled with English coal, belched out its smoke over the plantations of cotton, coffee, nutmeg, clove and pepper, while the steam wound its spirals round clumps of palm trees, among which were seen picturesque bungalows, here and there a sort of derelict monastery, called *vibari*, and marvellous temples decked in all the inexhaustible wealth of ornamentation of Indian architecture. Then, stretching out of sight, lay a vast expanse of jungle, the home of abounding snakes and tigers, terrified by the snorting screech of the engine; and after this the forests cleft by the line, and still frequented by elephants, that gazed with wistful eye as the train rushed past in its dishevelled flurry.

In the course of that morning, beyond Malligam station, the travellers crossed the fatal country so often stained with blood by the votaries of the goddess Kali. At no great distance rose Ellora with its beautiful pagodas, and far-famed Aurungabad, fierce Aurungzeb's capital, now no more than the chief town of one of the provinces detached from the Nizam's dominions. It was over this region that Feringhea, chief of the Thugs, king of the Stranglers, exerted his despotic power. These assassins bound together as members of an association that defied all detection, strangled victims of all ages in honour of the goddess of Death, without ever shedding blood, and there was a time when one could not have dug up a single spot on this soil without finding a corpse. The British Government has certainly found means to effect a considerable reduction in the number of these murders, but the dread association still exists and is still at work.

At half-past twelve the train stopped at Burhanpur, and Passepartout was able to buy a pair of Indian slippers ornamented with false pearls, for which he gave an exorbitant price, and which he proceeded to put on with unconcealed vanity. After a hasty lunch, our travellers started for Assurghur, running for a short time along the bank of the Tapti, a small river that empties itself into the Gulf of Cambray, near Surat.

Passepartout's state of mind at this juncture claims our attention. Up to the moment when he reached Bombay, he believed, not without some show of reason, that Bombay would be the end of it all. But now that he was being whisked along at full speed by rail across India, a sudden change came over him. He was the old Passepartout once more, full of the spirit of adventure and the wild imaginings of his youth. He began to take his master's project seriously, the bet became a reality, with this journey around the world within the strictly limited time as a logical consequence. He there and then began to worry over possible delays and such accidents as might happen on the way. He became, so to say, a party to this wager, and was much perturbed at the thought of the possible consequences of his unpardonable foolery of the day before. And, being much less unemotional than Mr Fogg, he was much more anxious. He kept counting the passing days, cursed the train whenever it stopped, and accused it of crawling, mentally blaming his master for not having promised the engine-driver a tip. The good fellow did not know that, while this was possible on the boat, it could not be done on the railway, where the rate of going is fixed by regulations. Toward evening they entered the defiles of the Sutpur Mountains, which separate Khaidish territory from Bundelkhand.

On the morrow, October 22, in reply to a question from Sir Francis Cromarty, Passepartout looked at his watch and said it was three o'clock in the morning. And, as this precious watch was still set by the Greenwich meridian, now some seventy-seven degrees west of them, it was, and was likely to be, four hours slow. Sir Francis corrected Passepartout's time, repeating what Fix had already told him. He tried to make him see that the watch should be set by each new meridian, and that, as he was constantly advancing eastward, that is to say meeting the sun, the days were shorter by as many times four minutes as there were degrees travelled through. The brigadier-general's explanation, whether understood or not, was completely thrown away on Passepartout, who obstinately refused to put his watch on. The stubborn fellow, obsessed by this perfectly harmless mania, kept it ever at London time.

At eight o'clock in the morning, the train stopped fifteen miles beyond Rothal, in the middle of an extensive glade, on the border of which were a few bungalows and workmen's huts. The guard in charge of the train passed along the carriages shouting,

'All change! All change!'

Phileas Fogg looked at Sir Francis Cromarty, who seemed amazed at this halt in the heart of a forest of tamarinds and khajours. Passepartout, equally surprised, jumped down on the line and came back almost at once shouting, 'Sir, that's the end of the railway!'

'Whatever do you mean?' asked Sir Francis Cromarty. 'I mean that the train does not go any farther!' The brigadier-general got out at once, and Phileas Fogg got out too, but in a leisurely way. Both questioned the guard. 'Where are we?' asked Sir Francis. 'At Kholby hamlet,' answered the guard. 'Do we stop here?' 'Of course; the railway isn't finished.' 'Not finished; what!' 'There is a section of some fifty miles to be laid from here to Allahabad, where the line begins again.'

'But the papers announced the opening of the line right through!'

'Well, sir, the papers made a mistake.'

'But you issue tickets from Bombay to Calcutta!' said Sir Francis Cromarty, who was getting angry.

'Certainly,' replied the guard, 'but the passengers are aware that they will have to find means of transport from Kholby to Allahabad.'

Sir Francis was furious; and Passepartout

would have felled the guard with pleasure, though the guard had nothing to do with it. He dared not look at his master.

'Sir Francis,' said Mr Fogg quietly, 'if you are agreeable, we will set about procuring the means of getting to Allahabad.'

'This sort of delay, Mr Fogg, will fatally affect your interests.'

'No, Sir Francis; it was foreseen.'

'Do you mean to say that you knew that the line . . . ?' 'Not at all, but I knew that some obstacle or other would crop up on my way. Now there is no particular damage done. I have two days to the good, which I must sacrifice. There is a boat leaving Calcutta for Hong-Kong at noon on the 25th, today is the 22nd; we shall get to Calcutta in time.' This reply was made with such perfect assurance that there was nothing more to be said.

It was only too true that there was no railway or sign of one beyond this place. The papers are like certain watches that have a craze for being fast. They had prematurely announced the completion of the railway. The majority of the travellers knew of this break in the line; on getting out of the train, they at once proceeded to secure every kind of conveyance to be found in the little town; four-wheeled palki-garis, carts drawn by zebus, a sort of humped oxen, travelling-cars that looked like pagodas on wheels, palan-quins, ponies, all these and other vehicles were pressed into service. The result was that Mr Fogg and Sir Francis Cromarty, after looking everywhere, came back having found nothing.

'I shall walk,' said Phileas Fogg.

Passepartout, coming up at this moment, heard him, and made an expressive grimace, as he looked down at his gorgeous but flimsy slippers. Very fortunately he too had been trying to find something, and, speaking with some diffidence, he said, 'Sir, I think I have found a conveyance.' 'What is it?' 'An elephant! An elephant belonging to an Indian who lives but a hundred yards from here.' 'Let us go and see the elephant,' replied Mr Fogg.

Five minutes later, Phileas Fogg, Sir Francis Cromarty and Passepartout reached a hut adjoining a paddock with a very high paling. The hut contained an Indian, and the paddock an elephant. At their request, the Indian took Mr Fogg and his two compan-ions into the paddock. There they found an animal, that was only half-domesticated, and that its owner had reared, not as a beast of burden, but as a beast of combat. With that object in view, he had begun to alter the naturally gentle disposition of the elephant so as to bring him gradually to that intense state of fury which the Hindus term *mulsh*. This he did by feeding him for three months on sugar and butter. The treatment may appear unlikely to produce such a result, but it is none the less used with success by trainers. Most fortunately for Mr Fogg, this elephant had only just commenced the diet, and *mulsh* had not broken out as yet.

Like all animals of the same kind, Kiouni — its name was Kiouni — could travel rapidly for a long time at a stretch, so, in default of every other sort of mount, Phileas Fogg determined to make use of him.

But elephants are not so plentiful as they were in India, and are therefore far from cheap. There is a very great demand for the males, which alone are suitable for circus contests. Moreover, as elephants rarely reproduce their species in the state of domesticity, the only means of supply is hunting.

Their owners, therefore, take the utmost care of them. When Mr Fogg asked the Indian if he was willing to let him have his beast on hire, the Indian refused flatly. Fogg persisted and offered the excessive sum of ten pounds an hour for the use of the beast. This was refused. Twenty pounds, forty pounds, nothing doing. Passepartout gave a jump at each advance. But the Indian was not to be tempted.

Yet the offer was handsome; for, supposing the elephant took fifteen hours to get to Allahabad, it would mean six hundred pounds for the owner. Phileas Fogg, absolutely unperturbed, then offered to purchase the beast, and straightway suggested a thousand pounds. The crafty native, possibly scenting a magnificent bargain, said he did not want to sell.

Sir Francis took Mr Fogg aside and advised him to think before proceeding with the matter. Phileas Fogg replied that he was not in the habit of acting without thinking; that, after all, the bet was a matter of twenty thousand pounds; that he could not do without the elephant, and that he must have it, even if he had to pay twenty times what it was worth.

Mr Fogg returned to the Indian, whose small eyes, aglow with greed, could not conceal the fact that with him it was only a question of how much he could get. Phileas Fogg offered first twelve hundred pounds, then fifteen hundred, then eighteen hundred, and finally two thousand. Passepartout, usually so red, was pale with emotion.

At two thousand pounds the Indian gave in.

'By my slippers!' exclaimed Passepartout. 'What price elephant-steak after this?'

The transaction once concluded, all they had to do was to find a guide, which proved to be a matter of less difficulty. A bright-looking young Parsee offered his services, which Mr Fogg accepted, promising him high remuneration, thereby stimulating his intelligence to greater exertion.

The elephant was brought out and equipped without delay. The Parsee, who was an expert mahout, covered the animal's back with a sort of saddle-cloth and fixed on either side a couple of rather uncomfortable litters. Phileas Fogg paid the Indian with banknotes drawn from the depths of the famous travelling-bag, an operation so painful to Passepartout that it seemed they were being extracted from his own bowels. Mr Fogg thereupon offered to carry Sir Francis Cromarty to Allahabad station, and the offer was accepted. One more traveller would not overtire the gigantic beast.

Provisions were procured at Kholby and, Sir Francis and Phileas Fogg having taken their seats in the howdahs, Passepartout placed himself astride between his master and the brigadier, and the Parsee perched himself on the elephant's neck. At nine o'clock they left the small town and made their way by the shortest cut into the thick forest of fan-palms.

12

In which Phileas Fogg and his companions venture across the forests of India, and the events that ensue

In order to shorten the journey, the guide left on his right the railway line still in the making. Being constantly obliged to avoid the capricious ramifications of the Vindhia Mountains, the line did not pursue a direct course, which it was Phileas Fogg's interest to take, as it would be the shortest. The Parsee, to whom the roads and paths of the locality were quite familiar, declared there would be a gain of twenty miles in striking across the forest, and they took his word for it. Phileas Fogg and Sir Francis Cromarty, up to their necks in the howdahs, were much shaken by the elephant's sharp trotting, for the mahout was driving fast. But they suffered with the most perfect British unconcern, talking little and hardly able to see each other.

Passepartout stuck on the animal's back and, receiving directly the full force of every jolt, was all the time trying to remember his master's recommendation and to keep his tongue from getting between his teeth, as in that position it would have been bitten in two. The worthy fellow, at one time flung onto the elephant's neck, at another on to his rump, was vaulting about like a clown on a spring-board. But he joked and laughed as he tossed about, and, from time to time, took a lump of sugar out of his bag, and the intelligent Kiouni received it at the end of his trunk, without a moment's interruption of his regular trot.

After two hours the guide stopped the elephant and gave him two hours' rest. The animal first quenched his thirst at a pond hard by, and then proceeded to devour the branches and shrubs about him. Sir Francis Cromarty was only too pleased with this halt. He was dead-tired. Mr Fogg looked as fresh and fit as if he had just jumped out of bed.

'He must be made of iron,' said the brigadier-general, looking at him admiringly. 'Of wrought-iron,' replied Passepartout, as he set about preparing a hasty breakfast.

At noon the Parsee gave the signal for departure. The country soon began to look very wild. The great forests gave place to copses of tamarinds and dwarf palms, after which came wide-spreading, arid plains, bristling with wretched shrubs and dotted with great boulders of syenite. The whole of this part of upper Bundelkhand, but little visited by travellers, is inhabited by a fanatical people hardened in the most terrible practices of the Hindu religion. The English have been unable to establish their rule efficiently over this region, subject as it is to the influence of the rajahs, whom it would have been no easy matter to reach in their inaccessible fastnesses in the Vindhia Mountains.

More than once troops of fierce-looking Indians were descried making wrathful gestures as they watched the great quadruped speeding by. But the Parsee avoided them as much as possible, for he thought it unsafe to meet them. They saw few animals in the course of that day; here and there a monkey or two, that scampered away making endless contortions and grimaces, to Passepartout's great delight.

Among many disturbing thoughts one in particular kept worrying him. He wondered what Mr Fogg would do with the elephant when they reached Allahabad. Would he take him with him? That was impossible. The cost of conveyance added to the purchase-price would make the beast quite ruinous. Would he sell him or set him free? It was only right that the estimable animal should be treated with proper consideration. Passepartout wondered what on earth he should do if Mr Fogg by any chance were to make him a present of the beast. He was much perturbed by this possibility.

The main range of the Vindhias was crossed at eight o'clock in the evening, and the travellers made a halt in a dilapidated bungalow at the foot of the northern slope. They had ridden about twenty-five miles that day, and they had another twenty-five before them to get to Allahabad. The night was cold, so the Parsee made a fire of dry branches, which was much appreciated. The provisions bought at Kholby supplied the supper, and the travellers ate like the dog-tired men they were. The conversation, begun in a few disjointed sentences, soon ended in loud snoring. The guide kept watch close to Kiouni, who went to sleep standing, leaning against the trunk of a thick tree. The night passed without any noteworthy incident. At times the silence was broken by the snarling of cheetahs and panthers, and the sharp tittering of monkeys. But, beyond noise, the carnivorous animals made no hostile demonstration against the occupants of the bungalow. Sir Francis Cromarty slept heavily, like a gallant soldier exhausted with fatigue. Passepartout had a somewhat restless night, dreaming that he was still tossing on the elephant's back. Mr Fogg slept as peacefully as if he had been in his own quiet home in Savile Row.

The journey was resumed at six in the morning, and the guide hoped to reach Allahabad station that very evening. So Mr Fogg would lose only a part of the forty-eight hours he had saved since the beginning of his venture.

Descending the last slopes of the Vindhias, Kiouni got into his stride, and about noon they arrived near the small town of Kallinger, on the Cani, a feeder of the Ganges. The guide passed at some distance from the town, as he was always careful to avoid inhabited places, feeling safer in those lonely plains which announce the first depressions of the basin of the great river. Allahabad was now only twelve miles away to the north-east. They stopped under a clump of banana trees, and greatly enjoyed the fruit, wholesome as bread, and 'luscious as cream,' as is the saying among travellers.

At two o'clock the guide entered a dense forest, across which he would have to travel for several miles. He preferred to remain under cover of the woods.

So far, at all events, there had been no unpleasant encounter, and it looked as if the journey would be successfully accomplished, when the elephant, showing signs of uneasiness, stopped dead.

It was then four o'clock. 'What is the matter?' asked Sir Francis Cromarty, looking out of his howdah. 'I don't know, sir,' replied the Parsee, listening attentively to a confused murmur that came along under the thick branches.

A few moments later the murmur became more distinct. It was now like a still very distant concert of human voices and brass instruments.

Passepartout was all eyes and ears.

Phileas Fogg uttered not a word, but waited patiently.

The Parsee jumped down, tied the elephant to a tree and disappeared in the thickest part of the wood. He returned a few minutes later, saying, 'It is a procession of Brahmins coming this way. We must avoid being seen, if possible.'

The guide untied the elephant and led him into a thicket telling the travellers to be sure not to dismount, and holding himself in readiness to mount quickly, should flight become necessary. But he was confident that the procession of the faithful would pass on without seeing him, as he was completely hidden by the dense foliage.

The discordant sound of voices and

instruments drew nearer. Monotonous chants mingled with the beating of drums and clanging of cymbals. The head of the procession soon made its appearance under the trees, some fifty yards away from the position occupied by Mr Fogg and his companions; and they could easily distinguish through the branches the strange performers of this religious ceremony.

First came the priests, wearing mitres and clothed in flowing embroidered robes.

They were surrounded by men, women and children singing a kind of dirge, interrupted at regular intervals by the tom-toms and cymbals. Behind them stood a hideous statue on a car with wide wheels, the spokes and felly of which represented serpents coiled about each other. This car was drawn by four richly-caparisoned zebus. The statue had four arms, the body coloured a dark red, haggard eyes, tangled hair, a lolling tongue and lips tinted with henna and betel. Its neck was circled by a collar of death's heads, its flanks by a belt of cut hands. It stood upright on a prostrate giant without a head.

Sir Francis Cromarty, who recognised the statue, whispered, 'It is the goddess Kali, the goddess of love and death.'

'Of death, possibly, but of love, never!' said

Passepartout. 'Horrible hag!'

The Parsee signed to him to be silent.

Around the statue a group of old fakirs, striped with ochre and covered with cross-wise cuts, from which their blood trickled drop by drop, were bestirring themselves with wild capers and frantic contortions. These stupid fanatics, at the great Hindu ceremonies, will still throw themselves under the wheels of the car of Juggernaut.

Next came a few Brahmins, in all the splendour of their oriental vestments, leading a woman who could scarcely stand. She was a young woman, with a skin as white as a European's. Her head, neck and shoulders, her ears, arms, hands and toes were weighed down with jewels, necklaces, bracelets, ear-rings and rings; and a tunic spangled with gold, and veiled with light muslin, showed the outline of her figure.

In violent contrast to the spectacle presented by this young woman were some guards who followed her, armed with naked sabres hanging from their waists, and long damascened pistols, and carrying a corpse on a palanquin.

This was the body of an old man, clothed in his gorgeous rajah's raiment. As in his lifetime, he wore a turban embroidered with pearls, a robe of silk and gold tissue, a sash of cashmere studded with diamonds, and the splendid weapons of an Indian prince.

Then came musicians and a rearguard of fanatics, whose yells at times drowned the deafening din of the instruments, and who closed the procession.

As Sir Francis Cromarty observed all this ceremony, his face bore a singularly sad expression, and, turning to the guide, he said, 'A suttee.' The Parsee nodded and raised a finger to his lips. The long procession slowly passed away under the trees, and soon its rear ranks disappeared in the depths of the forest.

Little by little the singing died down; yet a few cries were heard in the distance, then at last all this commotion gave place to profound stillness. As soon as the procession had disappeared, Phileas Fogg, who had heard the word uttered by Sir Francis Cromarty, asked what a 'suttee' was.

'A suttee, Mr Fogg,' answered the brigadier-general, 'is a human sacrifice, but a voluntary sacrifice. The woman you have just seen will be burnt tomorrow at early dawn.' 'Oh, the villains!' cried Passepartout, unable to restrain his indignation.

'What about that corpse?' asked Mr Fogg.

'It is the body of the prince, her husband, an independent rajah of Bundelkhand,' said the guide. 'What!' continued Phileas Fogg, in a perfectly calm tone of voice. 'Do these barbarous customs still prevail in India? Have not the English been able to put an end to them?' 'These sacrifices are no longer performed in the greater part of India,' replied Sir Francis, 'but we have no control over these wild regions, over this territory of Bundelkhand in particular. The whole district on the northern slope of the Vindhias is the scene of incessant murder and plundering.'

'Poor wretched woman!' muttered Passepartout, 'to be burnt alive!' 'Yes, burnt alive,' rejoined the brigadier; 'and you cannot imagine what she would have to suffer at the hands of her relatives, if she were not burnt. They would shave off her hair, and feed her on a scanty dole of rice; she would be spurned as an unclean creature, and be left to die in some corner like a mangy dog. So it is frequently the prospect of such a frightful existence, rather than love or religious fanaticism, that drives these poor wretches to self-immolation. Still it occasionally happens that this sacrifice is really voluntary, and it requires the forcible intervention of the Government to prevent it. For instance, a few years ago I was living in Bombay, when a young widow came and requested the governor's permission to be burnt with her husband's body. As you may imagine, the governor refused. Thereupon the widow left the town, took refuge with an independent rajah, and there gave effect to her resolution of self-sacrifice.'

As Sir Francis recorded this incident, the guide shook his head from time to time, and when the brigadier had finished, he said, 'The sacrifice that will take place tomorrow at sunrise is not a voluntary one.' 'How do you know?' 'Everybody in Bundelkhand knows the story,' answered the guide. 'The wretched woman appeared to be offering no resistance,' observed Sir Francis. 'That was because she had been intoxicated with the fumes of hemp and opium.' 'But where are they taking her?' 'To the pagoda of Pillagi, two miles from here. She will pass the night there, awaiting the hour of sacrifice.' 'And the sacrifice will take place when?' 'Tomorrow, at earliest dawn.'

So saying, the guide led the elephant out of the thick cover and scrambled up to his neck. But just as he was about to urge the animal forward by means of a peculiar whistle, Mr Fogg stopped him, and speaking to Sir Francis Cromarty, he said, 'What if we rescued this woman?' 'Rescued this woman, Mr Fogg!' cried the brigadier. 'I have still twelve hours to the good. I can devote them to this.' 'By Jove! You are a man of heart, then!' exclaimed Sir Francis. 'Occasionally,' replied Phileas Fogg quietly, 'when I have time.'

13

*In which Passepartout proves once more
that fortune favours the bold*

The project was a bold one, bristling with difficulties, perhaps impracticable. Mr Fogg was going to jeopardise his life or at the least his liberty, and consequently the success of his plans, but he did not hesitate; and he found a resolute ally in Sir Francis Cromarty. Passepartout was ready for anything, and entirely at the disposal of his master, whose idea excited him to enthusiasm.

He felt there was a warm heart and generous soul under that icy exterior, and began to love Phileas Fogg dearly.

What, now, would be the guide's decision? Would he not be inclined to side with the Hindus? If they could not secure his assistance, they must at any rate make sure of his neutrality. Sir Francis Cromarty frankly asked him what he would do. 'Officer,' replied the guide, 'I am a Parsee, and this woman is a Parsee. I am yours to command.' 'Good,' said Mr Fogg. 'But I must tell you,' resumed the Parsee, 'that we are not only running the risk of losing our lives, but of suffering horrible tortures, if we are caught, so judge for yourselves.' 'That's settled,' replied Mr Fogg. 'I think we must wait until it is dark, before setting to work.' 'I think so, too,' said the guide. The good Indian then proceeded to give them a few particulars concerning the victim. She was a celebrated beauty of the Parsee race, the daughter of a wealthy Bombay merchant. She had received a thoroughly English education in that city, and from her manners and attainments she would be taken for a European. Her name was Aouda. Being left an orphan, she was married against her will to this old rajah of Bundelkhand. Three months after, she became a widow and, knowing the fate that was in store for her, she escaped, but was at once recaptured, and doomed by the rajah's relatives, who were interested in her death, to this sacrifice from which apparently there was no escape.

This narrative only confirmed Mr Fogg and his companions in their generous resolution.

It was decided that the guide should direct the elephant towards the pagoda of Pillagi and get as near to it as possible.

Half an hour later, they halted under cover of a copse, five hundred yards from the pagoda, which was just visible, while the howls of the fanatics were distinctly heard.

The means of reaching the victim were then discussed. The guide was acquainted with the pagoda of Pillagi, in which he asserted the young woman was held captive. Would it be possible to get in by one of the doors, when the whole crowd was plunged in a drunken sleep, or would it be necessary to make a hole in one of the walls? The answer to this question could only be given at the time of action and on the spot. But one thing left no manner of doubt in their minds: it was that the abduction must be carried out that very night, and not after daybreak, when the victim was taken out to die. At that moment no human intervention could save her.

Mr Fogg and his companions waited for the night. As soon as it was dark, about six o'clock, they decided to make a reconnaissance around the pagoda. The last cries of the fakirs were just coming to an end. According to custom, the Indians must be heavily intoxicated with 'bang,' liquid opium mixed with infusion of hemp. It might, therefore, be possible to slip in between them and reach the temple.

Followed by Mr Fogg, Sir Francis and Passepartout, the guide made his way noiselessly through the forest. After crawling ten minutes under the branches, they came to the bank of a small stream, where, by the light of resin burning at the end of iron torches, they saw a pile of wood. This was the pyre, made of costly sandal, and already soaked in perfumed oil. On the top lay the embalmed body of the rajah, which was to be burnt, together with his widow. The pagoda, whose minarets were dimly seen rising above the tops of the trees, stood a hundred yards away from the pyre.

'Come,' whispered the guide. And with the utmost caution he silently slipped through the tall grass, followed by his companions.

Nothing now broke the stillness of night save the soughing of the wind in the foliage.

Ere long the guide stopped on the edge of a glade. The open space was lit up by a few torches, the ground covered with groups of men sleeping the heavy sleep of drunkenness. It looked like a field of battle strewn with the dead. Men, women and children lay huddled together. Here and there, there was still an occasional rattle from the throat of a drunkard or two.

In the background, encompassed by the forest, loomed the temple of Pillagi. But, to the guide's great disappointment, the guards of the rajahs, lighted by smoky torches, were keeping watch at the doors, and walking to and fro with drawn swords. It was reasonable to suppose that the priests, too, were watching inside.

The Parsee went no farther. Having recognised the impossibility of getting into the temple by force, he made his companions retrace their steps.

Phileas Fogg and Sir Francis Cromarty likewise saw that it was useless to attempt anything in this direction. They stopped and discussed the situation in whispers.

'Let us wait a while,' said the brigadier; 'it is only eight o'clock; it is possible these guards may also be overcome by sleep.' 'Yes, it is possible,' answered the Parsee. So Phileas Fogg and his companions lay down at the foot of a tree and waited. Time seemed to stand still. The guide left them now and again to see what was happening on the edge of the wood, but the guards were watching as before by the glimmer of the torches, and a dim light trickled through the windows of the pagoda. They waited thus till midnight, and there was no change; the guards still kept watch outside; to depend on their drowsiness was evidently hopeless. They had probably been spared intoxication from 'bang.' It therefore became necessary to adopt another plan and to gain access to the pagoda by making a hole in the wall.

The next thing to ascertain was whether the priests were watching by their victim as keenly as the soldiers at the door of the temple.

After a last consultation, the guide said he was ready to start, and was followed by Mr Fogg, Sir Francis and Passepartout. They made a rather long detour so as to get round to the back of the pagoda, and reached the foot of the walls by about half-past twelve, without having met anyone. No watch was kept on this side, but then there were absolutely no doors nor windows.

The night was dark. The moon in its last quarter scarcely left the horizon, which was shrouded with heavy clouds, and the height of the trees made the darkness deeper still. To have reached the walls was not enough, however; Phileas Fogg and his companions must manage to make an opening in them; and for this operation they had absolutely nothing but their pocket-knives. Fortunately the walls of the temple were built of bricks and wood, which could be pierced with little difficulty. Once the first brick was removed, the others would come out easily. They set to work as noiselessly as possible. The Parsee on one side and Passepartout on the other exerted themselves to loosen the bricks, so as to contrive an opening two feet wide. They were making good progress, when a cry rang out within the temple, to which almost at once other cries made answer from without. Passepartout and the guide stopped. Were they detected? Was that the alarm being given? The most elementary prudence bade them retire. So the four of them sought cover again in the wood, ready to get to work once more, should the alarm, real or otherwise, pass away. But guards now made their appearance at the back of the pagoda, and took up such a position as to make all approach impossible.

Here was a fatal obstacle. The disappointment of these four men, thus interrupted in their work of rescue, would be hard to describe; for, now that it was impossible to reach the victim, how could they hope to save her?

Sir Francis Cromarty was desperately angry, Passepartout was beside himself, and the guide had some difficulty in keeping him quiet. Fogg, cool as ever, waited on apparently unmoved.

'I suppose all we can do now is to go?' suggested the brigadier in an undertone. 'Yes, go we must, there is nothing else to be done,' answered the guide. 'Wait a bit,' said Fogg, 'I need not be at Allahabad before tomorrow, any time before midday.' 'But what can you hope for?' replied Sir Francis. 'It will be daylight a few hours hence and — ' 'The opportunity which is now slipping from us may occur again at the last moment.'

The brigadier wished he could have read Phileas Fogg's eyes. What had this cool Englishman at the back of his mind? Did he purpose to make a rush at the very moment when the young woman was about to die, and to snatch her openly from her executioners? This would be an act of utter folly, and he could not admit that the man was mad enough for that. Nevertheless Sir Francis consented to see the end of the terrible drama. But the guide did not leave his companions in their present place of concealment; he led them back to the front of the glade, whence, screened by a clump of trees, they surveyed the groups of sleeping humanity.

Meanwhile Passepartout, who had perched himself on the lowest branches of a tree, was revolving an idea which had first crossed his mind like a flash, and had now taken firm hold of it.

He had first said to himself that this idea was sheer madness, and now he kept muttering, 'Why not, after all? It's a chance — possibly the only chance; and with such a besotted crowd!' Passepartout, leaving his plan thus undefined, was soon slipping, with the litheness of a serpent, along the low branches, the ends of which were bent towards the ground.

The hours passed and lighter shades heralded the approach of dawn, though it was still very dark. The moment had come. The slumbering crowd rose as if from the sleep of death. The various groups began to bestir themselves. Tom-toms resounded; songs and cries broke out anew. The hour was at hand when the unfortunate woman must die. The doors of the pagoda burst open, and a brighter light escaped from the interior. Mr Fogg and Sir Francis Cromarty now caught sight of the victim in the vivid glare, as she was being taken out by two priests. It even seemed to them that the wretched woman, obeying the final prompting of the instinct of self-preservation, had shaken off the torpor of intoxication and was endeavouring to escape from her tormentors. Sir Francis Cromarty's heart gave a great throb, and, impulsively gripping Phileas Fogg's hand, he felt that it held an open knife. At this moment the crowd began to move. The young woman, who had fallen back into the state of torpor induced by the fumes of hemp, passed through the fakirs, who accompanied her with their religious bawling.

Phileas Fogg and his companions, mixing with the last ranks of the crowd, followed. In two minutes they reached the bank of the river, and stopped less than fifty paces from the pyre, on which lay the rajah's body. In the semi-obscurity they perceived the victim perfectly inert, lying beside her husband's corpse.

Then a torch was applied, and the wood, soaked with oil, blazed up at once. It was then that Sir Francis Cromarty and the guide held back Phileas Fogg, who, in a moment of generous frenzy, was in the act of dashing towards the pyre. But Phileas Fogg had already thrust them aside, when a sudden change came over the scene.

There was a cry of terror, and the whole multitude fell prostrate, stricken with dismay.

The old rajah, then, was not dead, for here he was rising suddenly like a phantom, taking up the young woman in his arms and coming down from the pyre enveloped in whirling clouds which gave him a spectral appearance!

The fakirs, guards and priests, seized with panic, lay there with their faces to the ground, not daring to lift their eyes and look upon such a miracle.

The insensible victim was carried along in the strong arms that held her, and for which she seemed a light burden.

Mr Fogg and Sir Francis were erect at the same place, the Parsee had bowed his head, and, doubtless Passepartout was no less dumbfounded.

The resuscitated man moved in this manner as far as Mr Fogg and Sir Francis, and there gave the abrupt order, 'Let us be off!'

It was none other than Passepartout, who had made his way to the pyre in the midst of the thick smoke, and, taking advantage of the darkness, which was still opaque, had snatched the young woman from the jaws of death! It was Passepartout who, playing his part with lucky audacity, was able to go right through the crowd during the ensuing panic!

A moment later all four had disappeared in the woods, and the elephant was taking them away at a speedy trot.

But the shouts and hubbub, and a bullet that made a hole in Phileas Fogg's hat, told them that their stratagem was discovered. On the blazing pyre the old rajah's body was now plainly visible, and the priests, recovering from their terror, and perceiving that an abduction had just been effected, rushed headlong into the forest, with the guards close behind them. A volley was fired at the captors, but in a few moments their rapid flight took them beyond the reach of bullets and arrows.

14

In which Phileas Fogg travels down the whole length of the beautiful Ganges without as much as thinking of seeing it

The bold abduction had been quite successful.

An hour later Passepartout was still chuckling over it, and Sir Francis Cromarty exchanged a vigorous handshake with the worthy fellow. His master simply said, 'Well done,' which, from such a man, was high praise. To this Passepartout replied that the whole credit of the affair was his master's. A 'quaint' idea had struck him, and that was all he had had to do with it. It made him laugh to think that for a short time he, Passepartout, the ex-gymnast, ex-sergeant of firemen, had been parted by death from a charming woman, and then become an embalmed old rajah!

As for the young Indian, she knew nothing of what had taken place. She was wrapped up in the travelling-rugs and reposing in one of the howdahs.

Meanwhile the elephant, directed with

unerring skill by the Parsee, was making rapid progress through the forest, though it was still dark; and an hour after leaving the pagoda of Pillagi, he was travelling at great speed across an immense plain. They halted at seven o'clock, and, as the young woman was still in a state of complete prostration, the guide made her drink a little brandy and water; but she was to remain in the grip of this stupor for some time longer. Sir Francis Cromarty, who knew the effects of intoxication produced by inhaling hemp fumes, had no anxiety on her account. But, while he felt quite sure the young Indian would come round, he showed far less confidence with respect to her future. He told Phileas Fogg plainly that, should Aouda remain in India, she would inevitably fall again into the hands of her executioners. These fanatics were to be found throughout the peninsula, and surely, in spite of the English police, they would manage to recapture their victim, were it in Madras, Bombay or Calcutta. And in support of his assertion, Sir Francis mentioned a similar case of recent occurrence. In his opinion the young woman would not be really safe until she had left India.

Phileas Fogg replied that he would keep this in mind and see what could be done. About ten o'clock the guide was at Allahabad;

the interrupted line started there again, and trains ran from Allahabad to Calcutta in less than twenty-four hours. Phileas Fogg would therefore arrive in time to take a boat due to leave Calcutta on the next day, October 25, at noon, for Hong-Kong.

The young woman was taken to a room at the station, and Passepartout was entrusted with the task of purchasing for her various requisites of a lady's toilet — a dress, a shawl, some furs, etc., in fact anything necessary that he could find. His master gave him unlimited credit for the purpose. Passepartout set out at once on his errand, exploring the streets of Allahabad, the 'city of God.' It is one of the most venerated in India, as it stands at the junction of the two sacred rivers, the Ganges and the Jumna, whose waters attract pilgrims from every part of the peninsula. It need scarcely be mentioned that, according to the legend of the Ramayana, the Ganges rises in heaven, and comes down to earth through Brahma's bounty.

While making his purchases, Passepartout saw a good deal of the city, once protected by a very fine fort, which is now a state prison. Allahabad, formerly an industrial and trading centre, has now neither commerce nor industry. Expecting to find a Regent Street with a Farmer and Co. close by, Passepartout looked about for a linen-draper, and saw none. He was at last able to get what he wanted at the second-hand shop of a tough old Jew, who sold him a dress of Scotch material, a large cloak, and a magnificent otter-skin pelisse, for which he readily gave seventy-five pounds. He then returned to the station, immensely pleased with himself.

Aouda was gradually recovering as the effect of the narcotics to which the priests of Pillagi had subjected her wore off, and her beautiful eyes were regaining all their Indian softness.

When the poet king, Usaf Uddaul, celebrates the charms of the Queen of Ahmehnagara, he says:

Her glossy hair evenly parted, encircles the harmonious lines of her soft white cheeks, radiant in their smooth freshness. Her brows, black as ebony, have the shape and potency of the bow of Kama, the god of Love; and beneath her long silken lashes, in the dark pupils of her large clear eyes, swim the purest reflections of celestial light, as in the sacred lakes of Himalaya. Her teeth, small, even and white, sparkle between her smiling lips like dewdrops in the half-closed heart of a pomegranate flower. Her

116

lovely little ears, of symmetric mould, her rosy hands, her small feet, rounded and dainty as lotus-buds, glitter with the brilliance of the finest pearls of Ceylon, the most splendid diamonds of Golconda. Her slim, supple waist, that one hand can circle, sets off the graceful bend of her rounded back and the rich beauty of her bust, where flowering youth displays the most perfect of its treasures; beneath the silken folds of her tunic, she seems to have been modelled in pure silver by the hand divine of Vicvacarma, the eternal statuary.

Without using all this poetic imagery, one may say that Aouda, the widow of the Bundelkhand rajah, was a charming woman in the full European acceptation of the word, and this is enough. She expressed herself in purest English, and the guide had not exaggerated when he affirmed that the young Parsee had been transformed by the manner of her upbringing.

The train was now about to leave Allahabad, and the Parsee guide was paid the sum agreed upon. Mr Fogg did not give a farthing more, which rather surprised Passepartout, who knew what his master owed to the man's devoted service. The Parsee had, in fact, willingly run the risk of losing his life in the Pillagi business, and, should the Hindus hear of this later, he would find it difficult to escape their vengeance.

The next thing was to dispose of Kiouni. What was to be done with an elephant bought at such a price? But Phileas Fogg had already settled the question. 'Parsee,' he said to the guide, 'you have been useful and devoted. I have paid you for your service, but not for your devotion. Would you like the elephant? If so, it is yours.'

The guide's eyes glowed.

'Your honour is giving me a fortune!' he exclaimed. 'Accept my offer,' replied Mr Fogg; 'I shall still be your debtor.'

'Splendid!' cried Passepartout. 'Take him, friend! Kiouni is a right-down good and plucky animal!' He then went up to Kiouni and offered him a few pieces of sugar, saying, 'Here you are, Kiouni; here you are.' The elephant gave a grunt or two of satisfaction, and, seizing Passepartout around the waist with his trunk, lifted him as high as his head. Passepartout, not in the least frightened, gave the animal a friendly pat, and was gently replaced on the ground, and then honest Kiouni's trunk-grip was returned by a hearty hand-grip from the worthy fellow.

A few minutes later, Phileas Fogg, Sir Francis Cromarty and Passepartout, having taken their seats in a comfortable carriage, in which Aouda occupied the best place, were running at full-speed on their way to Benares. The distance between the latter town and Allahabad is at most eighty miles, and the run took two hours.

During the journey the young Indian became herself completely. The effects of the stupefying fumes of the 'bang' had passed away.

What was her amazement on finding herself in this railway carriage, dressed in European garments, and in the company of travellers who were absolute strangers!

Their very first care was to restore her completely, and to this end, among many attentions, they made her drink a few drops of spirit. The brigadier then proceeded to inform her of what had happened to her. He dwelt on the devotion of Phileas Fogg, who had not hesitated to stake his life in order to save hers, and on the happy termination of the adventure, due to Passepartout's bold conception.

Mr Fogg let him speak without uttering one word, while Passepartout, immensely shy, said more than once, 'Not worth mentioning.'

Aouda thanked her deliverers effusively, more by her tears than by her words. Her glorious eyes were even better interpreters of her gratitude than her lips. Then, as her thoughts travelled back to the scenes of the suttee, and she looked once more on this land of India, where she had still so many dangers to face, she shuddered with terror.

Phileas Fogg, who perceived what was passing in her mind, tried to reassure her, and offered, in his coldest manner, to take her to Hong-Kong, where she could stay until the affair had blown over.

The offer was gratefully accepted. It so happened that Aouda had a relation living at Hong-Kong, a Parsee like herself, and one of the leading merchants in that city, which is quite English, though situated off the coast of China.

The train pulled up at Benares at half-past twelve. The Brahminical legends assert that this city stands on the site of ancient Casi, which, like Mahomet's tomb, was once suspended in space between the zenith and the nadir. But in these more realistic days, Benares, called the Athens of India by orientalists, rested quite prosaically on the ground, and Passepartout had a hurried view of its brick houses and wattling huts, giving the place a perfectly desolate aspect, absolutely without local colour.

Sir Francis Cromarty was not going beyond Benares; the troops he was rejoining were encamped a few miles away to the north of the town. He therefore bade Phileas Fogg farewell, wishing him all possible success, and expressing the hope that he might come again, in a less original but more profitable way. Mr Fogg lightly pressed his fingers in return. Aouda took leave of Sir Francis with much more emotion, saying she could never forget all she owed him. As for Passepartout, he was honoured with a hearty shake of the hand, which affected him so much that he asked himself where and when he could give his life for the brigadier. Then Sir Francis Cromarty left them.

After Benares, the railway followed the valley of the Ganges for a time. In sufficiently clear weather the travellers could see through the windows of their carriage the varied landscape of Behar; mountains clothed in verdure, fields of barley, maize and wheat, streams and pools teeming with greenish alligators, well-kept villages, and forests still green. A few elephants and some zebus, with their great humps, came down to bathe in the waters of the sacred river, and parties of Indians, men and women, piously performed their holy ablutions in spite of the advanced season and chilly temperature. These devotees, bitter foes of Buddhism, are fervent followers of the Brahminical religion, with its

121

three godheads, Vishnu, the sun god, Shiva, the divine impersonation of the natural forces, and Brahma, the supreme lord of priests and lawgivers. What must Brahma, Shiva and Vishnu have thought of this anglicised India, when some steamboat scurried screeching by, churning the sacred waters of the Ganges, scaring away the gulls that flitted about on its surface, the turtles teeming on its shores, and the faithful lying all along its banks!

The panorama passed before them like a flash, and its details were often hidden by a cloud of white mist. They had but a fleeting glimpse of the fort of Chunar, twenty miles south-east of Benares, an ancient stronghold of the rajahs of Behar; of Ghazipur and its important rose-water factories; Lord Cornwallis's tomb standing on the left bank of the Ganges; the fortified town of Buxar; Patna, a large manufacturing and commercial centre, the principal seat of the opium trade in India; Monghyr, a more than European town, being as English as Manchester or Birmingham, famous for its iron foundries, and its factories of edge-tools and side-arms, and whose high chimneys besmirched Brahma's sky with murky smoke — brutal assault upon the land of dreams.

Night came, and the train passed on at

full-speed in the midst of the roaring of tigers and bears and the howling of wolves, that scampered off before the engine; and nothing more was seen of the marvels of Bengal — Golconda, the ruins of Gour, Murshidabad, once a capital, Burdwan, Hugli, Chandernagore, that bit of French soil on Indian territory where the sight of his country's flag would have gladdened Passepartout's heart — night hid them all. Calcutta was reached at seven o'clock in the morning, and the boat about to sail for Hong-Kong would not weigh anchor before twelve. Phileas Fogg had five hours to spare. According to his time-table he was to arrive at the Indian capital on the 25th of October, twenty-three days after leaving London, and he had arrived on the appointed day. He was therefore neither behind nor before his time. Unfortunately the two days he had gained between London and Bombay had been lost, as we have seen, in the journey across the Indian peninsula, but we may reasonably suppose that Phileas Fogg did not regret them.

15

In which the bag containing the bank-notes is again lightened by a few thousand pounds

When the train stopped, Passepartout was the first to get down; then came Mr Fogg, who helped his fair young companion out of the carriage.

Phileas Fogg intended to go straight to the Hong-Kong boat, in order to see Aouda comfortably settled for the voyage. He was anxious to be with her until she left a country so full of danger for her.

Just as he was leaving the station, a policeman walked up to him and said, 'Mr Phileas Fogg?' 'That is my name.' 'Is this man your servant?' asked the policeman, pointing to Passepartout. 'Yes.' 'Be good enough to follow me, both of you.'

Mr Fogg showed not the slightest sign of surprise. This man was a representative of the law, and the law is sacred to all Englishmen.

Passepartout, being a Frenchman, tried to argue, but the policeman tapped him with his stick, and Phileas Fogg motioned to him to obey.

'May this young lady come with us?' asked Mr Fogg. 'She may,' replied the policeman.

Mr Fogg, Aouda and Passepartout were taken to a *palki-gari*, a sort of four-wheeled carriage for four people, drawn by two horses, and they were driven away. The *palki-gari* took about twenty minutes, and no one spoke on the way. They first passed through the 'black town,' with its narrow streets, between rows of hovels in which swarmed a squalid, ragged cosmopolitan population; then through the European town, with its cheery brick houses, and shady coco-nut trees, and its forest of masts. Although it was early morning, smart-looking men on horse-back and splendid equipages were already passing to and fro.

The *palki-gari* stopped before an unpretentious-looking house, which was obviously not a private residence. The policeman requested his prisoners to descend — I say prisoners because they really might be considered as such — and conducted them into a room with barred windows, where he said to them, 'You will appear before Judge Obadiah at half-past eight.' He then withdrew and shut the door.

'So we are trapped!' exclaimed Passepartout, limply sitting down on a chair.

'Sir,' said Aouda to Mr Fogg with ill-concealed emotion, 'you must leave me to my fate! It is on my account that you are being prosecuted; it is because you saved me.'

To this Phileas Fogg simply replied that the thing was not possible, that it was not admissible that he could be prosecuted for that suttee business, as the plaintiffs would never dare to come forward. There was a mistake somewhere. He added that, in any case, he would not abandon her, but would take her to Hong-Kong.

'But the boat leaves at twelve!' observed Passepartout. 'We shall be on board before twelve,' was all his imperturbable master replied, but it was said with such positive assurance, that Passepartout could not help saying to himself:

'Why, of course, we shall be on board before twelve!' But he felt anything but comfortable about it.

At half-past eight the door opened, and the policeman ushered the prisoners into the adjoining room. This was the court, and the part reserved for the public was occupied by a fairly numerous gathering of Europeans and natives.

Mr Fogg, Aouda and Passepartout sat

down on a bench opposite the seats reserved for the magistrate and the clerk of the court.

A moment after, Judge Obadiah, a stout, rotund-looking man, entered, followed by the clerk. He took down a wig hanging on a nail and put it on hurriedly.

'The first case,' said he; then, raising his hand to his head, he exclaimed, 'Hallo! This is not my wig!' 'No, my lord, it is mine,' answered the clerk.

'My dear Mr Oysterpuf, pray tell me how a judge is to pass a just sentence in a clerk's wig!'

They then exchanged wigs. During these preliminaries, Passepartout was fuming with impatience, for the hand of the big clock in the court-room seemed to be travelling around the dial at a terrible pace.

'The first case,' repeated Judge Obadiah. 'Phileas Fogg?' called out the clerk.

'Here,' answered Mr Fogg. 'Passepartout?' 'Here!' replied Passepartout. 'All right,' said the judge. 'Prisoners at the bar, the police have been looking for you on every train from Bombay for the last two days.' 'But what is the charge against us?' cried Passepartout, getting out of patience. 'This you will now be told,' replied the judge. 'I am an Englishman, sir,' said Mr Fogg, 'and am entitled to . . . ' 'Have you been ill-used?' interrupted the judge. 'Not in the least.'

'Well, then, bring in the plaintiffs.'

At the judge's order, a door swung open, and three priests were shown in by an usher.

'That is it, of course,' muttered Passepartout; 'there are the scoundrels who wished to burn our young lady!'

The priests remained standing before the judge, and the clerk read in a loud voice a charge of sacrilege against Phileas Fogg and his servant, who were accused of having violated a place consecrated by the Brahmin religion.

'You have heard the accusation?' the judge asked Phileas Fogg. 'Yes, sir,' replied Mr Fogg, consulting his watch, 'and confess' 'Ah! You confess?' 'I confess, and I am waiting for these three priests to confess in their turn what they intended to do in the pagoda of Pillagi.'

The priests looked at each other, apparently unable to understand anything of the defendant's statement. 'Certainly!' cried Passepartout indignantly; 'at the pagoda of Pillagi, in front of which they were about to burn their victim!'

The priests were again astounded, and the judge asked in amazement, 'What victim? Burn whom? In the heart of Bombay?' 'Bombay?' exclaimed Passepartout. 'Yes,

Bombay. This has nothing to do with the pagoda of Pillagi, but with the pagoda of Malabar Hill.'

'And as a proof,' added the clerk, 'here are the desecrator's shoes.' And he deposited a pair of shoes on his desk. 'My shoes!' exclaimed Passepartout, who, in his intense surprises could not keep back this impulsive cry.

The confusion which had taken place in the minds of master and man is obvious. They had clean forgotten this incident of the Bombay pagoda, for which they were now arraigned before the Calcutta magistrate.

Detective Fix, fully grasping all the advantage he could derive from that unfortunate affair, had postponed his departure by twelve hours, and had taken upon himself to advise the priests of Malabar Hill. He held out to them the prospect of heavy damages, knowing full well that the English Government treated this sort of offence with great severity. The next step he took was to send them off by the next train in pursuit of the culprit. But as a result of the time spent in rescuing the young widow, Fix and the Hindus arrived in Calcutta before Phileas Fogg and his servant, whom the magistrates, instructed by telegram, were to arrest as they stepped out of the train. One may imagine

Fix's disappointment on hearing that Phileas Fogg had not yet reached the capital. He naturally inferred that the thief he was tracking had stopped at one of the stations of the Peninsular Railway and taken refuge in the Northern Provinces. For twenty-four hours Fix looked out for him at the station, a prey to the most harassing anxiety. Imagine his exultation when, that very morning, he saw him get down from the train, howbeit in the company of a young woman whose presence he could not understand. He at once directed a policeman to take him into custody, and thus it was that Mr Fogg, Passepartout and the widow of the Bundelkhand rajah were brought before Judge Obadiah.

Had not Passepartout's attention been so engrossed by his case, he would have noticed the detective in a corner of the court, watching the proceedings with an interest which was quite intelligible, for he was in the same position at Calcutta as he had been at Bombay and Suez: he was still without the warrant. Judge Obadiah took note of the confession that had escaped Passepartout, who would have given all he had in the world to recall his rash utterance.

'The facts are admitted?' asked the judge.
'They are admitted,' replied Mr Fogg coldly.

'Inasmuch,' continued the judge, 'as English law makes a point of giving equal and strict protection to all the religions of the peoples of India, and as the offence is admitted by the man Passepartout, convicted of having desecrated with sacrilegious foot the floor of the Malabar Hill pagoda at Bombay, during the 20th of October, I condemn the said Passepartout to go to prison for fifteen days and to pay a fine of three hundred pounds.' 'Three hundred pounds!' cried Passepartout, to whom the fine alone was a matter of concern. 'Silence!' yelped the usher.

'And,' added Judge Obadiah, 'inasmuch as it is not substantially established that there was no connivance between the servant and his master, and as, in any case, the master must be held responsible for the doings of a paid servant, I condemn the said Phileas Fogg to eight days' imprisonment and a fine of one hundred and fifty pounds. Clerk, call up the next case.'

Passepartout was stunned by this sentence, which spelt ruin for his master. It meant the loss of a wager for twenty thousand pounds, and all because, like a silly fool, he had walked into that cursed pagoda.

Phileas Fogg, just as cool as if the judgement had nothing to do with him, had not even frowned. But, just as the clerk was calling up another case, he stood up and said, 'I am prepared to give bail.' 'That is your right,' replied the judge. Fix felt a cold shiver down his back, but regained his composure when he heard the judge declare, 'As Phileas Fogg and his servant are strangers, each of them will have to find bail for the enormous sum of one thousand pounds.'

Should Mr Fogg fail to serve his sentence, it would cost him two thousand pounds. 'Here is the money,' said Phileas Fogg; and from the bag in Passepartout's keeping he took out a bundle of banknotes, which he placed on the clerk's desk.

'This money will be returned to you when you leave prison,' said the judge. 'In the meantime you are liberated on bail.'

'Come along,' said Phileas Fogg to his servant.

'The least they can do is to return the shoes!' cried Passepartout angrily; whereupon the shoes were given back to him.

'A precious sum they have cost!' he muttered. 'More than a thousand pounds each! And they are not even comfortable!'

Passepartout, thoroughly disgusted with things, followed Mr Fogg, who offered his arm to Aouda. Fix still hoped that the thief would never make up his mind to forfeit the sum of two thousand pounds, and that he would serve his sentence of eight days' imprisonment. He therefore hurried out after Fogg.

Mr Fogg at once took a carriage for himself and his two companions, and they drove off. Fix thereupon ran behind the carriage, which soon stopped on one of the quays. Half a mile away, in the roadstead, the *Rangoon* lay at anchor, with the blue peter at the mast-head. Eleven o'clock was striking; Mr Fogg was an hour in advance of time.

Fix saw him get down from the carriage and put out in a small boat with Aouda and his servant. The detective stamped his foot with rage. 'The scoundrel is off once more!' he cried. 'Two thousand pounds gone! None more wasteful than a thief! I'll shadow him to the end of the world, if I must, but at this rate there will be nothing left of the stolen money.'

The detective had some ground for this conclusion, for, what with travelling expenses, bribes, elephant buying, bails and fines, Phileas Fogg had already frittered away more than five thousand pounds since leaving London, and the percentage on the sum recovered, assigned as a reward for the detectives, was constantly growing less.

16

In which Fix appears to know nothing of what is said to him

The *Rangoon*, one of the P. & O. liners plying in the Chinese and Japanese seas, was an iron screw-propelled boat, of seventeen hundred and seventy tons gross, and nominally of four hundred horse-power. She was as fast as the *Mongolia* but not so well appointed. So Aouda was not so comfortable as Phileas Fogg would have liked. But the passage was one of only three thousand five hundred miles, a matter of eleven or twelve days, and the young woman made a point of being easily pleased.

During the first days of the voyage, Aouda became better acquainted with Phileas Fogg, and lost no opportunity of showing him her intense gratitude; but all her protestations, apparently at least, left the phlegmatic gentleman perfectly cold; he listened, but neither by voice nor manner did he betray the slightest emotion. He took care that Aouda should have every possible comfort, and regularly came at certain hours to talk with her, or rather to hear her talk. While doing all that the strictest politeness could require, he behaved to her with just the graciousness and spontaneity that an automaton might have shown, whose movements had been contrived for the purpose.

Aouda was rather puzzled by this attitude, but Passepartout enlightened her to some extent on his master's eccentric character. He told her of the wager which was hurrying him round the world. This made Aouda smile, but, after all, she owed Phileas Fogg her life, and he could only gain in her estimation by being seen through the medium of her gratitude. The guide's narrative of her touching history was confirmed by Aouda herself. It was quite true that she belonged to the Parsee race, which holds the first rank among the natives. Many Parsee merchants have made great fortunes in India in the cotton trade. One of them, Sir James Jejeebhoy, received a title from the English Government, and Aouda was related to this wealthy person, who lived in Bombay. As a matter of fact, it was a cousin of his, Jejeeh by name, whom she hoped to join at Hong-Kong. Whether he would give her the protection and assistance she needed, she could not say. Mr Fogg assured her that there was no cause for anxiety, and that everything would be arranged mathematically, which was the very word he used. How far Aouda understood this horrible adverb it is hard to say, but her great eyes looked into Mr Fogg's, her great eyes, 'clear as the sacred lakes of Himalaya,' yet the unconscionable Fogg, reserved as ever, did not seem disposed to throw himself into the lake.

The first part of the voyage was accomplished in excellent conditions. The weather was mild, and throughout a long stretch of the immense bay the liner was favoured by wind and sea.

The *Rangoon* soon came in sight of Great Andaman, the principal island of the group, made conspicuous to navigators from a very great distance by its picturesque mountain, the Saddle-Peak, rising to a height of two thousand four hundred feet.

The ship passed fairly close inshore, but the savage aborigines of the island, rightly placed at the lowest grade of humanity, but wrongly termed cannibals, were not to be seen.

The panorama presented by these islands was superb. The foreground was a mass of forests of fan-palms, areca, bamboo, nutmeg, teak, gigantic mimosa and arborescent ferns, and behind this maze of greenery the mountains rose in graceful outlines against the sky. Along the coast swarmed in their thousands the precious swallows, whose edible nests are esteemed a great delicacy in the Celestial Empire. But all this varied landscape of the Andaman Islands was soon out of sight, and the *Rangoon* passed on rapidly towards the Straits of Malacca, through which she would enter the China seas.

And now, what was Detective Fix doing all this while, unfortunately faced as he was with the prospect of a compulsory voyage around the world? Leaving instructions at Calcutta that the warrant, should it arrive, was to be dispatched to him at Hong-Kong, he had managed to embark on the *Rangoon* without being seen by Passepartout, and he hoped to conceal his presence till the ship reached her destination. For it would be no easy matter to account for his being on board without arousing Passepartout's suspicions, as Passepartout could not but think he was still in Bombay. Nevertheless the force of circumstances induced him quite logically to change his mind and to renew his acquaintance with the worthy fellow; and it happened in this wise.

The one spot in the whole world on which all the detective's hopes and wishes were centred was Hong-Kong; for the boat's stay at Singapore would be too short to allow him to take effective steps there. The arrest must therefore be made at Hong-Kong, or the thief would escape him irretrievably.

Hong-Kong was English soil, but it was the last English soil they would touch. Beyond that, China, Japan, America, all held out to the man Fogg a practically safe retreat.

Should Fix at last find at Hong-Kong the warrant of arrest, which must have been sent after him post-haste, he would arrest Fogg and give him into the custody of the local police. It was quite simple. But beyond Hong-Kong, a mere warrant of arrest would not be sufficient; an extradition order would be necessary. That would mean endless delays and difficulties of all sorts, of which the rogue would take advantage to get away for good.

If his plans failed at Hong-Kong, it would be very difficult, if not quite impossible, to resume operations with any chance of success.

During the long hours which he spent in his cabin, Fix kept repeating to himself, 'One of two things — either the warrant will be at Hong-Kong, in which case I shall arrest my man; or it will not be there, and then I must at all cost find means to delay his departure. I failed at Bombay, I failed at Calcutta; if I fail at Hong-Kong, it is all up with my reputation. I must succeed, cost what it will. But, should it prove necessary, how on earth am I to delay the cursed fellow's departure!'

Should everything else come to naught Fix had quite made up his mind to tell Passepartout everything and show him the true character of his master. Passepartout, who without a doubt was no accomplice, when enlightened by this disclosure would most probably join hands with the detective, if only from fear of being himself implicated in Fogg's offence. But, after all, this was a risky expedient, not to be tried until everything else had failed, for one word from Passepartout to his master would be enough to ruin everything. The detective was in the midst of these sorely perplexing reflections, when the presence of Aouda on the *Rangoon* in Phileas Fogg's company opened up a vista of new possibilities.

Who was this woman? By what concurrence of circumstances had she become Fogg's companion? They had obviously met somewhere between Bombay and Calcutta; but where? Was this meeting of Phileas Fogg with the fair young traveller the result of chance, or was Fogg's journey across India undertaken with the express object of joining this charming damsel? For charming she was;

Fix had noticed the fact in the court-room at Calcutta.

Naturally the detective was intensely interested and puzzled. The possibility of a criminal elopement occurred to him. The possibility soon became a probability, and then a fixed idea, and he realised the great advantage he could derive from this state of affairs. Whether the young woman was married or not, it was a case of elopement, and, at Hong-Kong, it would be possible to create such difficulties for the culprit that no amount of money would set him free.

But he must act before the *Rangoon* reached Hong-Kong. The fellow had an abominable habit of jumping out of one boat into another, and might be a long way off before the matter was in hand. Fix must therefore warn the English authorities and signal the coming of the *Rangoon* before Fogg could get ashore. This was easy, since the ship stopped at Singapore, which is in telegraphic communication with the Chinese coast. However, before acting, and in order to work with greater certainty, Fix decided to question Passepartout. He knew it was easy enough to make him talk, and he made up his mind to remain concealed no longer, as there was no time to be lost. It was now the 30th of October, and the *Rangoon* was due at

140

Singapore on the morrow.

So Fix, leaving his cabin, went on deck with the intention of going up to Passepartout and being the first to show very great surprise. Passepartout was walking about on the forepart of the ship, when the detective rushed at him with the exclamation: 'What! you here on the *Rangoon!*' 'You on board, Mr Fix!' replied Passepartout, in amazement, as he recognised his fellow-passenger of the *Mongolia.* 'This beats me. I left you at Bombay, and here you are on the way to Hong-Kong! Are you, too, going round the world?'

'Oh, no,' replied Fix, 'I intend to stop at Hong-Kong — a few days at any rate.' 'I see,' said Passepartout, who seemed surprised for a moment. 'But how is it I have not seen you once on board since we left Calcutta?' 'Well, the fact is I have been a little queer, a bit sea-sick — I have been lying down in my berth — the Bay of Bengal does not suit me so well as the Indian Ocean. Is your master all right?' 'Perfectly well, and absolutely up to time; not a day late. By the way, Mr Fix, you didn't know that we had a young lady with us.' 'A young lady?' replied the detective, appearing to be completely at a loss to understand what was said to him.

Passepartout soon told him all about

himself. He gave him an account of the incident of the Bombay pagoda, of the purchase of the elephant for two thousand pounds, the suttee affair, the carrying off of Aouda, the sentence of the Calcutta court and their liberation on bail. Fix, who knew the latter part of these happenings, pretended to be completely ignorant of them all, and Passepartout went on talking about his adventures, carried away by the delight of finding a listener who appeared to be so interested in him.

'But,' asked Fix, 'what is the upshot of this going to be? Does your master intend to take this young woman to Europe?' 'Oh, no, Mr Fix, not at all! We are simply going to hand her over to the care of a relative of hers, a rich merchant of Hong-Kong.' 'No go!' said the detective to himself, concealing his disappointment. 'Will you accept a glass of gin, Mr Passepartout?' 'With pleasure, Mr Fix. We will drink in honour of our meeting on board the *Rangoon* — we could scarcely do less.'

17

Concerning a variety of things between Singapore and Hong-Kong

Passepartout and Fix met frequently after this, but the detective was extremely reserved, and made no attempt to make his companion talk. On one or two occasions only did he catch a glimpse of Mr Fogg, who rarely left the saloon, where he either kept Aouda company or took a hand at whist, in accordance with his unvarying habit.

Passepartout now began very seriously to reflect on the strange chance which had once more placed Fix on the same route as his master; he was surprised at the singular coincidence, and no wonder. Here was this very pleasant and certainly most obliging gentleman, first coming across them at Suez, then embarking on the *Mongolia*, landing at Bombay, with the avowed intention of staying there, and now cropping up again on board the *Rangoon*, on the way to Hong-Kong; in fact, dogging Mr Fogg's footsteps. What was this fellow Fix after?

The matter deserved consideration, and

Passepartout did some hard thinking, with the result that he was ready to wager his Turkish slippers, which he had very carefully preserved, that Fix would leave Hong-Kong when they did, and probably on the same boat.

Had Passepartout racked his brain for a century, he would never have guessed the nature of the detective's errand. He never could have imagined that Phileas Fogg was being shadowed around the earth as a thief.

But as it is in human nature to find an explanation for everything, Passepartout, by what seemed to him a flash of intuition, discovered a highly probable reason for Fix's abiding presence. Fix, he concluded, must be an agent sent by Mr Fogg's fellow-members of the Reform Club with orders to follow him closely and ascertain that he really travelled round the world along the route agreed upon.

'That's it! That's it!' repeated the good fellow to himself, very proud of his shrewdness. 'He's a spy sent by these gentlemen to track us! Not a very nice proceeding! To think of their having such an upright and honourable man as Mr Fogg watched by a spy! Ah, gentlemen of the Reform Club, you shall pay dearly for this!'

Delighted with his discovery, Passepartout decided, none the less, to say nothing about it to his master, lest he should be justly offended at this distrust on the part of his adversaries. But he resolved to chaff Fix, whenever he had the opportunity, with obscure allusions, yet without committing himself.

In the afternoon of Wednesday, the 30th of October, the *Rangoon* entered the Straits of Malacca, between the peninsula of that name and Sumatra. Most picturesque islets with very steep mountains hid the main island from view.

At four o'clock in the morning on the next day, the *Rangoon*, twelve hours in advance of her scheduled time, called at Singapore in order to take in a new supply of coal.

Phileas Fogg made a note of the gain, and this time went ashore to accompany Aouda, who expressed the desire to walk for some hours on land. Fix, to whom Fogg's every action appeared suspicious, followed him, taking care he himself should not be seen, while Passepartout, secretly much amused at Fix's slyness, went to make the usual purchases.

The island of Singapore is neither large nor imposing in appearance. There are no mountains, and therefore no sharp outlines. But despite its flatness, it is not lacking in charm. You might call it a park intersected with handsome roads. Mr Fogg and Aouda took a pretty carriage drawn by two of those smart horses imported from New Holland, and were driven through dense groves of palm trees with brilliant foliage, and clove trees on which the very bud of the half-open flower forms the cloves. Bushes of the pepper plant replaced the thorny hedges of European fields; sago-palms, great ferns with their magnificent branches lent variety to the gorgeous beauty of this tropical land; nutmeg trees with glistening leaves filled the air with their all-permeating scent. Troops of nimble, grinning apes peopled the woods, and possibly tigers were not rare in the jungle.

The fact that these terrible beasts of prey have not been utterly exterminated in such a comparatively small island may cause surprise, but their numbers are recruited from Malacca, whence they swim across the intervening strait.

After a two hours' drive in the country, Mr Fogg, who noticed very little of what he saw, brought back his companion to the town, a mass of squat, heavy-looking houses, surrounded by charming gardens luxuriant with the most luscious fruits of the earth, such as the pineapple and mangosteen.

At ten o'clock they re-embarked, unaware that they had been followed all the time by the detective, who likewise had gone to the expense of taking a carriage. They found Passepartout waiting for them on deck. The good fellow had bought several dozen mangosteens, a fruit of the size of an average apple, dark brown outside and bright red inside, and whose white flesh, as it melts in the mouth, gives your real epicure a delicious sensation like none other. He was only too pleased to offer them to Aouda, who was most gracious in her acceptance.

At eleven o'clock the *Rangoon*, having finished coaling, weighed anchor, and a few hours later her passengers lost sight of the high mountains of Malacca, with their forests where lurk the finest tigers in the world.

Some three hundred miles of sea separate Singapore from the island of Hong-Kong, a small English possession off the Chinese coast. It was important for Phileas Fogg that the voyage should not take more than six days, as he would then be in time to catch the boat due to leave Hong-Kong on November 6 for Yokohama, one of the chief ports of Japan.

The *Rangoon* was now heavily loaded, having taken on board a large number of passengers at Singapore, Hindus, Ceylonese, Chinese, Malays and Portuguese, who were mostly second-class travellers. The weather, which had been fine up till then, changed with the last quarter of the moon. The sea became rough, and the wind rose at times to half a gale, but very fortunately blew from the south-east, and was favourable to the ship's progress. When it was not too squally, the captain put up canvas. The *Rangoon*, rigged like a brig, often sailed under her two top-sails and fore-sail, and the double action of steam and wind gave her the greater speed. In this way, on a choppy and at times very trying sea, she forged ahead along the coasts of Annam and Cochin China.

The majority of the passengers were ill, but the *Rangoon* was more to blame than the sea. For the ships of the Peninsular and Oriental Company which ply in the China seas have a serious structural defect. The ratio between their draught when loaded and their depth was wrongly calculated, with the result that their power of resistance to the sea is small. Their watertight bulkheads are not large enough, so they are 'drowned,' as the sailors say; if they ship a few heavy seas, their behaviour is seriously affected. These vessels are therefore very inferior, though not necessarily as regards their motor and evaporating apparatus, to the types of the French Messageries, such as the *Impératrice* and the *Cambodge*. Whereas these vessels, according to the engineers' calculations, can ship a weight of water equal to their own, the boats of the P. & O. Company, the *Golconda*, the *Corea* and the *Rangoon*, would not ship the sixth of their own weight without sinking.

So in foul weather great precautions were necessary, and, at times, the captain had to lay the ship to, under easy steam. This meant a loss of time, by which Phileas Fogg seemed to be completely unaffected, but which aggravated Passepartout beyond measure. He blamed the captain, the engineer and the Company, and consigned to the devil all those who make it their business to convey travellers. It is just possible, too, that his impatience was provoked in no small measure by the thought of that gas-burner which was still on at his expense in the house in Savile Row.

'You seem to be in a great hurry to get to Hong-Kong,' Fix said to him one day. 'Yes, I am,' replied Passepartout. 'You think Mr Fogg is anxious to catch the boat for Yokohama?' 'Frightfully anxious.' 'You do believe in this mysterious journey around the world, then?' 'Absolutely. Don't you, Mr Fix?' 'No, I don't.' 'You sly dog!' replied Passepartout with a wink. This expression made the detective think. The epithet worried him, though he could not say why. Had the

Frenchman found him out? He was puzzled. But no one knew he was a detective; how could Passepartout have discovered that? Yet he could hardly have made use of such words unless he had something at the back of his head.

Passepartout ventured even further on another occasion; he simply could not help himself, his tongue ran away with him. 'Now, then, Mr Fix,' he said to his companion in a quizzing tone, 'shall we have the misfortune to leave you behind in Hong-Kong, when we get there?' 'Well,' answered Fix, rather uncomfortable, 'I can't say. It's just possible that . . . ' 'Ah,' broke in Passepartout, 'I should be so pleased if you would go on with us! Come, surely an agent of the Peninsular and Oriental Company cannot stop on the way, Bombay was your destination, and here you are now almost in China. America is not far away, and it is only a step from America to Europe.'

Fix, watching the other man's face intently, and seeing nothing but the most friendly benevolence there, thought it best to laugh with him. But Passepartout, feeling in the humour for banter, asked him whether his present job was a paying one.

'Yes, and no,' replied Fix, without wincing. 'There is good and bad business in it. But you must understand that I don't travel at my own expense.' 'Oh, you need not tell me that!' exclaimed Passepartout, laughing more heartily than ever.

This was the end of their conversation, and Fix returned to his cabin and began to think. He was evidently found out. In one way or another, the Frenchman had discovered that he was a detective. But had he told his master? What part was he playing in all this? Was he an accomplice or not? Had they wind of his object, in which case the game was up? The detective spent some hours in a state of great perplexity, sometimes thinking that all was lost; then hoping that Fogg knew nothing, and then again unable to decide what line of action to pursue.

Nevertheless, after a time he recovered his coolness of mind, and determined to deal frankly with Passepartout. Should he not be in a position to arrest Fogg at Hong-Kong, and should Fogg be taking steps to leave this English soil, the last they would touch, then he would tell Passepartout everything. One of two things: either the servant was the accomplice of his master, who in that case was aware of the measures taken against him, which made success very doubtful and reserve useless, or the servant had nothing to do with the theft, and it would then be his interest to leave the thief in the lurch.

Such was the respective positions of these two men, while above them Phileas Fogg soared in the majesty of his indifference. He was moving rationally around the world, regardless of the lesser planets that gravitated around him. And yet there was, not far away, what astronomers call a disturbing star, which ought to have produced certain tremors in the gentleman's heart. But it was not so; Aouda's charm failed to act, to Passepartout's great surprise; if any perturbations did exist, they would have been more difficult to calculate than those of Uranus which led to the discovery of Neptune.

This was a daily wonder to Passepartout, who read in Aouda's eyes such heartfelt gratitude to his master.

Very reluctantly he came to the conclusion that Phileas Fogg's heart was just capable of heroic conduct, but quite incapable of love.

As to the worries which the chances of the journey might have caused him, there was not a trace of any; whereas Passepartout lived in a state of perpetual alarm. One day, as he was leaning on the breast-rail of the engine-room, watching the powerful engine, he saw it race away from time to time, when, owing to a heavy pitch of the vessel, the screw was spinning round wildly in the air, and the steam rushing out through the valves; this made the good fellow very angry.

'Those valves are not sufficiently weighted!' he cried. 'We are not getting on at all! It's just like the English! If this were an American ship, we might blow up, but we should be going faster!'

18

*In which Phileas Fogg, Passepartout and
Fix attend to their business, each on his
own account*

During the latter days of the voyage, the
weather was rather rough. The wind, which
had settled in the north-west, delayed the
ship's progress, and made her roll heavily,
owing to her want of stability. The passengers
suffered a good deal from the long nauseating
waves which the wind churned up from the
open sea.

On the 3rd and 4th of November they
encountered almost a gale, which lashed
the sea with fury, and compelled the
captain to lay to for half a day, while the
ship was kept on her course with only ten
revolutions of her screw, and in such
manner as to receive the waves aslant. All
sail had been taken in, but even the rigging
was a great strain, as it laboured, whistling
in the squalls.

The ship's pace was, of course, considerably slowed, and it was reasonably estimated
that she would reach Hong-Kong twenty

hours behind time, and even more if the storm continued.

Phileas Fogg contemplated this raging sea, that seemed to be battling against him personally, with his usual serenity. His brow was not clouded for one moment, although a delay of twenty hours might be the cause of failure by making him miss the boat at Yokohama. But the man had no nerves; he was neither impatient nor annoyed. It really seemed as though this storm formed part of his programme and had been foreseen. When Aouda discussed this set-back with him, she found him calm as ever.

For Fix the matter had a very different aspect. The storm delighted him. His satisfaction would have been boundless, if the *Rangoon* had been forced to turn and run before the hurricane. All these delays fitted in with his schemes, for they would compel this man Fogg to remain a few days in Hong-Kong. At last the heavens themselves were taking a hand on his side with their gusts and squalls. True he was a little seasick, but what did that matter! While his body writhed in the grip of nausea, he heeded it not, for his spirit exulted with exceeding great joy. One can easily imagine with what ill-concealed wrath Passepartout went through this trying time. Earth and sea had hitherto seemed to be at his master's service; steamers and trains at his beck and call; wind and steam had joined forces in furthering his voyage. But now it looked as though the hour of disappointments had struck. Passepartout was as truly racked as if the twenty thousand pounds of the wager were to come from his own pocket. He was exasperated by the storm, infuriated by the squall, and ready to scourge the rebellious sea. Poor fellow! Fix took care not to let him see how delighted he was; and he was wise, for had Passepartout had an inkling of his secret satisfaction, Fix would have had a rough time of it. Throughout the storm Passepartout stayed on deck; it would have been quite impossible for him to remain below. He climbed up the masts and lent a helping hand everywhere with the clever agility of a monkey, to the astonishment of the crew. The captain, officers and sailors were worried by him with endless questions, and could not help laughing at seeing a man in such a flurry. He insisted on knowing how long the gale would last, whereupon he was told to go and consult the barometer, which still showed no sign of rising. He shook the barometer, but with no result, for neither shaking nor the curses which he heaped upon the irresponsible instrument had the least effect.

At long last, however, the hurricane abated, and during the 4th of November the sea became less rough; the wind shifted through two points of the compass to the south, and was once more favourable. Passepartout brightened up with the weather. The top-sails and lower sails were set, and the *Rangoon* proceeded once more at her highest speed. It was, however, impossible to make good all the time that had been lost. That could not be helped, and land was not signalled before the 6th, at five o'clock in the morning. According to Phileas Fogg's time-table the liner was to arrive on the 5th. He would therefore be twenty-four hours late, and would necessarily miss the connection with Yokohama.

At six o'clock the pilot stepped on board the *Rangoon* and went up on the bridge in order to steer the ship through the fair-way into Hong-Kong harbour.

Passepartout was dying to ask him if the Yokohama boat had sailed, but he dared not, preferring to keep a little hope to the last minute. He had confided his anxiety to Fix, who, sly fox that he was, tried to comfort him by telling him that if the worst came to the worst, Mr Fogg would take the next boat, but this, of course, only made Passepartout furious.

Mr Fogg, feeling none of Passepartout's

restraining apprehensions, consulted his *Bradshaw*, and asked the said pilot, in his quiet way, whether he knew when there would be a boat for Yokohama.

'At high tide tomorrow morning,' replied the pilot. 'Is that so?' said Mr Fogg, without showing the slightest surprise.

Passepartout, who heard this, would have been happy to embrace the pilot, whilst Fix would have gladly wrung his neck.

'What is the name of the ship?' asked Mr Fogg. 'The *Carnatic*,' replied the pilot. 'Was she not due to sail yesterday?' 'Yes, sir, but one of her boilers had to undergo repairs; so her departure was put off till tomorrow.' 'Thank you,' answered Mr Fogg, who then returned to the saloon, descending with that automatic step of his.

As for Passepartout, he gripped the pilot's hand, gave it a hearty squeeze and said: 'Pilot, you are a brick!'

Doubtless the pilot never knew why his answers were rewarded with this effusive demonstration. On hearing a whistle, he went up again on the bridge, and guided the steamer through the flotilla of junks, tankas, fishing-boats, and ships of every kind which crowded Hong-Kong harbour. At one o'clock the *Rangoon* was berthed, and the passengers were landing.

It cannot be denied that chance had been singularly kind to Phileas Fogg on this occasion. But for this necessary repair to her boilers, the *Carnatic* would have left on the 5th of November, and the passengers for Japan would have had to wait eight days for the sailing of the next boat. True, Mr Fogg was twenty-four hours late, but this loss of time could not affect adversely the remainder of the journey, for the steamer plying between Yokohama and San Francisco ran in direct connection with the Hong-Kong boat, and could not sail before her arrival. Of course, they would leave Yokohama twenty-four hours late, but the voyage through the Pacific lasts twenty-two days, and in that time it would be easy to make good these twenty-four hours. So Phileas Fogg, thirty-five days after leaving London, was twenty-four hours behind his time-table.

As the *Carnatic* would not leave Hong-Kong before five o'clock next morning, Mr Fogg had sixteen hours to attend to his business in that town: that is to say, to arrange for Aouda's future. On landing, he offered her his arm and took her to a palanquin.

On his inquiring for some hotel, the men mentioned the Club Hotel, and the palanquin moved on, followed by Passepartout, and twenty minutes after they reached their destination. A room was engaged for the young woman, and Phileas Fogg, having seen that she had all she wanted, told her he was going to try and find the relative in whose care he was to leave her, and directed Passepartout to remain at the hotel until he returned, that she should not be left there alone.

Mr Fogg then drove off to the Stock Exchange, feeling sure that a person who ranked among the richest merchants of the town must be well known there.

Mr Fogg applied to a broker for the information he desired, and was told by this broker, who knew the merchant Jejeeh, that he had left China two years before. Having made his fortune, he had gone to Europe to live; to Holland, it was thought, which was natural, as he had had a great deal to do with that country in the course of his commercial career.

Phileas Fogg returned to the Club Hotel, and at once asked if he could see Aouda. Going straight to the point, he informed her that her relative was no longer in Hong-Kong, but was probably living in Holland.

Aouda at first said nothing; then, passing her hand over her forehead, she remained thinking a while, whereupon in her gentle voice she said, 'What am I to do, Mr Fogg?' 'It is very simple,' he replied. 'Return with us to Europe.' 'But I cannot abuse your . . . ' 'You abuse nothing, and your presence does not interfere in the least with my plan. Passepartout?'

'Sir.' 'Go and engage three cabins on the *Carnatic*.'

Passepartout hurried out on his errand, delighted that he was not to lose the company of the young woman who always treated him with great kindness.

19

*In which Passepartout takes too keen
an interest in his master, and the
consequence*

Hong-Kong is a small island which was
secured to England by the Treaty of Nanking,
after the war of 1842. In a few years the
colonising genius of Great Britain created
upon it the important seaport town of
Victoria. The island is situated at the mouth
of the Canton River, not more than sixty
miles from the Portuguese city of Macao, on
the opposite shore. In the commercial
struggle between the two settlements, Hong-
Kong necessarily defeated her rival, and now
the greater part of the Chinese transit trade
is carried on through the English town.
With docks, hospitals, wharves, warehouses,
a Gothic cathedral, a Government house,
macadamised streets, Hong-Kong looks
exactly like a busy town in Kent or Surrey
transported through the globe to this Chinese
locality, almost at the Antipodes.

Passepartout, his hands in his pockets,
made his way towards Victoria Port, gazing at

the palanquins, the hand-chairs with sails, still in favour in the Celestial Empire, and the crowds of Chinese, Japanese and Europeans that thronged the streets. It was all very much like Bombay, Calcutta or Singapore over again. There is thus, so to speak, a trail of English towns all round the world.

Passepartout, arriving at Victoria Port, at the mouth of Canton River, found a swarming mass of ships of every nation — English, French, American, Dutch, some of them men-of-war, Japanese or Chinese boats, junks, sampans, tankas, and even flower-boats, dotting the water like so many floating flower-beds. As he strolled, Passepartout observed a certain number of natives dressed in yellow, all very old. On going into a barber's shop to get shaved in the Chinese fashion, he was told by the local Figaro, who spoke English fairly well, that these old people were octogenarians at least, and that in consequence they were entitled to wear yellow, the imperial colour. This struck Passepartout as very funny, though he did not quite know why. After his shave, he proceeded to find the quay whence the *Carnatic* would sail, and saw Fix walking to and fro. He was not surprised at finding the detective there, but noticed that his face showed signs of intense disappointment.

'Good!' said Passepartout to himself. 'Things are not going well for the gentlemen of the Reform Club.' He went up to Fix with his sunny smile, appearing not to notice his companion's chagrin.

It was not without good reason that the detective was cursing the infernal bad luck that dogged his steps. Still no warrant! It was evident that the warrant was being dispatched after him, and that it would not get to him unless he could remain a few days in this town. Now Hong-Kong was the last English territory on the route, and this man Fogg would escape him for good and all, if he failed to find some device for keeping him here.

'Well, Mr Fix, have you made up your mind to come with us as far as America?' asked Passepartout. 'Yes,' replied Fix through clenched teeth. 'Come, come!' cried Passepartout, breaking into a loud guffaw. 'Didn't I know that you could not leave us? Come and book your passage; come along.' Thereupon they went together to the Company's office and engaged cabins for four persons.

The clerk informed them that the *Carnatic's* repairs were finished, and that the ship would consequently sail that very evening at eight o'clock, and not next morning, as had been announced.

'All the better!' replied Passepartout. 'This will fit in excellently with my master's plans. I will go at once and let him know.'

At this moment Fix decided on an extreme measure, and determined to tell Passepartout everything, as it was perhaps the only means at his command for keeping back Phileas Fogg a few days at Hong-Kong.

When they left the office, Fix offered his companion a drink. Passepartout, having plenty of time, accepted the invitation. There was a pleasant-looking tavern on the quay, and they went in and found themselves in a large, well-decorated room, at the far end of which was a camp-bed, covered with cushions, and on this bed lay a certain number of persons asleep. Some thirty customers were seated at small tables made of plaited rushes. A few were draining mugs of English beer or porter; others jugs of spirits, gin or brandy. Most of them were also smoking long red-clay pipes stuffed with small pellets of opium mingled with attar of roses. From time to time one of the smokers, overcome by the fumes, would slip under the table, and the waiters, taking him by the head and feet, carried him away and deposited him on the camp-bed beside a fellow-sleeper. About twenty of these inebriates were thus laid out on the bed, side by side, in the last stage of stupefied intoxication.

Fix and Passepartout perceived that the place they were in was a smoking-house, a haunt of those besotted, emaciated, idiot wretches to whom England, in her commercialism, sells every year ten million four hundred thousand pounds' worth of that fatal drug called opium. A mournful revenue this, raised from one of the most deadly vices of humanity!

The Chinese Government has in vain tried to put a stop to the evil by stringent laws. The use of opium was at first strictly confined to the wealthy, but it gradually reached the lower classes, and the havoc it worked could not be arrested. Opium is smoked everywhere and on all occasions in the Middle Kingdom. Men and women are addicted to this deplorable craze, and once accustomed to inhale these fumes, they cannot leave off the habit without experiencing horrible spasms of the stomach. A great smoker can smoke as many as eight pipes a day, but he dies in five years.

It was one of these dens, of which there are any number even in Hong-Kong, that Fix and Passepartout entered to get something to drink. Passepartout had no money, but he readily accepted his companion's friendly offer, intending to return the compliment on some future occasion.

Two bottles of port were ordered, to which the Frenchman did ample justice, whilst Fix, drinking more cautiously, observed him with the closest attention. They chatted about one thing and another, and in particular about Fix's splendid idea of booking a berth on the *Carnatic*. Talking of the ship reminded Passepartout of her sailing some hours before the time announced, so, the bottles being empty, he got up to go and inform his master.

Fix detained him. 'One moment,' he said. 'Why do you wish me to stay, Mr Fix?' 'I want to talk to you about a serious matter.' 'A serious matter!' exclaimed Passepartout, drinking a few drops of wine left at the bottom of his glass. 'Well, we can talk about that tomorrow. I have no time today.' 'Stay,' replied Fix, 'this concerns your master.' On hearing this, Passepartout looked at Fix attentively, and the expression on his face struck him as being so strange that he sat down again and said, 'Well, what is this that you have to say to me?' Fix laid his hand impressively on his companion's arm, and, lowering his voice, said, 'You have found me out?' 'Of course I have!' said Passepartout, smiling. 'Then I am going to tell you everything — ' 'Now that I know everything, my friend! No, I cannot call it very clever.

However, go ahead. But let me tell you at once that those gentlemen have gone to very useless expense.' 'Useless!' said Fix. 'That's all very well! You evidently don't know how large the sum is.' 'Yes, I do,' replied Passepartout. 'Twenty thousand pounds.' 'Fifty-five thousand!' returned Fix, pressing the Frenchman's hand. 'What!' cried Passepartout, 'do you mean to say Mr Fogg dared! — Fifty-five thousand pounds! — Well, then, that's all the more reason for not losing a moment,' he added, getting up once more. 'Fifty-five thousand pounds!' resumed Fix, making Passepartout sit down again, and ordering a bottle of brandy, 'and if I am successful, I shall get two thousand pounds. I will give you five hundred, if you will help me.' 'Help you?' cried Passepartout, whose eyes were almost out of their sockets. 'Yes; help me keep this man Fogg here in Hong-Kong for a few days.'

'Eh, what!' cried Passepartout; 'it is not enough for them to send a man on my master's track and suspect his honour; now they want to put obstacles in his way! I blush for these gentlemen!' 'Whatever do you mean?' asked Fix. 'What I mean is that this is nothing but a shabby trick. They might just as well plunder Mr Fogg and pick his pockets!' 'Well, that is just what we hope to do sooner or later.'

'Then it's a case of foul play!' cried Passepartout, getting more and more excited under the effect of the brandy which Fix kept on pouring out to him, and which he drank without noticing what he was doing. 'It's regular foul play! And gentlemen, too! Colleagues!' Fix was getting more and more bewildered. 'Colleagues!' exclaimed Passepartout. 'Members of the Reform Club! Let me tell you, Mr Fix, that my master is an honest man, and that when he makes a bet, he means to win it honourably.'

'But who on earth do you think I am?' asked Fix, looking at him intently. 'You're an agent of the Reform Club, of course. And your business is to check my master's journey. This is so humiliating a proceeding that I have taken great care not to tell Mr Fogg what you were up to, although I found you out some time ago.' 'Doesn't he know?' asked Fix eagerly. 'He knows nothing,' replied Passepartout, once more draining his glass.

The detective passed his hand across his forehead, thinking what he should say next, and wondering what to do. Passepartout's mistake seemed quite genuine, but made his plan all the more difficult of execution. The fellow obviously spoke in perfect good faith, and was not his master's accomplice, as Fix might have feared.

'Well, then,' he said to himself, 'since he is not his accomplice, he will help me.'

Once again the detective decided on a line of action, having no time to wait, as at any cost he must arrest Fogg at Hong-Kong. 'Listen,' said Fix sharply. 'Hear me out attentively. I am not what you imagine; that is, I am no agent of the members of the Reform Club — '

'Pooh!' broke in Passepartout, looking at him with an air of mockery.

'I am a police-inspector, sent out on special duty by Scotland Yard — ' 'You a police-inspector?' 'Yes, I am,' resumed Fix; 'and I will prove it. Here is my warrant.' Thereupon the official took a paper from his pocket-book and showed his companion a warrant signed by the head of the London Police. Passepartout, absolutely dumbfounded, gazed at Fix, unable to utter a word. 'Fogg's wager,' continued Fix, 'is nothing but a blind, which has taken you all in, you and his fellow-members of the Reform Club. He found it useful to secure your unconscious complicity.' 'But why?' exclaimed Passepartout.

'Listen. On the 29th of last September, a theft of fifty-five thousand pounds was committed at the Bank of England by a person whose description was fortunately obtained. Now this description is in every feature a true one of the man Fogg.'

'What nonsense!' cried Passepartout, striking the table with a bang of his powerful fist. 'My master is the most honourable man in the world!'

'What do you know about it?' answered Fix. 'How can you know the man? You entered his service the very day of his departure, and he left in a hurry, on a senseless pretext, without luggage, and taking with him a huge sum in banknotes. And yet you make bold to maintain he is an honest man!' 'Yes, yes,' repeated the poor fellow mechanically.

'Do you want to be arrested as his accomplice?' Passepartout buried his distorted countenance in his hands. He dared not look the detective in the face. Phileas Fogg a thief! The saviour of Aouda, a man so eminently generous and brave, a thief! And yet how black things looked against him! Passepartout strove to reject the suspicions which were stealing into his mind. He refused to believe his master guilty.

'Well, what do you want of me?' he said, controlling his feelings by a supreme effort.

'This is the point,' replied Fix. 'I have tracked Fogg as far as here, but I have not yet received the warrant of arrest for which I applied in London. You must therefore help me to keep him back here in Hong-Kong.' 'You want me to — !' 'And I will share with you the reward of two thousand pounds to be given by the Bank of England.' 'Never!' replied Passepartout, who tried to rise, but fell back, feeling that both his reason and his strength were leaving him.

'Mr Fix,' he stammered, 'even though everything you have told me were true, though my master were the thief you are looking for, which I deny, I have been, and am still in his service. I have never seen him anything but good and generous. I betray him! Never! No, not for all the gold in the world. They don't eat that sort of bread where I come from.' 'You refuse?' 'I refuse.' 'Then take it that I have said nothing, and let us drink on it.' 'All right, let us drink!'

Passepartout felt he was getting more and more intoxicated. Fix, seeing that, come what might, he must separate him from his master, decided to incapacitate him completely. There were a few pipes filled with opium on the table. Fix slipped one of these into Passepartout's hand. He seized it, raised it to his lips, lit it, drew a few puffs out of it, and collapsed, stupefied by the narcotic.

'At last!' said Fix, seeing Passepartout down and out. 'That man Fogg will not be informed in time of the hour of sailing of the *Carnatic;* and, if he does get away, he will at all events go without that cursed Frenchman.'

He then paid the bill and left the tavern.

20

In which Fix comes into contact with Phileas Fogg

While this was taking place at the opium-den, Mr Fogg, little suspecting the danger that threatened him, was walking leisurely with Aouda in the streets of the English quarter. Aouda having accepted his offer to take her to Europe, a great many things, made necessary by such a long voyage, had to be thought of. An Englishman like Mr Fogg might possibly travel round the world with a carpet-bag, but a lady could not undertake such a journey in the same way. Clothing and other objects needed for prolonged travel had to be procured. Mr Fogg accomplished his task with characteristic composure, and whenever the young widow offered apologies or objections, feeling embarrassed by so much kindness, he invariably replied: 'It will conduce to the success of my journey; it is all part of my programme.'

Having made their purchases, they returned to the hotel and dined at a sumptuous table d'hôte; after which Aouda, feeling rather tired, shook hands with her impassive deliverer, as is the English custom, and retired to her room. Mr Fogg spent the whole evening immersed in the reading of *The Times* and *Illustrated London News*.

If anything could have surprised him, it would have been the failure of his servant to appear at bedtime. But, as he knew the boat would not leave for Yokohama until the next morning, the matter caused him no anxiety. Next morning Passepartout did not answer his master's bell, and Mr Fogg was told that his servant had not returned to the hotel. What he thought of it, no one could have told, for all he did was to take his travelling-bag, send word to Aouda, and order a palanquin.

It was then eight o'clock; at half-past nine it would be high tide, and the *Carnatic* would then be able to leave port. The palanquin having arrived, Mr Fogg and Aouda got into this comfortable conveyance, and their luggage followed them in a wheel-barrow. Half an hour later the travellers descended on the quay, and Mr Fogg was told that the *Carnatic* had sailed the day before. He had expected to find the liner and his servant, and now he was forced to face the loss of both. But his face showed not the slightest sign of disappointment, and as Aouda looked at him anxiously,

175

all he said was, 'It is a mere incident, madam; nothing more.' At this moment a man who had been observing him attentively came up to him. It was Fix, who bowed, saying, 'Were you not, sir, like myself a passenger on the *Rangoon*, which arrived yesterday?' 'Yes, I was, sir,' replied Mr Fogg coldly, 'but I have not the honour — ' 'Excuse me, but I expected to find your servant here.' 'Do you know where he is, sir?' asked Aouda eagerly. 'What!' replied Fix, feigning surprise, 'is he not with you?' 'No,' answered Aouda. 'We have not seen him since yesterday. I wonder if he sailed on the *Carnatic* without us?' 'Without you, madam?' replied the detective. 'But, excuse my question, was it your intention, then, to go by this boat?' 'Yes, sir.' 'It was mine too, and I am extremely disappointed. Her repairs being completed, the *Carnatic* left Hong-Kong twelve hours sooner than she was expected to do, and without notice, and now we shall have to wait a week for the next boat.'

As he uttered the words, 'a week,' Fix felt his heart leap with joy. A week! Fogg kept back a week in Hong-Kong! This would give him time to receive the warrant. At last luck was showing itself favourable to the representative of the law.

One can imagine what a stunning blow he received when he heard Phileas Fogg say in his cool, quiet tone of voice: 'But it seems to me there are other ships besides the *Carnatic* in Hong-Kong harbour.' And Mr Fogg, offering his arm to Aouda, made his way to the docks in search of a ship about to sail.

Fix followed in a state of amazement; it looked as though he were tied to this man by a thread.

Chance, however, quite seemed to have deserted the man it had hitherto served so well. For three hours Phileas Fogg thoroughly searched the docks, having decided to charter a ship, if necessary, to convey him to Yokohama. But all the vessels he saw were either loading or unloading, and consequently could not make ready for sea. Fix began to hope again.

Nevertheless Mr Fogg, not in the least disconcerted, was about to continue his search, even at Macao, when he was accosted by a sailor on the outer harbour.

'Is your honour looking for a boat?' asked the sailor, uncovering. 'Have you a boat ready to sail?' asked Mr Fogg. 'Yes, your honour, a pilot-boat, No. 43 — the best one of the lot.' 'Is she a fast boat?' 'Her speed is from eight to nine knots an hour, near as can be. Would you like to see her?' 'Yes.' 'You'll be pleased with her, sir. You want to go for a trip?' 'No, for a voyage.' 'A voyage?' 'Will you undertake to carry me to Yokohama?'

On hearing this proposal the sailor stood with his arms limp at his sides and his eyes wide open. 'Your honour is joking?' he said.

'No. I have missed the *Carnatic*, and I must be at Yokohama on the 14th at latest, to take the boat for San Francisco.' 'I am sorry,' replied the sailor, 'but the thing is impossible.' 'I am prepared to give you a hundred pounds a day, and a bonus of two hundred pounds, if I get there in time.'

'Are you in earnest?' asked the pilot. 'Very much in earnest,' answered Mr Fogg. The pilot stood aside, looking at the sea; he was evidently pulled one way by the desire to earn a huge sum of money, and another by the fear of venturing so far away. Fix was on the rack. Mr Fogg, turning to Aouda, said to her, 'You are not afraid, madam?' 'Not with you, Mr Fogg,' she replied.

The pilot now came forward, fidgeting with his hat. 'Well, pilot?' said Mr Fogg. 'Well, your honour,' he replied, 'I cannot endanger my men, myself and you, by undertaking such a long voyage on a boat of scarcely twenty tons, and at this time of the year. Besides, we should not get there in time, for it is sixteen hundred and fifty miles to Yokohama.' 'Not more than sixteen hundred,' said Mr Fogg. 'That makes no difference.' Fix breathed freely. 'But,' continued the pilot, 'we might possibly manage it another way.' Fix choked. 'What way?' asked Phileas Fogg. 'By going to Nagasaki, in the extreme south of Japan, a distance of eleven hundred miles, or even to Shanghai, which is eight hundred miles from this port. The latter voyage would not take us far from the Chinese coast, which would be a great advantage, all the more that the currents run northward.' 'Pilot,' answered Phileas Fogg, 'it is at Yokohama that I must take the American mail-boat, not at Shanghai or Nagasaki.'

'Why not?' replied the pilot. 'The San Francisco boat does not start at Yokohama. Yokohama and Nagasaki are ports of call, but the port of departure is Shanghai.' 'Are you sure of that?' 'Quite sure.' 'When does the boat leave Shanghai?' 'On the 11th, at seven o'clock in the evening. This gives us four days to do it in. Four days make ninety-six hours, so that with an average speed of eight knots an hour, if we are in luck, if the wind remains in the south-east, and if the sea is calm, we can cover the eight hundred miles between here and Shanghai.' 'When can you start?' 'In an hour. I just want time enough to buy provisions and get under sail.' 'Done! You are the skipper of the boat?' 'Yes, I am John Bunsby, master of the *Tankadere*.' 'Would you like some earnest-money?' 'If it is not inconvenient to your honour.' 'Take these two hundred pounds on account.' Then Phileas Fogg turned round and said to Fix, 'Sir, if you care to avail yourself of — ' 'I was just going to ask this favour of you,' replied Fix resolutely. 'All right; we shall be on board in half an hour.' 'But what about your poor servant?' said Aouda, who was excessively worried by Passepartout's disappearance. 'I shall do all I possibly can for him,' answered Phileas Fogg. Fix, nervous, restless and fuming, went to the pilot-boat, and Mr Fogg and Aouda made their way to the Hong-Kong Police Station, where Mr Fogg gave Passepartout's description and left sufficient money to take him back to France. Similar steps were taken at the French consulate, and, after going to the hotel to fetch their luggage, they returned in the palanquin to the outer harbour. At three o'clock punctually, pilot-boat No. 43, with her crew on board and her provisions stowed away, was ready to set sail.

The *Tankadere* was a beautiful little schooner of twenty tons, long in the beam, with fine bows and graceful lines. She looked like a racing yacht. Her shining brass and galvanised ironwork, her deck white as ivory, all pointed to the care and skill with which her master, John Bunsby, kept her seaworthy and smart. Her two masts leaned backward a little; she carried spanker, foresail, fore-staysail, jibs, and could put up canvas to run before the wind. She was obviously a very fast sailer, and, as a matter of fact, she had won several prizes in pilot-boat races. The crew of the *Tankadere* was composed of the skipper, John Bunsby, and four men, fearless seamen, who in all weathers ventured out in search of ships in need of them, and were perfectly familiar with the Chinese seas. John Bunsby, a man of forty-five or so, sturdy, sunburnt, keen-eyed, with a strong face, thoroughly steady and devoted to his business, would have inspired confidence in the most timid.

Phileas Fogg and Aouda went on board, whither Fix had preceded them.

Aft the hood led down the hatchway to a square cabin, the sides of which bulged out so as to form cots above a circular divan. In the middle stood a table lighted by a swinging-lamp. There was not much room, but everything was neat.

'I am sorry I have nothing better to offer you,' said Mr Fogg to Fix, whose only answer was a bow. The detective felt something like humiliation at benefiting thus by Fogg's kindness. 'Certainly,' he thought, 'the man is a polite rascal, but a rascal none the less.'

The sails were hoisted at ten minutes past three, and the English flag fluttered at the schooner's gaff. As the passengers sat on deck, Mr Fogg and Aouda looked once more at the quay, in the hope of seeing Passepartout turn up. Fix was by no means free from anxiety, for chance might have brought to this very spot the unfortunate fellow whom he had treated so abominably, and in that case an explanation and indignant reproaches would have followed, which must have proved anything but advantageous for the detective. But the Frenchman was not to be seen; doubtless he was still in the grip of the stupefying narcotic.

Skipper John Bunsby having at last gained the open sea, the *Tankadere* took the wind under her spanker, foresail and jibs, and leaped forward over the waves.

21

In which the master of the Tankadere
runs great danger of losing a
bonus of two hundred pounds

This voyage of eight hundred miles, on a craft of twenty tons, was a dangerous venture, especially at that time of the year. The Chinese seas are generally rough and liable to sudden squalls of terrible violence, particularly during the equinox; and it was still early November. It would undoubtedly have been to the pilot's advantage to take his passengers to Yokohama, since he was paid so much per day. But he would have been very rash in attempting such a long voyage in these conditions; it was bold enough, not to say foolhardy, to sail up the coast as far as Shanghai. But John Bunsby had full confidence in his *Tankadere*, which rose to the wave like a gull, and he was perhaps justified.

During the last hours of the day, the *Tankadere* made her way through the capricious channels of Hong-Kong, and, whether under full sail or close-hauled, or with wind astern, she behaved admirably.

'Pilot,' said Phileas Fogg, just as the schooner was coming out into the open sea, 'I need not urge upon you the necessity for making all possible speed.' 'Your honour can leave that to me,' replied John Bunsby. 'We are carrying all the canvas the wind will let us. Our jibs, far from helping, would only make her labour and reduce her pace.' 'This is your job, not mine, pilot, and I trust you.'

Phileas Fogg, with body erect and legs well apart and firmly planted like a sailor, watched the heavy sea without faltering. The young woman, seated aft, was not unmoved, as she gazed on that ocean, already darkened in the twilight, whose fearsome perils she was facing on a frail vessel. Above her head stretched the white sails, hurrying her through space like huge wings, for the schooner seemed to be lifted by the wind and actually flying.

Night came. The moon was entering her first quarter, and her feeble light would soon flicker out altogether behind the misty horizon. Clouds were driving up from the east, and had already overcast a part of the heavens. The pilot had hung out his lights, a very necessary precaution in these seas crowded with ships making port. Collisions were of frequent occurrence and, at the speed she was going, the schooner would have been shattered by the slightest shock.

Fix, in the fore part of the ship, was buried in thought. Knowing Fogg's uncommunicative disposition, he remained apart; all the more that he disliked talking to this man whose assistance he had accepted. The future, too, claimed his attention. It seemed a certainty that Fogg would not stop at Yokohama, but would at once take the boat for San Francisco, so as to get to America, where the vast extent of the country would ensure for him both impunity and security. Phileas Fogg's plan, he thought, was simplicity itself. Instead of sailing from England to the United States, like an ordinary malefactor, the fellow had taken a very roundabout way, travelling through three-quarters of the globe, in order to reach the American continent the more surely, where, having thrown the police off his track, he would enjoy in peace the thousands of pounds stolen from the bank. But once they landed in the United States, what was he, Fix, going to do? Should he let the man go? No; a hundred times no! He would hold on to him until he obtained an extradition order. It was his duty, and he would fulfil it to the end. At all events there was now one thing in his favour. Passepartout was no longer with his master. After Fix's confidential revelations, it was more than ever necessary that they never should come together again.

Phileas Fogg also was thinking about Passepartout, and his very strange disappearance. Looking at the matter in every way, he came to the conclusion that it was not impossible that, through some misunderstanding, the poor fellow had at the last moment embarked on the *Carnatic*. This was also Aouda's opinion. She felt keenly the loss of this honest servant to whom she owed so much. There was, then, just a possibility that they might find him at Yokohama, and it would be easy to ascertain whether he had arrived there on board the *Carnatic*. About ten o'clock it began to blow. It might have been wise to take in a reef, but the pilot, after scanning the sky with great care, left the ship rigged as she was. As a matter of fact, the *Tankadere* carried canvas admirably, for she drew a great deal of water, and everything was in readiness to take in sail, in case of a sudden squall.

At midnight Phileas Fogg and Aouda went below. Fix was there already, lying on one of the cots. The pilot and his men remained all night on deck. On the next day, November 8, at sunrise, the schooner had sailed more than a hundred miles. The log, repeatedly consulted, showed an average speed of between eight and nine miles. With every sail taking the wind fully, the *Tankadere* was making the best speed of which she was capable. Should the wind hold as it was, the chances were in her favour.

During the whole of that day the *Tankadere* kept fairly close to land, where the currents helped her. The coast was not more than five miles distant on her port quarter. Its irregular outline was occasionally visible when the mist cleared. As the wind blew from the land, the sea was not so heavy, which was fortunate for the schooner, for small vessels labour a great deal in the swell, which breaks their speed, or, as sailors say, 'takes the life out of them.' The breeze abated a little and set in from the south-east. The pilot put up the jibs, but two hours after they had to be taken down again, for the wind freshened anew.

Mr Fogg and Aouda, happily proof against sea-sickness, ate the ship's preserves and biscuit with a good appetite. Fix was invited to join them, and could not refuse, as he knew that food was as necessary for the human stomach as ballast for the ship's hold, but it galled him. To travel at this man's expense and live on his provisions struck him as being rather unfair; still, eat he must, and eat he did, though it was only a snack. When the meal was over, he thought it his duty to take Fogg apart, and said, 'Sir,' — the word blistered his lips; it was all he could do not to collar this 'gentleman.' 'Sir, it was very kind of you to offer me a passage, but, although I am not in a position to spend as freely as you do, I must insist on paying my share — ' 'Don't mention it, sir,' replied Mr Fogg. 'Indeed, I absolutely must — ' 'No, sir,' repeated Fogg in a tone which admitted of no reply. 'This is only one item in my general outlay.' Fix felt as if he would choke; he bowed and went to lie down at full length on the fore-deck. He never spoke another word for the rest of that day.

Meanwhile they were going fast, and John Bunsby was in high hope. He told Mr Fogg more than once that they would get to Shanghai in time, to which Mr Fogg merely answered that he depended upon it. Moreover the whole crew of the little schooner worked with a will; the worthy fellows being greatly stimulated by the attractive reward to be gained. There was not a sheet but was properly taut, not a sail but was vigorously set. The man at the helm could not have been blamed for a single yaw. The seamanship would not have been more strictly correct in a race of the Royal Yacht Club regatta.

In the evening the log showed a run of two hundred and twenty miles since leaving

Hong-Kong, and Phileas Fogg might hope that, on reaching Yokohama, he would have no loss of time to record in his diary, and in that case the first serious mishap he had experienced since his departure from London would probably not interfere at all with his success.

Before dawn next morning the *Tankadere* was sailing right into the straits of Fo-Kien, which separate the large island of Formosa from the Chinese coast, and she crossed the Tropic of Cancer. The sea was very trying in the straits, which are full of eddies formed by the counter-currents. The schooner laboured greatly amid the chopping waves, which broke her progress, and it became very difficult to stand on deck.

At daybreak the wind began to blow harder, and the sky showed signs of a coming gale. The barometer, too, announced an early change of weather by its daily vagaries, the mercury rising and falling fitfully. And the sea in the south-east was seen to rise in long surges, ominous of storm. The evening before, the sun had gone down in a red mist, in an ocean sparkling with phosphorescent light.

The pilot, having long scanned the threatening appearance of the heavens, muttered something between his teeth. At a certain moment, happening to be near Mr Fogg, he said to him in a low voice: 'May I tell your honour frankly what is in my mind?' 'Of course,' replied Phileas Fogg. 'Well, we are in for a squall.' 'Will it come from the north or the south?' asked Mr Fogg quietly. 'From the south. Look, there's a typhoon on the way.' 'It's all right; if it's a typhoon from the south, it will blow us in the right direction,' answered Mr Fogg. 'If that is the way you look at it, I have nothing more to say,' replied the pilot.

John Bunsby's forebodings proved only too well-grounded. At a less advanced season of the year the typhoon — to use a celebrated meteorologist's words — would have passed away like a luminous cascade of electric flames, but at a time of winter equinox it was to be feared that it would break out with great fury.

The pilot took his precautions in advance. All sails were furled and the yards lowered on deck. The poles were struck and the boom taken in. The hatches were securely battened down, so that not a drop of water could get into the hull. A single triangular sail, a storm-jib of strong canvas, was hoisted as a fore-stay-sail, so as to keep the schooner's stern to the wind. Then they waited.

John Bunsby strongly urged his passengers

to go below; but to be confined in a small space almost without air, and tossed about by the surge, was anything but pleasant. Mr Fogg and Aouda, and even Fix, refused to leave the deck.

The raging storm of rain and wind fell upon them about eight o'clock. Though she had but one little bit of sail, the *Tankadere* was lifted like a feather by this wind, which defies accurate description when it blows its worst. To compare its velocity to four times the speed of a locomotive going on full steam would be short of the truth. During the whole of that day the vessel scudded northward, carried along by the monstrous waves, fortunately not lagging behind them in speed.

Twenty times she was on the point of being overwhelmed by the mountainous seas that rose behind her, but a skilful shift of the helm by the pilot prevented the catastrophe. The passengers were at times smothered in spray, but bore it stoically. Fix cursed, without a doubt, but Aouda, her eyes never leaving her companion, whose coolness filled her with admiration, showed herself worthy of him, and, unafraid, faced the tempest at his side. As for Phileas Fogg, the typhoon might have been a detail in his programme.

Up till now the *Tankadere* had held her course to the north, but towards evening the wind, as was to be feared, veered threequarters and blew from the northwest. The schooner, now broadside on to the waves, was horribly shaken. The sea struck her with a violence simply appalling for anyone who does not know how solidly all the parts of a ship are knit together. At nightfall the gale increased in fury. Seeing that the hurricane grew worse as the darkness grew more dense, John Bunsby became seriously alarmed; and, thinking it might be time to put into some port, he consulted his men, after which he approached Mr Fogg, and said, 'I think, your honour, we should do well to make for one of the ports on the coast.' 'I think so too,' replied Mr Fogg. 'Ah!' said the pilot. 'Now which shall it be?' 'There is but one for me,' answered Mr Fogg quietly. 'And which is that?' 'Shanghai.' For some moments the pilot failed to understand the meaning, the purposeful tenacity of the answer. Then he exclaimed, 'Well, yes, your honour is right. Shanghai it will be!' So the *Tankadere* was steadfastly kept on her northward course. It was a perfectly terrible night; that the small craft did not capsize was a miracle. She was twice swept by the seas, and everything would have been washed overboard had the gripes failed.

Aouda was thoroughly exhausted, but not one complaint escaped her lips. Repeatedly Mr Fogg had to rush to her help against the violence of the waves.

Day reappeared. The storm was still raging with extreme fury, but the wind now returned to the south-east. This was a favourable change, and the *Tankadere* once more forged ahead on this vile sea whose waves now clashed with those that sprang from the new direction of the wind. Caught in the trough of these conflicting surges, any boat less stoutly built would have been crushed out of existence.

From time to time one caught glimpses of the coast through rifts in the mist, but there was not a ship in sight. The *Tankadere* alone kept at sea.

At noon there were some signs that the wind was abating, and, as the sun went down on the horizon, the lull became more marked. The storm had been too violent to last very long. The passengers, who were now dead-beat, could take a little food and rest a while. The night was comparatively quiet. The pilot made some use of his sails, and the schooner made considerable progress. On the next day, the 11th, at daybreak, after examining the coastline, John Bunsby was able to declare that Shanghai was not a hundred miles off. A hundred miles, and this was the last day they had to cover the distance. Mr Fogg had to reach Shanghai that very evening, otherwise he would miss the boat to Yokohama. But for the storm, which had caused a loss of several hours, he would at this moment have been within thirty miles of Shanghai port.

The breeze was slackening perceptibly; unfortunately the sea was slackening too. All sails were set; jibs, stay-sails, flying-jib, every bit of canvas was out, and the sea foamed under the boat's stem. By twelve o'clock the *Tankadere* was not more than forty-five miles away from her destination. Six hours remained in which to make the port before the departure of the Yokohama boat.

All on board were in a state of painful suspense. Everybody, no doubt with the exception of Phileas Fogg, felt his heart throb with impatience. Everybody wanted to get to port in time at any cost. It was absolutely necessary that the little schooner should keep up an average speed of nine miles an hour, and the wind went on dropping! It was a fitful breeze, blowing from land in capricious gusts, which left the sea quite smooth as soon as they had passed. Still, the *Tankadere* was so light, her upper sails of fine material caught every flurry so well that John Bunsby, with a helpful current behind him, found himself at six o'clock no more than ten miles from the mouth of Shanghai River; the town is at least twelve miles farther up.

At seven o'clock they were still three miles from Shanghai. The pilot let fall an angry oath as he saw the bonus of two hundred pounds slipping from his grasp. He looked at Mr Fogg. Mr Fogg was quite unmoved, though at this moment his whole fortune was at stake.

At this moment, too, a long, black, spindle-shaped object, crowned with a plume-like tuft of smoke, appeared on a level with the water. It was the American liner leaving at the appointed time.

'Curse it!' cried John Bunsby, thrusting away the helm with a jerk of despair.

'Signal her,' said Phileas Fogg quietly.

A small brass cannon lay on the foredeck of the *Tankadere*, for the purpose of making signals in foggy weather. This gun was loaded to the muzzle, but, just as the pilot was about to apply a red-hot coal to the touch-hole, Mr Fogg said to him, 'Put your flag at half-mast.' The flag was lowered at half-mast, which was a signal of distress. It was reasonable to hope that the American ship, on seeing it, would alter her course for a moment so as to stand by the pilot-boat.

'Fire!' said Mr Fogg. And the report of the small brass cannon burst upon the air.

22

In which Passepartout sees that, even at the Antipodes, it is wise to have some money in one's pocket

The *Carnatic*, having left Hong-Kong on November 7, at half-past six in the evening, directed her course at full speed towards Japan. She carried a full cargo, and her full complement of passengers. Two quarter-deck cabins were unoccupied, those which had been engaged by Phileas Fogg.

Next morning the men in the bow of the ship were somewhat surprised to see a passenger, who looked half-dazed, whose step was shaky and hair ruffled, come out of the second-class hatchway and totter as far as some spars, on which he sat down.

The passenger was no other than Passepartout. What had happened was this.

A few moments after Fix left the opium-den, two attendants lifted Passepartout, fast asleep, and carried him to the bed reserved for smokers. But three hours later, pursued even in his nightmares by a fixed idea, Passepartout woke up and struggled against the stupefying action of the narcotic. The thought of duty unfulfilled shook off his torpor. He left the drunkards' bed and, stumbling, supporting himself against the walls, falling and getting up again, but ever irresistibly impelled by a sort of instinct, he came out of the den, shouting as in a dream, 'The *Carnatic*! the *Carnatic*!' The liner lay close by with steam up, ready to start. Passepartout had only a few yards to go. He rushed on to the gangway, went as far as the foredeck and there fell down insensible, at the very moment when the *Carnatic* was casting off. Sailors are used to scenes of this kind, so two or three carried the poor fellow down into a second-class cabin, and, when he awoke next morning, he was a hundred and fifty miles from China.

Thus it was that on that morning Passepartout found himself on the deck of the *Carnatic*, and came up to open his lungs to the fresh sea-breeze. The air sobered him. He began to collect his thoughts, which he found anything but easy work. At last he recalled the happenings of the day before, Fix's revelations, the opium-den, etc.

'Certainly,' said he to himself, 'I was made abominably drunk! What is Mr Fogg going to say? Anyhow I did not miss the boat, which is the main thing.' Then he thought of Fix: 'As for that fellow, I hope and believe we are rid of him, and that he did not dare follow us on the *Carnatic* after his proposal to me. A police-inspector, a detective on the track of my master, accused of robbing the Bank of England! What utter nonsense! Mr Fogg is no more a thief than I am a murderer.' Ought he to tell his master? Was it advisable to inform him of the part Fix was playing in this matter? Would it not be better to wait until Mr Fogg reached London, and then let him know that an agent of the Metropolitan Police had been shadowing him around the world? How they would laugh over it! Yes, that was the best course; no doubt of it. At all events, it was worth considering. But the first thing to do was to go to Mr Fogg, and obtain his pardon for the outrageous conduct of which he had been guilty.

The sea was rough and the boat rolled heavily, so the good fellow, getting on his feet, managed to reach the after-deck, not without difficulty, as his legs were still very unsteady. He saw nobody on deck who was like his master or Aouda. 'That's all right,' he said, 'Aouda has not got up yet, and Mr Fogg has probably found a partner and is playing whist as usual.' Thus soliloquising, he went down to the saloon. Mr Fogg was not there. The only thing to be done was to ask the purser which was Mr Fogg's cabin. The purser told him he didn't know of any passenger of that name. 'I beg your pardon,' continued Passepartout insistently, 'the man I mean is a tall gentleman, who is very reserved and talks very little, and has a young lady with him.'

'We have no young lady on board,' replied the purser. 'But here is the list of the passengers. See for yourself.'

Passepartout read the list through. His master's name was not there. He was staggered; then an idea flashed through his mind. 'I am not mistaken, I am on the *Carnatic* all right, am I not?' 'Yes,' answered the purser. 'Bound for Yokohama?' 'Certainly.' Passepartout had feared for one moment that he had got into the wrong boat. But, if it was true he was on the *Carnatic*, it was equally true his master was not. Passepartout collapsed in an armchair; it was a crushing blow. Then, all of a sudden, the whole thing dawned on him. He remembered that the hour of sailing of the *Carnatic* had been advanced, that he was to have informed his master of the fact, and that he had failed to do so. It was his fault, then, that Mr Fogg and Aouda had missed the boat.

Yes, it was his fault, but it was still more the fault of the traitor who, in order to separate him from his master and keep the latter in

Hong-Kong, had tempted him to drink to intoxication! He now quite understood the detective's trickery. By this time Mr Fogg was ruined to a certainty, for his bet was lost; he was arrested, possibly in prison!

At this thought Passepartout tore his hair. Ah! if ever Fix should fall into his hands, what a settling of scores there would be! After a time Passepartout shook off his overwhelming depression and became calm enough to consider his position, which was anything but pleasant. Here was he, a Frenchman, on the way to Japan. He was bound to get there; how should he get back? His pocket was empty. He hadn't a shilling, not a penny! But his passage had been paid for in advance, so that he had five or six days in which to make up his mind. His consumption of food and drink during this passage would beggar all description. He ate for his master, for Aouda and for himself. He ate as if Japan, the land on which he would soon set foot, were a howling wilderness, where no food whatever could be found.

On the 13th the *Carnatic* entered the port of Yokohama on the morning tide. Yokohama is an important port of call in the Pacific. All boats carrying mails or passengers between North America, China, Japan and the Malaysian Islands, put in there. It is situated in the Bay of Yeddo, at a short distance from that huge city, the second capital of the Japanese Empire, once the residence of the Tycoon, in the days when the civil emperor existed, and a rival of Meako, the great city which is the seat of the Mikado, the spiritual emperor, descended from the gods.

The *Carnatic* took up her moorings in Yokohama harbour alongside the quay, near the custom-house, in the midst of a multitude of ships of all nations.

Passepartout set foot on this curious land of the Sons of the Sun without feeling the least excitement. Having nothing better to do than let chance take him where it would, he started to walk haphazard about the streets. He found himself at first in a perfectly European town, of which the houses with low fronts were adorned with verandas, under which ran graceful peristyles. This part of Yokohama covered, with its streets, squares, docks and warehouses, the whole space between the 'promontory of the Treaty' and the river. Here, as at Hong-Kong and Calcutta, swarmed a medley of all races, Americans, English, Chinamen, Dutchmen, merchants prepared to sell and buy anything. The Frenchman, in the midst of this crowd, felt as completely stranded as if he had been dropped among the Hottentots.

There was certainly one way in which Passepartout could get assistance: he could go to the French or English consul at Yokohama. But he was loath to tell his story, so intimately connected with his master's. Before having recourse to this extreme measure, he resolved to exhaust all other possible means of facing his desperate position.

Having wandered about the European quarter without meeting with the slightest luck, he made his way into the native part of the city, determined, if necessary, to push on to Yeddo.

The Japanese quarter of Yokohama is called Benlen, from the name of a sea goddess worshipped on the neighbouring islands. There Passepartout saw beautiful avenues of fir and cedar trees, sacred gates of strange architecture, bridges hidden under bamboos and reeds, temples sheltering in the wide-spread gloom of secular cedars, convents within whose walls the priests of Buddhism and the sectaries of Confucius led a negative existence, unending streets in which one might have gathered a regular harvest of pink-complexioned and red-cheeked children, little people who looked as if they had been cut out of some native screen, and who were disporting themselves in the midst of short-legged poodles and yellowish tailless cats, with lazy, wheedling ways.

The streets were alive with people going to and fro, processions of bonzes beating their monotonous tom-toms, yakoonins, custom-house and police officers in pointed hats encrusted with lacquer, and carrying two swords hanging from their belts, soldiers clothed in blue cotton stuff with white stripes, and armed with percussion guns, men-at-arms of the Mikado, cased in their silken doublets, hauberks and coats of mail, and numbers of other military men of all ranks; for in Japan the soldier's profession is as highly respected as it is despised in China. Then Passepartout saw mendicant friars, long-robed pilgrims, ordinary civilians, with smooth, ebony-black hair, big heads, long busts, thin legs, of short stature, whose complexion varied from dark copper tints to dull white, but was never yellow like the Chinaman's; for the two races have essentially different characteristics. Among the carriages, palanquins and barrows fitted with sails, the 'norimons' with sides of lacquer, the soft luxurious 'cangos,' regular litters made of bamboo, a few women were seen making their way through the traffic, with small steps of their small feet, shod in canvas shoes, straw sandals or clogs of ornamented wood. They were not good-looking, these flat-chested women with childish eyes, and teeth blackened to suit the prevailing fashion, but they wore gracefully their national garment, the 'kimono,' a sort of dressing-gown fastened across with a broad silk sash tied in an enormous knot behind, which up-to-date Parisian ladies seem to have borrowed from the women of Japan.

Passepartout strolled about for some hours in the midst of this motley multitude, sometimes looking at the quaint, gorgeous shops, the bazaars with their crowded display of the Japanese jeweller's tinsel, the eating-houses, decked with streamers and banners, which he was not in a position to enter, and those teahouses in which the fragrant hot water is drunk by the cupful with 'saki,' a liquor obtained from fermented rice, and those comfortable smoking-houses where a very fine tobacco is smoked — not opium, the use of which is almost unknown in Japan.

Presently Passepartout found himself in the country, in the midst of immense paddy-fields. There, not on shrubs but on trees, the full-blown blossoms of dazzling camelias were putting forth their last colours and perfumes, and, within bamboo enclosures, cherry trees, plum trees, and apple trees, which the natives grow rather for their blossom than for their fruit, and which forbidding scarecrows and loud whirligigs protect from the beaks of sparrows, pigeons, ravens, and other voracious birds. Every majestic cedar had a large eagle, every weeping willow spread its foliage over some heron, gloomily perched on one leg; and on all sides were crows, ducks, hawks, wild geese, and numbers of cranes, on which the Japanese confer nobility, and which in their eyes symbolise long life and happiness.

As he wandered about, Passepartout noticed a few violets in the grass. 'Good!' said he, 'there's my supper.' He smelt them and found them quite odourless. 'No luck!' thought he.

The good fellow had certainly taken care to eat as much as he possibly could before leaving the *Carnatic*, but after walking about all day he felt the pangs of hunger. He had observed that the flesh of sheep, goats and pigs was absolutely wanting in the butchers' stalls, and, knowing as he did that it is sacrilege to kill cattle, which are strictly reserved for the needs of agriculture, he came to the conclusion that meat was scarce in Japan, and he was right. But, in default of butcher's meat, he would have done quite well with the joints of wild boar or deer, the partridges or quails, the poultry or fish which, together with the produce of the paddy-fields, make up almost the whole culinary resources of the Japanese. However, he had to put a good face on the matter, and decided he would not look for food till the morrow.

Night came; Passepartout returned to the native quarter, and wandered about the streets lit by many-coloured lanterns, watching the troops of dancers going through their wonderful performances, and the astrologers in the open collecting the crowd around their telescopes. Then he saw the harbour again, spangled with the lights of fishermen, who were attracting the fish with the glow of blazing resin.

The streets were at last deserted, and instead of the crowd, the yakoonins appeared on their rounds. These officers in their splendid costumes, and surrounded by their retinue, looked like ambassadors. Whenever Passepartout came across one of these dazzling patrols, he observed humorously: 'Hallo! Here's another Japanese embassy on its way to Europe!'

23

*In which Passepartout's nose assumes
inordinate length*

On the morrow Passepartout, tired out and
famished, reflected that he must get something to eat, no matter how, and the sooner
the better. If everything else failed he could of
course sell his watch, but he would have
starved before doing that. So, now or never,
the good fellow must make use of the
powerful, if not melodious voice, with which
Nature had gifted him. He knew a few
French and English catches, which he
resolved to try on the Japanese, feeling sure
they must be fond of music, since they did
everything to the accompaniment of cymbals,
tom-toms and drums.

They could not fail to appreciate the
performance of a European virtuoso. As it
was perhaps rather early in the morning for a
concert, it was possible that the dilettanti,
startled out of their slumbers, might pay the
singer with other coin than that which bears
the effigy of the Mikado. Passepartout
therefore decided to wait a few hours. As he

went along, he reflected that he would look too well dressed for a strolling artist, and it then occurred to him to change his garments for old clothes more suitable to his condition. Moreover, this exchange should leave a balance, by means of which he could at once satisfy his hunger.

This resolution once taken, the next thing was to carry it out. After a long search, Passepartout succeeded in discovering a native dealer in old clothes, to whom he explained what he wanted. The dealer liked the European costume, and Passepartout left his shop rigged out in an old Japanese robe and a kind of corded turban, faded with age. As an offset, a few small silver coins jingled in his pocket. 'That's all right,' he thought; 'I shall imagine it is carnival time.'

Passepartout's first care, after he was thus 'Japanesed,' was to find a tea-house of modest appearance, where he breakfasted on the remains of a fowl and a few handfuls of rice, like a man for whom dinner was as yet an unsolved problem.

'Now,' said he to himself, when he had eaten his fill, 'I must take good care not to make a fool of myself. I can't help myself by selling this old outfit for one still more Japanese. I must therefore see what I can do to get out of this Land of the Sun as soon as

I possibly can; the memories I shall take away will be anything but pleasant.'

It then occurred to him to pay a visit to the boats about to leave for America. His idea was to offer his services as cook or servant in return for his passage and food. Once at San Francisco he would find some way of getting out of his difficulties. The thing that mattered was to cross the four thousand seven hundred miles that separate Japan from the New World.

Passepartout, who was not the man to dilly-dally with an idea, at once directed his steps towards the docks. But as he drew nearer to his destination, his project, which had seemed so simple when he first conceived it, appeared more and more impossible of realisation. Why should they require a cook or a servant on board an American liner? And what sort of confidence would he inspire in such a rig-out? What recommendations could he produce in support of his application? What references could he give? As these thoughts were passing through his mind, his eyes fell upon an immense placard carried by a sort of clown through the streets of Yokohama. This placard was in English and ran as follows:

HONOURABLE WILLIAM BATULCAR'S TROUPE

LAST PERFORMANCES
Before their Departure for the United States
of the

LONG, LONG NOSES
Under the Special Patronage of the God Tingou

GREAT ATTRACTION!

He followed the poster-bearer, and was soon once more in the Japanese part of the city. A quarter of an hour later he stood before a large building at the top of which fluttered several clusters of streamers, and bearing on its outside walls, in crude garish colours but without perspective, the picture of a whole company of jugglers.

This was the Honourable Batulcar's establishment. The man was a sort of American Barnum, the manager of a troupe of buffoons, jugglers, clowns, acrobats, equilibrists and gymnasts, who, according to the placard, was giving his last performances before leaving the Empire of the Sun for the States of the Union. Passepartout stepped in under a peristyle leading into the building, and asked to see Mr Batulcar, who at once came forward in person.

'What do you want?' said he to Passepartout, whom he at first took for a native.

'Do you require a servant?' asked Passepartout. 'A servant!' exclaimed the Barnum, stroking the thick grey goatee that covered the nether part of his chin. 'I have two obedient and faithful servants, that have never left me, and serve me for nothing, on condition I feed them — here they are,' he added, showing him his two sturdy arms, lined with veins as large as the strings of a double-bass.

'So I can be of no use to you?' 'None.' 'It's deuced bad luck! It would have suited me so well to have gone away with you.'

'Look here,' said the Honourable Batulcar, 'you are no more a Japanese than I am a monkey! Why are you dressed in this fashion?'

'A man dresses as best he can.' 'That's true enough. You're a Frenchman, eh?' 'Yes, a Parisian of Paris.' 'Then you surely know how to make funny faces?' 'As to that,' replied Passepartout, somewhat nettled to see that his nationality had suggested such a question, 'we Frenchmen can certainly make funny faces, but no better than the Americans.'

'I guess that's right — well, if I can't take you as a servant, I can take you as a clown. You understand, my friend; in France they exhibit foreign buffoons, and in foreign countries French buffoons.' 'Is that so?'

'And you're a strong fellow, eh?' 'Yes, particularly when I have had a good feed.' 'Can you sing?' 'Yes,' replied Passepartout, who had once sung his part in a few street concerts. 'But can you sing with your head down, a spinning-top on the sole of your left foot, and a sword balanced on the sole of your right foot?' 'Why, of course I can!' answered Passepartout, recalling the first performances of his early years. 'You see, everything depends on that,' replied the Honourable Batulcar.

The engagement was concluded there and then. Passepartout had at last found employment. He was engaged as a Jack-of-all-work in the celebrated Japanese troupe. It was not a very gratifying position, but within a week he would be on his way to San Francisco.

The performance, so noisily announced by the Honourable Batulcar, was to commence at three o'clock, and soon the fearsome instruments of a Japanese orchestra, drums and tom-toms, were thundering at the door. Needless to say, Passepartout had had no time to prepare a part, but he was to lend the support of his broad and robust shoulders in the wonderful feat of the 'human cluster' accomplished by the Long Noses of the god

Tingou. This great attraction was to close the performance.

Before three o'clock the large hall was invaded by the spectators. Europeans, Chinese, Japanese, men, women and children, made a rush for the narrow benches and the boxes facing the stage. The musicians had taken up their position inside, and the full orchestra of gongs, tomtoms, bones, flutes, tambourines and big drums was working frantically.

The performance was much the same as all acrobatic displays; but there is no denying that the Japanese are the finest equilibrists in the world. One man, with nothing more than his fan and bits of paper, performed that most graceful trick of the butterflies and the flowers. Another, with the odorous smoke of his pipe, rapidly traced in the air a series of bluish words, which made up a compliment to the audience. A third juggled with some lighted candles, which he extinguished one after the other as they passed before his lips, and relit one from the other without interrupting his fascinating jugglery for one moment. Yet another produced, by means of spinning-tops, the most extraordinary combinations; under his touch these humming things seemed to assume a life of their own in their endless gyration; they ran along pipe-stems and the edges of sabres, and along wires, that looked no thicker than hairs, stretched across the stage; they careered round the brims of large crystal vases, climbed up bamboo ladders, scattered about into all corners, and produced weird harmonic effects by combining their various pitches of tone. The jugglers tossed them up, and they went on spinning in the air; they hurled them like shuttlecocks with wooden battledores, and still they went on spinning; they thrust them into their pockets, and when they took them out they were spinning as before until at a given moment the release of a spring made them spread out into gerbes.

There is no need to describe the astounding feats of the acrobats and gymnasts. The performances with the ladder, the pole, the ball, the barrels, etc., were executed with remarkable precision. But the chief attraction of the show was the exhibition of the Long Noses, astounding equilibrists, unknown as yet to Europe.

The Long Noses form a peculiar company under the special patronage of the god Tingou. Attired like heroes of the Middle Ages, they sported a magnificent pair of wings at their shoulders. But their chief distinctive feature was the long nose which adorned the face, and even more the use to which it was put. These noses were actually bamboo canes, five, six, or even ten feet long: some straight, others curved, some smooth, others covered with little knots. It was on these appendages, firmly fastened, that all their balancing feats were performed. A dozen of these followers of the god Tingou lay flat upon their backs, and their fellow-actors settled on their noses, placed as straight as lightning-conductors, jumping and tumbling from one to the other, and performing the most amazing feats. As a grand finale, special mention had been made of the human pyramid, in which some fifty Long Noses were to represent the Car of Juggernaut. But, instead of forming this pyramid by using their shoulders as the supports of the structure, the Honourable Batulcar's artistes were to use nothing but their noses. It so happened that one of those who formed the base of the Car had left the troupe, and, as all that was required was strength and skill, Passepartout had been selected to take his place. The good fellow felt truly sorry for himself when — sad reminiscence of his youth — he donned his garb of the Middle Ages, adorned with many-coloured wings, and a nose six feet long was adapted to his face, but, all said and done, this nose meant bread and cheese, so he cheered up, went upon the stage, and took his place beside those who were to represent the base of the Car of Juggernaut. They all lay down flat on their backs, their noses pointing skyward. A second set of equilibrists took up its position on these long appendages, then a third established itself on top, and then a fourth, and on these noses that met just at their tips, a human structure soon rose to the very borders of the theatre.

The applause was more frantic than ever, and the instruments of the orchestra had just broken out like so many claps of thunder, when the pyramid tottered, the balance being destroyed through the failure of one of the noses at the base, and the structure collapsed like a house of cards.

Passepartout was the man at fault, for, leaving his post, he had suddenly cleared the footlights unassisted by his wings, clambered up to the right-hand gallery, and fallen at the feet of one of the spectators, crying out, 'Ah, my master! My master!' 'What, you here?' 'Yes, I, and no mistake.' 'Well, then, my friend, come with us at once to the boat.'

Mr Fogg, Aouda, who was with him, and Passepartout hurried out through the lobbies, but outside they found the Honourable Batulcar, who was furious, and claimed damages for the 'breakage' of the pyramid. His wrath was soothed by Mr Fogg, who threw a handful of banknotes to him. At half-past six, just as the American boat was about to leave, Mr Fogg and Aouda stepped on board, followed by Passepartout, with his wings still on, and the six-feet-long nose, which he had not yet succeeded in removing from his face.

24

The voyage across the Pacific Ocean

What happened when the *Tankadere* arrived in sight of Shanghai scarcely needs telling. The signals of distress had been seen from the Yokohama boat, and the captain, observing a flag at half-mast, had directed his course towards the little schooner. A few minutes later, Phileas Fogg, paying the sum agreed upon for his passage, handed to the skipper, John Bunsby, five hundred and fifty pounds. Then he, Aouda, and Fix got on board the steamer, which at once resumed her route for Nagasaki and Yokohama.

Phileas Fogg arrived at his destination on the morning of the 14th of November, at scheduled time, and, leaving Fix to attend to his business, went to the *Carnatic*, where he was told, to Aouda's great delight — and perhaps to his own, though he betrayed no sign of it — that the Frenchman, Passepartout, had actually arrived the day before.

Phileas Fogg, who was due to leave for San Francisco that very evening, set out at once in search of his servant. He applied without success to the French and English consuls, and, having wandered about the streets of Yokohama without coming across Passepartout, was beginning to despair of finding him, when chance, or possibly a kind of presentiment, led him into the Honourable Batulcar's theatre. Without a doubt, he would never have recognised his servant in that fantastic, heraldic garb; but the latter, lying with his face upwards, caught sight of his master in the gallery.

He made an involuntary movement, which brought his nose out of position, thereby upsetting the balance of the 'pyramid,' with the consequences that we know.

So much Passepartout learnt from Aouda herself, who then told him the details of the voyage from Hong-Kong to Yokohama on the *Tankadere*, with a man called Fix.

Passepartout heard the name Fix without wincing. He did not think the moment had come to let his master know what had passed between the detective and himself. So, when giving an account of his own adventures, he simply expressed keen regret for having been accidentally overcome by the intoxication of opium in a smoking-house at Hong-Kong. Mr Fogg, having heard this narrative coldly, answered not a word, but advanced his servant a sufficient sum to allow him to procure on board garments more becoming than those he wore. Within an hour the worthy fellow had cut off his nose and shed his wings, and had nothing about him that recalled the follower of the god Tingou.

The boat about to sail from Yokohama to San Francisco belonged to the Pacific Mail Steamship Company, and was called the *General Grant*. She was a very large paddle-wheel steamer of two thousand five hundred tons, well fitted up and very fast. A huge beam rose and fell regularly above the deck; a piston-rod was jointed to one of its extremities, and to the other that of a connecting-rod, which, converting the rectilinear into circular motion, acted directly on the paddle-shaft. The *General Grant* was rigged like a three-masted schooner, and had a large spread of canvas, which greatly assisted her steam-power. As her speed was twelve miles an hour, she would not take more than twenty-one days to cross the Pacific. Phileas Fogg had therefore good reason for thinking that he would reach San Francisco by the 2nd of December, New York by the 11th, and London by the 20th — anticipating thus by a few hours the fateful date of the 21st of December.

There was a very fair number of passengers

on board, some Englishmen, many Americans, a whole crowd of coolies emigrating to America, and a certain number of officers of the Indian Army, who were spending their leave in making the tour of the world.

The voyage, from a sailor's point of view, was quite uneventful; the boat, supported on her large paddles, steadied by her great spread of sail, rolled but little. The Pacific Ocean about justified its name.

Mr Fogg was as calm and reserved as ever. His young companion felt more and more that the ties which bound her to her protector were other than those of mere gratitude. The silent, yet more generous nature of the man impressed her more than she thought, and almost unconsciously she was giving way to feelings to which her inscrutable companion seemed absolutely impervious. And apart from sentiment, Aouda took the keenest interest in Mr Fogg's plans, and worried over any mishaps that might endanger the success of the journey. She often chatted with Passepartout, who saw well enough what was going on in Aouda's heart, guarded though she was. The good fellow, whose attitude towards his master was now one of perfectly blind faith, could never speak highly enough of Phileas Fogg's uprightness, generosity and unselfishness. He likewise calmed Aouda's apprehensions concerning the termination of the journey, assuring her that the worst was over, telling her again and again that they had left behind them those fantastic lands of China and Japan, and were on their way back to civilised countries, and that a train from San Francisco to New York, with a transatlantic liner from New York to London, would, without a doubt, enable them to complete this impossible journey round the world within the stipulated time.

Nine days after leaving Yokohama, Phileas Fogg had traversed exactly one half of the terrestrial globe, for, on the 23rd of November, the *General Grant* crossed the hundred and eightieth meridian, in the southern hemisphere, and was therefore at the very antipodes of London. Mr Fogg, it is true, had taken up fifty-two out of eighty available days, and had only twenty-eight left. But, though he was only half-way by the difference of meridians, one must not forget that he had really travelled over more than two-thirds of the total distance to be accomplished; for consider what roundabout journeys he had been obliged to make, from London to Aden, from Aden to Bombay, from Calcutta to Singapore, and from Singapore to Yokohama.

Anyone following without deviation the

fiftieth latitude, which is that of London, would not have travelled over more than twelve thousand miles, roughly speaking; whereas Phileas Fogg had been compelled by the unmethodical means of transport at his disposal to undertake a journey of twenty-six thousand, of which he had now, on the 23rd of November, accomplished about seventeen thousand five hundred. Now, however, the route was direct, and Fix was no longer there to multiply obstacles in his way!

It also happened, on this 23rd of November, that Passepartout was greatly elated. It will be remembered that the obstinate fellow had stubbornly refused to make any alteration in the London time of his precious family watch, holding that the time of all the countries he passed through was wrong. Now, on this day, although he had never put his watch on or back, it agreed exactly with the ship's chronometer. One can easily imagine Passepartout's exultation. With what pleasure he would have jeered at Fix, if he had been there! 'What buncombe that rascal told me about the meridians, the sun, the moon and what not!' repeated Passepartout. 'Eh, what! if people of that sort had their way, there would be some funny clocks and watches about! I knew well enough that, some day or other, the sun would settle to go by my watch!'

What Passepartout did not know was that, if the dial of his watch had been divided into twenty-four hours, like Italian clocks, he would have had no reason to exult, for at nine a.m. on board the ship the hands of his timepiece would have shown nine p.m., that is to say, the twenty-first hour after midnight, or a difference exactly equal to that between London and the hundred and eightieth meridian. But, had Fix been able to explain this purely physical effect, Passepartout would undoubtedly have been unable to admit it, even if he had understood. And in any case, if, supposing the impossible to have happened, the detective had unexpectedly appeared on board at that moment, Passepartout, moved by just wrath, would very probably have discussed with him a totally different subject, and in an entirely different manner.

But where was Fix at that moment? He was actually on board the *General Grant*. On arriving at Yokohama, the detective, leaving Mr Fogg, whom he expected to meet again during the day, had gone straight to the British consulate. And there he at last found the warrant, which had followed him from Bombay, and was already forty days old. It had been dispatched from Hong-Kong by the *Carnatic*, the very boat on which he was supposed to be. The detective's disappointment may well be imagined. The warrant was now useless. The man Fogg, having left English soil, could only be arrested on an extradition order.

'Very well,' thought Fix, swallowing his wrath, 'my warrant is of no use here, but it will be good in England. There is every indication that the rogue intends to return home, in the belief that he has thrown the police off his track. Very well, I shall follow him all the way there. As for the money, Heaven grant there may be some left! But what with travelling, bribes, law-suits, fines, elephants, expenses of all sorts the fellow has already got through more than five thousand pounds. Anyhow, the Bank has plenty of money!'

Having made up his mind, he at once embarked on the *General Grant*, and was already on board when Mr Fogg and Aouda arrived. He was astounded at seeing Passepartout, for he recognised him in his heraldic attire. He forthwith hid himself in his cabin, to avoid an explanation which might spoil everything. Owing to the large number of passengers, he was confident of escaping his enemy's notice, when, on that very day, he found himself face to face with him on the foredeck. Without a word, Passepartout flew at him, seized him by the throat, and, to the great delight of certain Americans, who at once proceeded to bet on him, he administered to the wretched Fix a magnificent thrashing, thereby proving the great superiority of French over English boxing. When Passepartout had finished he felt relieved, as it were, and composed himself. Fix got up in a somewhat battered condition, and, looking at his adversary, said to him coldly, 'Have you done?' 'Yes, for the present.' 'Then come and have a word with me.' 'A word with you! You want me — ' 'In your master's interest.'

As though subdued by the detective's coolness, Passepartout followed him, and they went and sat down right in the bow of the ship.

'You have given me a hiding,' said Fix. 'That's all right, I expected it. Now attend to what I say. So far I have been Mr Fogg's adversary; I am now playing on his side.' 'At last!' exclaimed Passepartout, 'you believe he is an honest man?' 'No,' replied Fix coldly, 'I believe he is a rogue. Hush! don't move, and let me speak. So long as Mr Fogg was on English soil, it was my interest to keep him back, until I should receive a warrant. I spared no effort to this end. I set the Bombay priests at him; I got you intoxicated at Hong-Kong; I separated you from your master; I made him miss the Yokohama boat — ' Passepartout heard all this with clenched fists. 'Now,' resumed Fix, 'Mr Fogg seems to be on his way back to England. Well, I shall follow him there. But henceforth I shall exert myself just as zealously to remove all difficulties from his path as I have hitherto done to multiply them. As you see, my game is no longer the same, and for the simple reason that my interest requires a change. I may add that your interest is the same as mine, for in England, and in England only, shall you know whether you are serving a criminal or an honest man.' Passepartout, who had listened to Fix with close attention, was convinced that he was perfectly honest in what he said.

'Are we going to be friends?' asked Fix. 'Friends, no,' replied Passepartout; 'allies, yes; but conditionally, for at the slightest sign of treachery I shall wring your neck for you.' 'That's agreed,' said the detective quietly.

Eleven days later, on the 3rd of December, the *General Grant* steamed into the Bay of the Golden Gate and reached San Francisco.

So far Mr Fogg had neither gained nor lost a single day.

25

Which contains a cursory view of
San Francisco on the day of a
political meeting

At seven in the morning Phileas Fogg, Aouda
and Passepartout set foot on the American
continent, if this name can properly be given
to the floating quay on which they disem-
barked. These quays, rising and falling with
the tide, facilitate the loading and unloading
of ships. Clippers of all sizes, steamers of
every nationality, and those steamboats with
several decks, one over the other, which ply
on the Sacramento and its tributaries, are
moored alongside these floating quays. And
there also are piled up the commodities
produced by a commerce extending to
Mexico, Peru, Chili, Brazil, Europe, Asia, and
all the islands of the Pacific.

So overjoyed was Passepartout at having at
last reached American soil, that he thought it
right to land by means of a perfect
somersault. But when he came down on the
quay, the flooring of which was worm-eaten,
he very nearly went right through. Much

228

taken aback at the manner in which he had 'set foot' on the New World, the worthy fellow uttered a tremendous cry, which frightened away a multitude of cormorants and pelicans, the customary denizens of movable quays.

The moment Mr Fogg landed, he inquired at what time the first train for New York would start, and was told six o'clock in the evening. So Mr Fogg had a whole day to spend in the Californian capital. He ordered a carriage for Aouda and himself, and this conveyance, for which he paid three dollars, drove off to the International Hotel, with Passepartout on the box. From his commanding position, Passepartout observed the great American city with much curiosity. He saw wide streets, even rows of low houses, churches and chapels in Anglo-Saxon Gothic style, huge docks, warehouses like palaces, some made of wood, others built of brick; in the streets there were numbers of vehicles: omnibuses, 'cars,' tramways, and on the crowded pavements, not only Americans and Europeans, but Chinese and Indians; in fact enough people to make up a population of more than two hundred thousand inhabitants.

Passepartout was greatly surprised; he expected to see the legendary city of 1849, the city of the bandits, incendiaries and assassins, who had rushed to the conquest of the gold-nuggets, the huge *omnium gatherum* of all nondescripts, in which men gambled for gold-dust, with a revolver in one hand and a knife in the other. But those 'spacious days' had gone for ever. San Francisco now looked what it was, a great commercial city. The lofty tower of the town hall, where the watchers are on the look-out, commanded the whole network of streets and avenues, which intersected each other at right angles, and in the midst of which lay verdant squares, while beyond was a Chinese town, that seemed to have been imported from the Celestial Empire in a toy-box. No more sombreros, no more red shirts as worn by placer hunters, no more plumed Indians, but a number of silk hats and black coats, worn by gentlemen endowed with feverish activity. Certain streets, like Montgomery Street, which corresponds to Regent Street in London, the Boulevard des Italiens in Paris, and Broadway in New York, were lined with magnificent shops, which displayed in their windows the products of the whole world.

When Passepartout reached the International Hotel, he felt just as if he had never left England. The ground-floor of the hotel was taken up by an immense 'bar,' a sort of refreshment-room open gratis to all passers-by. Dried meat, oyster soup, biscuit and cheese were distributed free to the consumer, who only paid for what he drank, whether ale, port or sherry. This Passepartout thought 'very American.'

The hotel restaurant was comfortable, and Mr Fogg and Aouda, taking their seats at a table, were copiously served in Lilliputian dishes by negroes of darkest hue.

After breakfast, Mr Fogg, accompanied by Aouda, proceeded to go to the English consulate to have his passport *visaed*. On coming out of the hotel he found his servant, who asked him if it would not be wise, before taking the train, to buy a few dozen Enfield rifles or Colt revolvers, as he had heard of Sioux and Pawnees holding up the trains just like ordinary Spanish brigands. Mr Fogg answered that it was an unnecessary precaution, but he left him free to do as he thought fit, and directed his steps towards the consul's office.

He had not walked two hundred yards when, 'by the merest chance,' he found himself face to face with Fix. The detective expressed the utmost surprise. What! had Mr Fogg and he crossed the Pacific together without meeting on board! Well, anyhow Fix felt it a great honour to meet once more the gentleman to whom he owed so much, and, as he must needs return to Europe for business reasons, he would be delighted to continue his journey in such pleasant company. Mr Fogg replied that the honour would be his, and Fix, who was most anxious not to lose sight of him, asked if he might see this curious city of San Francisco with him. The request was granted, and Aouda, Phileas Fogg and Fix were soon sauntering about the streets together. Before long, they found themselves in Montgomery Street, which was crowded with the lower orders. On the pavements, in the middle of the road, on the tramway rails, in spite of the incessant traffic of coaches and omnibuses, at the shop-doors, at all the windows, and even on the roofs, the people swarmed. Poster-bearers were going about through the crowd; flags and streamers fluttered in the wind, and shouts burst forth on every side:

'Hurrah for Kamerfield!'

'Hurrah for Mandiboy!'

It was a political meeting. This, at least, was Fix's opinion, which he imparted to Mr Fogg, saying: 'It might be well, sir, to keep out of this mob. There's nothing but blows to be got out of mixing with it.' 'Yes, indeed,' replied Mr Fogg, 'and blows, though political, are blows for all that.' Fix thought proper to smile at this remark, and, so as not to be caught in the crush, they all three took up a position at the top of a flight of steps leading to a terrace that overlooked Montgomery Street.

In front of them, on the other side of the street, between a coal wharf and a petroleum store, stood a large committee room in the open, towards which the various currents of the crowd seemed to converge.

Of the reason and object of this meeting Phileas Fogg had not the slightest idea. Was it to elect some high military or civil official, the governor of a State or a member of Congress? The extraordinary excitement and impassioned interest of the citizens justified the conjecture. At this moment there was a great commotion in the crowd. All hands were raised; some were firmly clenched and seemed to rise and fall swiftly in the midst of the cries — doubtless an energetic way of casting a vote. The throng swayed to and fro. The banners wavered, disappeared for a moment, then reappeared in tatters. The human waves came as far as the steps, and the mass of heads billowed on the surface like a sea suddenly stirred up by a squall. The number of black hats grew rapidly less, and most of them seemed below normal height.

'It is evidently a meeting,' suggested Fix,

'and the question at issue must be a most exciting one. I should not be surprised if it were still about the Alabama dispute, although it is settled.' 'Possibly,' replied Mr Fogg in his quiet way. 'At all events,' continued Fix, 'two champions are face to face — Mr Kamerfield and Mr Mandiboy.'

While Aouda, leaning on Phileas Fogg's arm, was gazing in astonishment at this tumultuous scene, and Fix inquired of one of his neighbours the cause of such popular excitement, the general commotion became more violent. There was a more frantic burst of hurrahs, seasoned with abuse; the staffs of the banners were converted into weapons; hands disappeared to make room for fists everywhere. From the tops of the carriages and omnibuses, now at a standstill, there was a liberal exchange of blows. Everything was good enough to hurl at an opponent. Boots and shoes described very low trajectories, and occasionally there was an impression that the revolver was adding its national bark to the bawling of the multitude. The seething mass drew nearer, and ebbed on to the lower steps. One of the parties had evidently been repulsed, but mere spectators could not tell whether Mandiboy or Kamerfield had the upper hand.

'I think it would be wise for us to retire,'

suggested Fix, who did not want to see 'his man' knocked about or get into a scrape. 'If all this has anything to do with England, and we are recognised as Englishmen, we shall have a bad time in the scuffle.' 'An English subject — ' replied Phileas Fogg, but could not finish his sentence, for, behind him, from the terrace to which the steps led, broke out terrific shouts of 'Hurrah! Hip, Hip, Hurrah for Mandiboy!' It was a party of electors coming to the rescue, and taking the supporters of Kamerfield in flank.

Mr Fogg, Aouda, and Fix found themselves between two fires; it was too late to escape. This torrent of men, armed with loaded sticks and clubs, was irresistible. Phileas Fogg and Fix were dreadfully hustled, in their endeavour to protect the young woman. Mr Fogg, as cool as ever, tried to make use of his fists, those natural means of defence of every Englishman, but in vain. A huge fellow with a red goatee, a ruddy complexion, and broad shoulders, who seemed to be the leader of the party, raised his dread fist over Mr Fogg, to whom he would have done serious harm had not Fix devoted himself and taken the blow in his stead. An enormous swelling at once appeared under the detective's silk hat, which assumed the shape of a muffin-cap.

'Yankee!' said Mr Fogg, glancing at his

enemy with the utmost contempt. 'Englishman!' replied the other. 'We shall meet again!' 'When you please.' 'Your name?' 'Phileas Fogg. And yours?' 'Colonel Stamp Proctor.'

Thereupon the tide swept by; Fix was knocked down, but got up again without any serious hurt. His overcoat had been divided into two unequal parts, and his trousers were like those breeches of which it is the fashion among certain Indians to remove the seat before putting them on. Aouda was unharmed; Fix alone had suffered, and bore the mark of the American's fist. As soon as they were out of the crowd, Mr Fogg thanked the detective.

'Don't mention it,' replied Fix; 'but come along.' 'Where?' 'To a slop-shop.' Nor was this visit superfluous, for both Phileas Fogg and Fix were in rags. They might have been fighting on behalf of Messrs Kamerfield and Mandiboy.

An hour after, they returned to the International Hotel with respectable hats and clothes. Passepartout was there, waiting for his master, armed with half a dozen central-fire six-chambered revolvers, fitted with daggers. When he caught sight of Fix with Mr Fogg, his brow darkened; but he brightened up again when Aouda told him briefly what had occurred. It was obvious Fix was no longer an enemy; he was an ally, and was keeping his word.

Dinner over, a coach was procured to take the travellers and their luggage to the station. As he was getting in, Mr Fogg said to Fix, 'You have not seen this Colonel Proctor again, have you?' 'No,' answered Fix. 'I shall return to America to find him,' said Phileas Fogg calmly. 'It would not be proper for an Englishman to stand such treatment.'

The detective smiled, but said nothing. Mr Fogg, apparently, was one of those Englishmen who, while thoroughly opposed to duelling in their own country, are quite prepared to fight abroad in defence of their honour.

At a quarter to six the travellers were at the station and the train was ready to leave. As he was about to get in, Mr Fogg saw a porter, went up to him and said, 'Was there not a certain amount of rioting in San Francisco today?' 'It was a meeting, sir,' replied the porter. 'But I thought I observed a good deal of commotion in the streets.' 'It was only a meeting arranged for an election.' 'The election of a commander-in-chief, I suppose?' 'No, sir, a justice of the peace.'

Having received this reply, Phileas Fogg took his seat, and the train steamed out at full speed.

26

*In which Phileas Fogg and his compan-
ions travel by the Pacific Express*

'From Ocean to Ocean,' the Americans say;
and these words ought to be the general
designation of the grand trunk line which
crosses the United States of America at their
broadest part. As a matter of fact, however,
the Pacific Railroad is really divided into two
distinct lines: the Central Pacific, between
San Francisco and Ogden, and the Union
Pacific, between Ogden and Omaha. Five
different lines converge upon Omaha, which
is thus in frequent communication with New
York.

Thus, at the present moment New York
and San Francisco are joined together by an
unbroken band of metal, which is not less
than three thousand seven hundred and
eighty-six miles long. Between Omaha and
the Pacific, the railway crosses a vast tract
which is still the haunt of Indians and wild
beasts, and which the Mormons began to
colonise about 1845, when they had been
expelled from Illinois. In the most favourable

circumstances, the journey from New York to San Francisco formerly took six months; it now takes seven days.

It was in 1862 that, in spite of the opposition of the Southern members of Congress, who wanted a more southerly route, it was settled that the railroad should lie between the forty-first and forty-second parallels. President Lincoln, so long remembered with affectionate regret, himself made Omaha, in the State of Nebraska, the terminus of the new network of railway lines.

The work was begun at once, and carried on with American energy, which eschews alike scribbling and red-tape; nor was the line to suffer in any way from the rapidity with which it was laid. The work progressed in the prairie at the rate of a mile and a half a day. An engine, running on the rails laid down the day before, brought the rails to be laid on the morrow, and advanced upon them as they were laid.

The Pacific Railroad is met by several branch lines — in Iowa, Kansas, Colorado and Oregon. On leaving Omaha, it runs along the left bank of the Plate River as far as the mouth of the northern branch, then follows the southern branch, crosses the Laramie territory and the Wahsatch Mountains, passes round the Great Salt Lake and reaches Salt

Lake City, the capital of the Mormons, dives into the Tuilla Valley, skirts the American Desert, Mounts Cedar and Humboldt, Humboldt River, and the Sierra Nevada, and descends, via Sacramento, to the Pacific. The gradient never exceeds a hundred and twelve feet to the mile, even through the Rocky Mountains.

Such was the long artery which trains travel over in seven days, and which would enable Mr Phileas Fogg — at least, so he hoped — to leave New York for Liverpool on the 11th.

The carriage which he occupied was a sort of long omnibus resting upon two trains, each of which consisted of four wheels and whose mobility makes it possible to take sharp curves. The carriages were not divided into compartments; two rows of seats were arranged perpendicularly to the axis, and between these ran a passage leading to the dressing-rooms and lavatories, with which each carriage was provided. Throughout the whole length of the train, the carriages communicated with each other by means of platforms, so that the passengers could walk from one end of the train to the other. There were saloon-cars, balcony-cars, dining-cars, and refreshment-cars. The one thing lacking was theatre-cars, but even these will be supplied some day.

There was a constant stream of people selling books and papers, and of venders of drinkables, eatables and cigars, doing a good business.

When the travellers left Oakland station, at six o'clock, it was already night, a night cold and black; the heavens were overcast with clouds that threatened snow. The train was not going at a great pace; allowing for the stoppages, it was not doing more than twenty miles an hour; but that was speed enough to take it across the United States in accordance with the time-table.

There was but little talking in the carriage and the passengers soon became sleepy. Passepartout happened to be sitting next to the detective, but he did not speak to him. After what had lately happened, their relations had grown distinctly cold; there was no longer any sympathy or intimacy between them. Fix behaved in exactly the same manner, but Passepartout was extremely reserved, and prepared to strangle his former friend on the slightest suspicion of trickery. Snow began to fall an hour after they left the station, a fine snow, which fortunately could not impede the train's progress. Nothing could be seen through the windows but a boundless white sheet, which made the steam unravelling its coils over it look greyish.

At eight o'clock a steward entered the car and informed the passengers that it was bedtime. In a few minutes the carriage, which was a sleeping-car, was converted into a dormitory. The backs of the seats were lowered, neatly-packed couches were spread out by means of an ingenious device, berths were rapidly improvised, and each traveller soon had a comfortable bed at his service, in which he was screened from prying eyes by thick curtains. The sheets were spotless and the pillows soft. It only remained to go to bed and sleep. This everybody proceeded to do, just as if he had been in the comfortable cabin of a liner. Meanwhile the train was running at full speed across the State of California.

The country between San Francisco and Sacramento is mostly flat. This part of the line, the Central Pacific, first started from Sacramento and was produced eastward to meet the railroad from Omaha. From San Francisco to the capital of California the line ran in a direct north-easterly course, skirting American River, which empties itself into San Pablo Bay. The hundred and twenty miles that separate these two important cities were crossed in six hours, and towards midnight, while soundly asleep, the travellers passed through Sacramento. So they saw nothing of this important town, the seat of the Californian Government, nothing of its fine quays, wide streets, magnificent hotels, and squares and churches.

Having left Sacramento and advanced beyond the junctions of Rochin, Auburn, and Colfax, the train entered the mountain system of the Sierra Nevada. It was seven o'clock in the morning when it steamed through Cisco station. An hour later the dormitory resumed its ordinary appearance, and the travellers caught glimpses of the picturesque scenery of this mountainous region. The railway track followed the capricious exigencies of the Sierra, at one time clinging to the mountain side, at another hanging on the brink of a precipice, avoiding sharp angles by describing bold curves, plunging into narrow gorges with apparently no outlet. The engine, sparkling like a reliquary, with its great head-light throwing yellow beams, its silvery dome, and its cow-catcher protruding like a spur-ram, mingled its whistling and roaring with the noise of torrents and waterfalls, and sent its smoke writhing about the sombre boughs of pines.

There were few, if any, tunnels or bridges on the route. The railway did no violence to

Nature by straight cuts in order to go the nearest way: it worked round the mountains.

The train entered the State of Nevada through the Carson Valley about nine o'clock; it was still running in a north-eastern direction. At twelve it left Reno, where the travellers had twenty minutes for breakfast.

From this point the railroad, skirting Humboldt River, struck north for some miles, following the course of the river. Then it turned eastward and kept close to the river until it reached the Humboldt Range, where the stream has its source, almost in the extreme east of Nevada.

After breakfast, Mr Fogg, Aouda and their companions resumed their comfortable seats in the carriage, and observed the varied scenery that passed before their eyes: vast prairies, mountains standing out on the horizon, and creeks with their seething, foaming waters. At times a great herd of buffaloes, massing in the distance, looked like a moving dam. These innumerable hosts of ruminants often oppose an insuperable barrier to the passage of trains. Thousands of these animals have been seen filing past across the rails, in serried ranks, for hours together. The engine is then forced to stop and wait until the road is clear again. And the very thing happened on this occasion. About three o'clock in the afternoon, a herd of ten or twelve thousand head of buffalo blocked the way. The engine, after slackening speed, tried to drive its spur-ram into the flank of the immense column, but the impenetrable mass brought it to a standstill.

These ruminants, improperly called buffaloes by the Americans, advanced with their tranquil step, at times bellowing loudly. They were larger than the bulls of Europe, short in the legs and tail, had prominent withers forming a muscular bump, horns wide apart at the base, head, neck and shoulders covered with long, flowing hairs.

To try and stop such a migration was out of the question. When bisons have settled on a line of march, nothing on earth can arrest or alter their course. It is a torrent of living flesh which no dam can keep back.

The travellers watched this curious sight from the platforms; but Phileas Fogg, to whom time must have been more precious than to anyone else, never left his seat, but waited philosophically until it should please the buffaloes to move out of the way. Passepartout was furious at the delay caused by this agglomeration of animals; it would have given him the greatest pleasure to have discharged his arsenal of revolvers upon them.

'What a country!' he exclaimed, 'where trains are stopped by mere cattle, that go along in a procession, and will no more hurry than if they were not interfering with the traffic! Egad! I should very much like to know if Mr Fogg has allowed for this mischance in his programme! And what of this engine-driver, who has not the pluck to send his engine at full speed through these obstructing beasts!'

The engine-driver had been very wise in not attempting to overthrow the obstacle. He would, no doubt, have crushed the first buffaloes struck by the spur-ram, but, no matter how powerful the engine might be, it would soon have been stopped, and the train would have infallibly been thrown off the metals and remained helpless. The best thing to do therefore was to wait patiently, and then make up for lost time by accelerating the train's speed. The march of the bisons lasted three full hours, and the line was not clear before nightfall, when the last ranks of the herd were crossing the rails, and the first were disappearing below the southern horizon.

It was eight o'clock when the train ran through the defiles of the Humboldt Range, and half-past nine when it entered the territory of Utah, the curious land of Great Salt Lake and the Mormons.

27

In which Passepartout attends, at a speed of twenty miles an hour, a course of Mormon history

During the night of the fifth of December, the train ran in a south-easterly direction for about fifty miles; then, going up a like distance to the north-east, it drew near to Great Salt Lake.

About nine o'clock in the morning, Passepartout went out on the platform to take the air. The weather was cold, the sky grey, but it was snowing no longer. The sun's disc, magnified by the mist, looked like an enormous gold coin, and Passepartout was busy calculating its value in pounds sterling, when his attention was diverted from this useful occupation by the appearance of a somewhat strange personage.

This man, who had taken the train for Elko station, was tall, very dark, with black moustache, black stockings, a black silk hat, a black waistcoat, black trousers, a white tie and dog-skin gloves. He looked like a parson, and was going from one end of the train to the other, sticking, by means of wafers, on the door of each car a manuscript notice. Passepartout drew near and read one of these notices, which was to the effect that Elder William Hitch, Mormon missionary, taking advantage of his presence on train No. 48, would give a lecture on Mormonism in car No. 117, from eleven to twelve o'clock, and that he invited all gentlemen to hear him, who cared to learn about the mysteries of the religion of the 'Latter Day Saints.'

'I shall go without fail,' said Passepartout to himself, who knew practically nothing of Mormonism, except the polygamous habits on which the society rests. The news spread rapidly through the train, which was carrying some hundred passengers. At most thirty of them, drawn by the attraction of a lecture, were seated in car No. 117 by eleven o'clock.

Passepartout was in the front row of the faithful, but neither his master nor Fix took the trouble to go.

At the appointed hour Elder William Hitch rose, and, in a voice betraying anger, as if he had been contradicted in advance, exclaimed, 'I tell you that Joe Smith is a martyr, that his brother Hiram is a martyr, and that the persecutions of the prophets by the United States Government will also make a martyr of

248

Brigham Young. Who would dare to assert the contrary?'

Nobody ventured to gainsay the missionary, whose fanaticism contrasted with his naturally calm facial expression. No doubt his wrath arose from the fact that Mormonism was at that moment subjected to severe trials. The United States Government had succeeded, with considerable trouble, in subduing these independent fanatics. It had made itself master of Utah, and compelled it to obey the laws of the Union, after imprisoning Brigham Young on a charge of rebellion and polygamy. Ever since, the disciples of the prophet redoubled their efforts and, while biding their time, opposed words to the claims of Congress. Apparently Elder William Hitch was proselytising on the very railway trains. Then, throwing impassioned force into his narrative by voice and gesture, he told the story of Mormonism from biblical times: how that, in Israel, a Mormon prophet of the tribe of Joseph published the records of the new religion and bequeathed them to his son Morom; how, centuries later, a translation of this precious book in Egyptian script was written by Joseph Smith, Junior, a Vermont farmer, who revealed himself as a mystical prophet in 1825; and how, finally, a heavenly messenger appeared to him in a luminous forest and gave unto him the records of the Lord.

Just then a few persons, not particularly interested in the missionary's retrospective account, left the carriage; but William Hitch, continuing his lecture, related how Smith, Junior, gathering together his father, his two brothers, and a few disciples, founded the religion of the 'Latter Day Saints' — a religion which has been accepted not only in America, but in England, Scandinavia and Germany, and numbers among its followers not only artisans, but many members of the liberal professions — how a temple was erected at a cost of two hundred thousand dollars and a town built at Kirkland; how Smith became a daring banker, and received from a humble mummy showman a papyrus containing a narrative written by Abraham, and others, famous Egyptians.

As Hitch's story was getting rather tedious, the ranks of his hearers were now thinned again, and the audience was reduced to some twenty persons. But the Elder, undeterred by this desertion, went on telling in detail how Joe Smith became bankrupt in 1837; how the ruined shareholders covered him with tar and rolled him in feathers; how he turned up again, more honourable and more honoured than ever, a few years later, at Independence, in Missouri, and the head of a flourishing community of at least three thousand disciples, when, pursued by the hatred of the gentiles, he fled into the far West.

There were now ten people in the audience, one of whom was honest Passepartout, who was listening intently. Thus he learnt that, after long persecutions, Smith reappeared in Illinois, and founded in 1839, on the banks of the Mississippi, the settlement of Nauvoo-la-Belle, which attained a population of twenty-five thousand souls, and of which he became mayor, chief justice, and commander-in-chief; that he was a candidate for the Presidency of the United States in 1843, and that finally he was lured into an ambush at Carthage, thrown into prison, and murdered by a gang of masked men.

By this time Passepartout was the only person left in the carriage, and the Elder, looking him straight in the face, fascinating him with his eloquence, reminded him that, two years after Smith's assassination, his successor, the inspired prophet, Brigham Young, left Nauvoo, and settled on the shores of Salt Lake, where in a beautiful and fertile country, on the route of emigrants crossing Utah on their way to California, the new colony, thanks to the principles of polygamy

251

practised by the Mormons, had grown and flourished exceedingly.

'And,' added William Hitch, 'that is why the jealousy of Congress has worked against us! why the soldiers of the Union have trodden the soil of Utah! why our chief, the prophet Brigham Young, has been put in prison, in defiance of all justice! Shall we yield to brute force? Never! Driven out of Vermont, driven out of Illinois, driven out of Ohio, driven out of Missouri, driven out of Utah, we shall yet find some land of freedom on which to pitch our tents. And you, my faithful one,' added the Elder, fixing a wrathful stare upon his one and only hearer, 'shall you pitch yours under the shadow of our flag?' 'No,' answered Passepartout bravely, and he too fled, leaving the fanatic to rant in the desert.

During the lecture the train had made rapid progress, and, about half-past twelve, it reached the north-west corner of Great Salt Lake. Thence the passengers commanded an extensive view of this inland sea, which is also called the Dead Sea, and into which flows an American Jordan. It is a magnificent lake, framed in by grand, broad-based crags, encrusted with white salt; a splendid expanse of water, which once covered a greater area; its shores having gradually risen in course of time, have thereby decreased its surface, while increasing its depth.

Salt Lake, about seventy miles long and thirty-five wide, is three thousand eight hundred feet above sea-level. Very different from Asphaltic Lake, which lies twelve hundred feet below the sea, it contains a considerable amount of salt, and its water holds a quarter of its weight of solid matter in solution; its specific gravity, as compared with distilled water, being as 1170 is to 1000. So fishes cannot live in it, and those which are washed into the lake by the Jordan, the Weber and other streams, soon perish. It is not a fact, however, that the density of the water is such that a man cannot dive into it.

The country around the lake was very well cultivated, for the Mormons are skilled agriculturists. Six months later, ranches and corrals for domestic animals, fields of corn, maize, and sorghum, luxuriant meadows, hedges of wild rose trees, clumps of acacias and euphorbias, would have met the eye on all sides; but now the ground was powdered over by a thin layer of snow.

The train arrived at Ogden at two o'clock, and the travellers alighted, as they would not leave again before six. Mr Fogg, Aouda and their two companions, having plenty of time, paid a visit to the City of the Saints, connected with Ogden by a small branch line. Two hours would be sufficient to see the town, American in every respect, and therefore built on the pattern of all the towns in the Union, like great chess-boards with long cheerless lines, and the 'sombre sadness of right angles,' as Victor Hugo expresses it. The founder of the City of the Saints succumbed to that craving for symmetry which is a distinctive characteristic of the Anglo-Saxons. In this strange land, where men are undeniably not on a level with their institutions, everything is done 'squarely,' cities, houses, and follies.

By three o'clock the travellers were strolling in the streets of this town, which stands between one bank of the Jordan and the first heights, the Wahsatch Range. They noticed few, if any, churches; the only monuments were the prophet's habitation, the court-house and the arsenal; they saw houses built of bluish bricks, with verandas and galleries, surrounded with gardens and bordered with acacias, palms and carob trees. A clay and pebble wall, built in 1853, encompassed the town; and in the main street, where the market is held, there were a few hotels decked with flags, and among them was Salt Lake House.

To Mr Fogg and his companions the place

did not appear to be very populous. The streets were nearly empty, except in the neighbourhood of the Temple, which they did not reach before they had passed through several quarters surrounded by palings. The women were fairly numerous, which is accounted for by the peculiar constitution of Mormon households. It would not be correct, however, to say that all Mormons are polygamous. Men are free to do as they please in that matter. But it should be said that the women of Utah are particularly anxious to become wives, because, according to the religion of Utah, female celibates are not admitted to the joys of the Mormon heaven. These poor creatures appeared to be neither well-off nor happy. A few, the wealthiest, doubtless, wore black silk jackets open at the waist, under a hood or very simple shawl. The others had nothing but print dresses.

Passepartout, who held decided views on the subject, could not see without a sort of dismay these Mormon women, two or more of whom were entrusted with the happiness of a single Mormon man. His common sense made him feel special pity for the man. It seemed to him a terrible thing to have to guide so many ladies at once through the vicissitudes of life, to have to lead them as a team up to the Mormon paradise, with the prospect of joining them there for eternity in the company of the glorious Smith, who no doubt was the shining light of that blissful abode. No, no, such a life did not appeal to him; and — he was possibly mistaken — it occurred to him that the ladies of Great Salt Lake City cast rather disquieting glances at his person.

Very fortunately his stay in the City of the Saints was not to be a long one. At a few minutes before four, the travellers were at the station again and went back to their places in the train.

The whistle sounded; but, just as the driving wheels of the engine, gliding on the rails, were beginning to impart a certain speed to the train, loud cries of 'Stop! Stop!' were heard. A train, once started, does not stop for passengers. The man who uttered these cries was evidently a belated Mormon. He rushed up breathless, and as, fortunately for him, the station had neither gates nor barriers, he was able to tear along the line, jump on the footboard of the last carriage, and drop panting on one of the seats.

Passepartout, who had watched these gymnastic incidents with considerable excitement, went up to have a look at this laggard, and was greatly interested when he heard that the headlong flight of this citizen of Utah was simply the outcome of a domestic quarrel. When the Mormon had recovered his breath, Passepartout ventured to ask him politely how many wives he had all to himself. This hurried Hegira had led him to suppose the man had a score at least.

'One, sir,' replied the Mormon, raising his arms to heaven; 'one, and that was enough!'

28

*In which Passepartout was unable to
make anyone listen to reason*

On leaving Ogden station and Great Salt
Lake, the train ran on a northerly course for
an hour, as far as Weber River, having
travelled about nine hundred miles from San
Francisco. From this point it struck east again
across the bold Wahsatch Mountains. It was
in the district included between these
mountains and the Rocky Mountains, properly so called, that the American engineers
had to contend against their most serious
difficulties; and for this part of the railroad
the Government's grant amounted to forty-
eight thousand dollars per mile, whereas it
was not more than sixteen thousand dollars
for laying the line on the flat country. But the
engineers, as we have pointed out before, did
not hack their way through natural obstacles,
so much as overcome them by skilfully
turning them, so that, in order to reach the
great basin, one single tunnel, fourteen
hundred feet long, was pierced in the whole
course of the railroad.

So far, the line had reached its highest elevation at the Great Salt Lake. From this point it described a very long curve, descending towards Bitter Creek Valley, and rose again up to the watershed between the Atlantic and the Pacific. There were many streams in this mountainous region; the Muddy, the Green, and others had to be crossed on culverts. Passepartout's impatience became greater and greater as he drew nearer to the goal. Fix, too, longed to be out of this country so full of obstacles. He feared delays, dreaded accidents, and was more anxious than Phileas Fogg himself to set foot on English soil.

The train stopped at Fort Bridger station at ten o'clock in the evening, and left again almost at once; twenty miles farther on it entered the State of Wyoming, formerly Dakota, following the whole length of Bitter Creek Valley, whence drain part of the waters which form the hydrographic system of Colorado. On the morrow, December 7, there was a quarter of an hour's stop at Green River station. During the night there had been a fairly heavy fall of snow, mixed with rain and half-melted, which could not impede the train's progress. But the bad weather worried Passepartout none the less, for the snow accumulating on the track would clog the wheels of the carriages, and would certainly be a possible cause of failure.

'Well, but what a mad idea it was to travel in winter!' he said to himself. 'Why on earth could not my master wait for the summer? It would have given him a better chance.'

At this very moment, when the worthy fellow was thinking of nothing but the state of the sky and the lower temperature, Aouda was a prey to worse anxiety, which had a totally different cause. A few travellers had got out of their carriage and were walking about on the platform of Green River station, awaiting the departure of the train, when she recognised one of them through the window as Colonel Stamp Proctor, the American who had treated Phileas Fogg with such gross rudeness at the San Francisco meeting. To avoid being seen, Aouda drew back instantly from the window.

The young woman was greatly alarmed by this incident. The man, who, dispassionate as his manner might be, gave her, day by day, proofs of the most absolute devotion, had become very dear to her.

Truly she did not quite realise how deep was the sentiment with which her deliverer inspired her, and to which she still gave the name of gratitude, but, though she knew it not, there was more than gratitude. So a pang shot through her heart when she recognised the unmannerly bully, from whom Mr Fogg intended sooner or later to demand satisfaction for his conduct. Of course, Colonel Proctor's presence in the train was a mere coincidence, but there he was, and everything must be done to prevent Phileas Fogg from getting sight of his adversary.

When the train had started, Aouda seized a moment when Mr Fogg was dozing to inform Fix and Passepartout of her discovery. 'What!' exclaimed Fix. 'This fellow Proctor is in the train! Well, you need not worry, madam; before settling accounts with that fellow — with Mr Fogg — he will have to deal with me! It seems to me that I was the most aggrieved party in that affair!'

'And, what is more,' added Passepartout, 'leave him to me, I'll tackle him, colonel as he is.'

'Mr Fix,' continued Aouda, 'Mr Fogg will never allow anyone to avenge him. He is quite capable of returning to America to find this bully. He has said so himself. If he sees Colonel Proctor, we shall not be able to prevent a duel, which might have deplorable consequences. He must not see him.' 'You are right, madam,' answered Fix; 'a duel might ruin everything. Victorious or not, Mr Fogg would be delayed, and — '

'And,' added Passepartout, 'that would be playing the game of the gentlemen of the Reform Club. In four days we shall be in New York. Well, if my master does not leave his car for four days, one may hope that chance will not bring him face to face with this cursed American; confound him! Surely we shall manage to prevent him — '

The conversation was interrupted. Mr Fogg had just woke up. and was looking at the landscape through the snow-flecked window. But some little time after, without being heard by his master or Aouda, Passepartout said to the detective: 'Do you mean to say you would really fight for him?' 'There is nothing I shall not do to bring him back alive to Europe,' replied Fix quietly, in a tone that denoted inflexible determination. Passepartout felt something like a shiver run through him, but his belief in his master remained unshaken.

Now was there any means whatever of keeping Mr Fogg in this compartment, so as to prevent all possibility of a meeting between him and the colonel? This should not present much difficulty, for Mr Fogg was neither restless nor curious. In any case the detective found this means, for a few minutes later he said to Mr Fogg, 'Time seems endless, travelling in a train, does it not, sir?' 'Yes,' replied Mr Fogg, 'but it passes all the same.' 'You used to play whist on board the liners?' 'Yes,' answered Phileas Fogg, 'but here it would not be an easy matter; I have neither cards nor people with whom to make a four.' 'As for cards, we could surely buy some. They sell everything on American trains. And if by chance this lady plays — ' 'Of course I do, sir,' replied Aouda eagerly. 'I know whist; it is part of an English education.' 'I flatter myself I am a pretty good whist-player,' resumed Fix. 'So that with three of us and a dummy — ' 'All right, sir,' replied Phileas Fogg, delighted to get back to his favourite game, even in a train.

Passepartout was dispatched to find the steward, and soon returned with two packs, scoring slips, counters, and a board covered with cloth. Everything was there; they began to play. Aouda had a very fair knowledge of the game; and Mr Fogg, severe critic as he was, paid her some compliments on her playing. As for the detective, he was simply a first-rate player, and quite a match for Mr Fogg. 'Now,' thought Passepartout, 'we have got him. He won't stir.'

At eleven o'clock in the morning the train reached the dividing ridge of the watersheds of the two oceans, at a spot called Bridger Pass, seven thousand five hundred and twenty-four feet above sea-level, one of the highest points attained by the line as it crosses the Rocky Mountains. After a run of about two hundred miles, the travellers would at last reach the plains which sweep on and on to the Atlantic, and are so well adapted by Nature to the laying of a railway.

On the watershed of the Atlantic river-system the first streams, tributaries, direct or indirect, of the North Platte River, were already on their way. The whole northern and eastern horizon was shrouded by that immense semicircular curtain, the northern portion of the Rocky Mountains, the highest of which is Laramie Peak. Between this curved boundary of the mountains and the railway were far-spreading, well-watered plains. On the right rose one above the other the first slopes of the group of mountains which reach down southward to the sources of the River Arkansas, one of the great tributaries of the Missouri. At half-past twelve the travellers caught a glimpse of Fort Halleck, which commands the district. In a few more hours they would be across the Rocky Mountains. It was therefore reasonable to expect that no untoward event would mark the passage of the train through this difficult country. The snow had stopped, and dry cold was setting in. Big birds, scared by the engine, flew right away; no wild beast, whether bear or wolf, was to be seen on the plain, which presented the aspect of the desert in its boundless nakedness.

Mr Fogg and his partners had enjoyed a comfortable lunch, served in their carriage, and had just returned to their endless whist, when a violent whistling was heard, and the train stopped.

Passepartout put his head out of the window, but saw nothing to account for this stoppage; there was no station in sight.

Aouda and Fix feared for a moment that Mr Fogg might take it into his head to get down on the line, but all he did was to say to his servant: 'Just go and see what is the matter.'

Passepartout jumped down from the carriage; some forty passengers had already left their seats; among them was Colonel Stamp Proctor. The train was stopped before a red signal which blocked the way. The engine-driver and the guard had got down and were talking excitedly with a watchman, whom the station-master at Medicine Bow, the next station, had sent to meet the train. Some of the passengers had come up and were taking part in the discussion, one of them being Colonel Proctor, who was conspicuous for his loud tone of voice and hectoring manner.

Passepartout, on joining the group, heard the watchman saying, 'No! it is impossible to pass! The bridge at Medicine Bow is shaky, and would not bear the weight of the train.' The bridge in question was a suspension bridge over rapids a mile away from the spot where the train had stopped. According to the watchman, it was in a ruinous condition, several of the chains were broken, and it was impossible to venture across. The watchman's assertion that the train could not get over this bridge was therefore no exaggeration. Moreover, it is safe to say that, when Americans, so casual as a rule, show signs of caution, it would be the height of folly not to be cautious too. Passepartout, who did not dare to inform his master of what was happening, listened with clenched teeth, motionless as a statue.

'Look here!' cried Colonel Proctor. 'I suppose we are not going to be left here to take root in the snow?' 'Colonel,' replied the guard, 'we have telegraphed to Omaha for a train, but it is not likely that it will get to Medicine Bow in less than six hours.' 'Six hours!' cried Passepartout. 'Certainly,' replied the guard. 'In any case it will take us all that time to get to the station on foot.' 'But it is only a mile away from us,' observed one of the passengers. 'A mile, yes, but on the other side of the river.' 'How about getting across in a boat?' asked the colonel. 'That's impossible. The creek is swelled by the heavy rain. It is a rapid, and we shall have to walk ten miles to the north in a roundabout way to find a ford.' The colonel let fly a volley of oaths, finding fault with the Company and the guard, and Passepartout, who was furious, was very near joining him in his denunciations. Here was a material obstacle which all his master's banknotes would be powerless to surmount. Nor were Passepartout and the colonel the only people to give vent to their disappointment.

When the passengers realised that, apart from the loss of time, they would have to trudge fifteen miles over the snow-covered plain, there was such a hubbub, such exclamations and shouts, that Phileas Fogg's attention must have been drawn had he not been completely absorbed by his game. Passepartout now felt, however, that his master must be told, and, with hanging head, was proceeding towards the carriage, when the engine-driver, a typical Yankee, by name Forster, called out, 'Gentlemen, there might be a way of getting over.'

'Over the bridge?' asked a passenger. 'Yes,

over the bridge.' 'With our train?' asked the colonel. 'With our train.' Passepartout stopped, and listened greedily to the engine-driver.

'But the bridge is in a ruinous condition!' rejoined the guard. 'No matter,' replied Forster. 'My idea is that, if we sent the train on at its highest speed, we should stand a chance of getting over.' 'The deuce!' said Passepartout. But a certain number of the passengers were at once tempted by the proposal. Colonel Proctor in particular was delighted with it, and the crazy fellow thought the thing quite practicable. He even supported his belief by quoting the fact that engineers had thought of sending single-car trains over rivers, without bridges, by putting on full steam. In the end, all those who were interested in the matter fell in with the engine-driver's opinion. 'We have fifty chances out of a hundred of getting over,' said one. 'Sixty!' said another. 'Eighty! Ninety!'

Passepartout was astounded, and, though ready to attempt anything to get across Medicine Creek, he thought the proposed effort rather too American.

'And,' thought he, 'there's a much more simple way, and it has not even occurred to these people! Sir,' said he to one of them, 'the engine-driver's idea seems to me somewhat risky, but — ' 'Eighty chances!' replied the passenger, turning his back on him. 'Yes, I know,' answered Passepartout, addressing another, 'but on second thoughts — ' 'There's no need of second thoughts,' replied this American, with a shrug of his shoulders, 'since the engine-driver assures us that we shall get over!' 'Yes, of course,' returned Passepartout, 'we shall get over, but it might be more prudent — ' 'What's this? Prudent!' cried Colonel Proctor, who, on overhearing the word, became frantically excited. 'At full speed, don't you understand? At full speed, man!' 'I know — I see,' repeated Passepartout, who was never allowed to finish his sentence, 'but it would be — I won't say more prudent, since the word offends you, — more natural at any rate — ' 'What's all this? What does the chap mean by natural? What's the matter with him?' cried people all round him. The poor fellow could get nobody to listen to him. 'Are you afraid?' asked Colonel Proctor. 'Afraid, I!' cried Passepartout. 'All right, I shall just show these people that a Frenchman can be as American as they are!'

'Take your seats! Take your seats!' shouted the guard. 'Yes, yes, take your seats! Take your seats!' repeated Passepartout. 'We'll do it at

269

once; but, all the same, they can't prevent my thinking that it would have been more natural to send us travellers first across the bridge on foot, and then the train.' But nobody heard this sensible reflection, nor would anyone have acknowledged its soundness.

The passengers returned to their places; Passepartout went back to his seat without saying anything about what had happened. The whist-players had no thought for anything but their game.

The engine whistled loud and long; the engine-driver, reversing, backed the train for nearly a mile, on the principle of the jumper, who takes a long run before leaping.

Then there was a second whistle, and the train moved forward again, faster and faster, and soon the speed was terrific. All that was heard was one continuous screech from the engine, whose pistons were doing twenty strokes per second; smoke came out of the axle-boxes. There was a sort of feeling that the train was flying bodily at a hundred miles an hour, and was no longer resting on the rails; gravity was almost cancelled by velocity.

And over they went, in a flash! Of the bridge they saw nothing; the train, it may fairly be said, leaped from one bank to the other, and shot five miles beyond the station before the engine could be brought to a standstill.

But hardly was the river crossed, when the bridge, now completely ruined, collapsed, and crashed into the rapids of Medicine Bow.

29

*In which is given an account of various
incidents which happen only on the
railroads of the union*

The train pursued its course that same
evening, meeting with no mishap, passed Fort
Saunders, crossed Cheyenne Pass and came
to Evans Pass. The railroad here reached the
highest point of the whole track, eight
thousand and ninety-one feet above the level
of the ocean. The travellers had now only to
descend to the Atlantic over boundless plains,
levelled by Nature.

At that spot on the Grand Trunk the
branch line started for Denver, the chief town
of Colorado, a country rich in gold and silver
mines, where already more than fifty
thousand people have settled.

Thirteen hundred and eighty-two miles
had now been travelled over from San
Francisco in three days and three nights. Four
nights and four days, in all probability, would
bring the travellers to New York. So Phileas
Fogg was still within the prescribed time-
limit.

During the night Walbach Camp was passed on the left. Pole Creek flowed parallel to the line and followed the rectilinear frontier between the States of Wyoming and Colorado. At eleven o'clock they entered Nebraska, then passed near Sedgwich and touched Julesburgh, situated on the southern branch of the Platte River. It was here that the inauguration of the Union Pacific Railroad took place on the 23rd of October, 1869, the chief engineer being General J. M. Dodge. Two powerful engines brought nine wagons of invited guests, one of whom was Vice-President Thomas C. Durant. Ringing cheers enlivened the scene; and Sioux and Pawnees treated the spectators to an Indian sham-fight, followed by a display of fireworks. There, too, was published on that great occasion, by means of a portable press, the first number of the *Railway Pioneer*. Thus was celebrated the inauguration of this great railway, an instrument of progress and civilisation, thrown across the desert and destined to link together towns and cities not yet in existence. The whistle of the locomotive, more potent than the lyre of Amphion, would soon bid them rise from America's soil.

Fort MacPherson was left behind at eight o'clock in the morning. A space of three hundred and fifty-seven miles separates this place from Omaha. The line running near the left bank of the southern branch of the Platte River followed the capricious windings of the stream. At nine o'clock the travellers arrived at the important town of North Platte, built between the two arms of the great river, which join again around it to form one artery, a large tributary whose waters mingle with those of the Missouri, a little above Omaha.

The one hundred and first meridian was passed. Mr Fogg and his partners were busy with the cards once more, and no one, not even the dummy, complained of the length of the journey. Fix had begun by winning a few guineas, which he was now in a fair way to lose, but he was just as keen as Mr Fogg. That morning luck was particularly kind to the latter. Trumps and honours rained down upon him. At one moment, having thought out a bold plan, he was about to play a spade, when a voice from behind his seat was heard saying, 'I would play a diamond.'

Mr Fogg, Aouda, and Fix looked up, and lo and behold, there was Colonel Proctor! Stamp Proctor and Phileas Fogg knew each other at once.

'Halloo, Britisher!' exclaimed the colonel; 'so you're the man who wants to play a spade!' 'And who plays it,' replied Phileas

Fogg coolly, putting the ten of that suit on the table. 'Well, it is my pleasure that it should be a diamond,' returned Colonel Proctor in an angry tone of voice. He then made as if he would snatch the card that had been played, and added: 'You know nothing about this game.' 'There is another at which I may perhaps show greater skill,' said Phileas Fogg, rising from his seat. 'You can try your hand at that one whenever you please, son of John Bull,' replied the churlish fellow.

Aouda turned pale, and her heart stood still. She grasped Phileas Fogg's arm, but was gently forced back. As the American stared at his adversary in the most insulting manner Passepartout would have flung himself upon him, but Fix got up, went to Colonel Proctor and said, 'You forget, sir, that I am the man you must deal with, for I am the man you not only insulted but struck!'

'Mr Fix,' said Mr Fogg, 'pardon me, but this concerns me, and no one else. When the colonel maintained that I was wrong in playing a spade, he put a fresh insult upon me, and he shall give me satisfaction for it.'

'When you please, and where you please,' replied the American, 'and with whatever weapon you please.' Aouda made vain efforts to restrain Mr Fogg, and the detective tried in vain a second time to make the quarrel his.

Passepartout was preparing to throw the colonel out of the window, but was checked by a sign from his master: Phileas Fogg left the carriage, and the American followed him on to the platform.

'Sir,' said Mr Fogg to his adversary, 'I am in a great hurry to return to Europe; the slightest delay would affect me very seriously.' 'Well, and what is that to me?' returned Colonel Proctor. 'Sir,' continued Mr Fogg very politely, 'after our encounter at San Francisco, I intended to come back and find you in America, as soon as I had settled the business which calls me to the old continent.' 'Really!' 'Will you arrange a meeting for six months hence?' 'Why not six years?' 'I say six months,' replied Mr Fogg, 'and I shall be there punctually.' 'All this is to put me off!' cried Stamp Proctor. 'It must be now or never.' 'Very good. You are going to New York, I suppose?' 'No.' 'To Chicago?' 'No.' 'To Omaha?' 'What difference does it make to you? Do you know Plum Creek?' 'No,' replied Mr Fogg. 'It is the next station. We shall be there in an hour. There will be a ten minutes' stop. Ten minutes is time enough to exchange a few revolver shots.' 'All right,' replied Mr Fogg. 'I will stop at Plum Creek.' 'I shouldn't wonder if you stayed there for good,' added the American with the utmost insolence.

276

'Who knows?' retorted Mr Fogg, returning to his carriage, as unruffled as ever.

The first thing he did was to reassure Aouda, telling her that blusterers were never to be feared. He then requested Fix to act as his second in the impending duel. Fix consented; he could hardly do otherwise; and Phileas Fogg calmly continued his interrupted game, playing a spade, as if nothing had happened.

At eleven o'clock the engine's whistle announced that Plum Creek station was near. Mr Fogg got up and went out on the platform, followed by Fix. Passepartout accompanied him, carrying a pair of revolvers. Aouda remained in the carriage, pale as death.

Another door opened at this moment, and Colonel Proctor likewise came forward on the platform, followed by his second, a Yankee of the same kidney. But just as the two opponents were about to step down to the line, the guard rushed up shouting, 'You can't get down, gentlemen!' 'Why not?' asked the colonel. 'We are twenty minutes late, so the train won't stop.' 'But I have to fight a duel with this gentleman.'

'I am sorry,' replied the guard, 'but we are off at once. There's the bell!' The bell was actually ringing, and the train started. 'I am really more than sorry, gentlemen,' said the guard, apologising again; 'in any other case it would have been in my power to oblige you. But, after all, since you have not had time to fight here, why shouldn't you fight on board the train?' 'This gentleman will possibly object,' sneered Colonel Proctor. 'I have not the slightest objection,' answered Phileas Fogg.

'Well, of one thing there can be no manner of doubt, this is America,' thought Passepartout, 'and the guard is quite the high-class gentleman!' And muttering thus to himself, he followed his master. The two principals with their seconds, preceded by the guard, passed through the carriages to the rear of the train. There were not more than nine or ten passengers in the last carriage, and the guard asked them to be so good as to leave it vacant for a few minutes, as two gentlemen wished to settle an affair of honour. This request seemed most natural to the passengers, who withdrew to the platforms, professing themselves only too happy to oblige.

The carriage, some fifty feet long, was very suitable for the purpose. The two combatants could advance against each other in the gangway between the seats, and shoot with perfect comfort. Never was a duel more easily arranged. Mr Fogg and Colonel Proctor, each equipped with two six-chambered revolvers, went into the carriage. Their seconds, who remained outside, shut them in. They were to open fire at the first whistle of the engine. After a space of two minutes, whatever remained of the two gentlemen would be removed from the carriage. What could be more simple? In fact it was all so simple that Fix and Passepartout felt their hearts beating as if they would burst.

They were thus waiting for the whistle, the signal agreed upon, when suddenly the air was rent with savage yells, accompanied by detonations, which did not come from the carriage reserved for the duellists, but extended all along the train, right up to the fore part. Cries of terror came from inside the carriages. Colonel Proctor and Mr Fogg came out at once, revolver in hand, and rushed to the fore part of the train, where shots and shrieks were loudest. They had at once understood that the train was being attacked by a band of Sioux. This was not the first attempt of these bold Indians; they had held up trains more than once. Some hundred of them had, as they always did, jumped on to the footboards, without waiting till the train should stop, and climbed into the carriages as a clown mounts a galloping horse.

These Sioux were armed with guns. Hence

the reports, to which the passengers, who were almost all armed, replied with revolver-shots. The first thing the Indians did was to rush to the engine, where they half-killed the driver and stoker with blows of their tomahawks. A Sioux chief, wishing to stop the train, but not knowing how to work the handle of the regulator, opened wide the throttle-valve instead of closing it, and the engine bolted at a terrific speed.

Having at the same time swarmed up the carriages, the Sioux were running about like infuriated apes over the roofs, bursting the doors open and fighting hand to hand with the passengers. Out of the luggage-van, which had been broken into and plundered, the packages were flung upon the line. Cries and shots were incessant.

The travellers defended themselves bravely. Some of the carriages were barricaded and sustained a siege, just as if they had been real movable forts carried along at a hundred miles an hour.

Aouda showed great courage from the very beginning of the attack, defending herself heroically with a revolver, firing through the broken windows whenever a savage appeared before her. Some twenty Sioux fell mortally wounded to the track, and those who slipped from the platforms onto the rails were crushed like worms under the wheels of the carriages.

Several passengers, who had received serious hurt from the bullets or tomahawks, lay on the seats.

It was necessary to end the struggle, which had already lasted ten minutes and must result in a victory for the Indians, if the train could not be pulled up. Fort Kearney station was not two miles distant. But, if the train went beyond Fort Kearney, where there was an American garrison, it would be in the hands of the Indians before the next station could be reached.

The guard, who was fighting beside Mr Fogg, fell, struck by a bullet; whereupon he cried, 'Unless the train can be stopped within five minutes, we are lost!'

'Stopped it shall be,' said Phileas Fogg, who prepared to rush from the carriage. 'Stay, sir,' cried Passepartout, 'that is my job!'

The plucky fellow was too quick for Phileas Fogg, and, opening a door without being seen by the Indians, managed to slip under the carriage. Then, while the struggle went on, while the bullets crossed each other over his head, he made his way under the carriages with the agility and litheness of his old acrobatic days; clutching hold of the chains, helping himself along by means of the brakes and edges of the sashes, creeping from one carriage to the other with marvellous skill, he reached the front part of the train without being seen, for he was invisible. There, hanging by one hand between the luggage-van and the tender, he used the other to separate the safety-chains; but, owing to the force of traction, he would never have unscrewed the coupling-pin. Fortunately, a violent jolt of the engine snapped the pin, and the train, parted from the engine, was gradually left behind, while the engine itself raced ahead with increased velocity.

Carried on by the force it had acquired, the train did not stop for some minutes, but the brakes were applied inside the carriages and it came to a standstill less than a hundred yards from Kearney station. The soldiers of the fort, attracted by the firing, hurried up. The Sioux did not wait for them. The whole lot of them scampered away before the train had quite stopped.

But when the passengers were counted on the station platform, it was found that several were missing, one of whom was the brave Frenchman whose devotion had just saved them.

30

*In which Phileas Fogg simply
does his duty*

Three passengers, including Passepartout, had disappeared. As yet, it was impossible to say whether they had been killed during the conflict, or taken prisoners by the Sioux. The wounded were fairly numerous, but it was found that none were fatally hurt. One of the worst cases was Colonel Proctor, who had fought bravely and been struck down by a bullet in the groin. He was removed to the station with others whose condition required immediate attention.

Aouda was safe; and Phileas Fogg, who had been in the thick of the fight, had not a scratch. Fix had received a slight wound in the arm, but Passepartout was missing, and silent tears showed Aouda's grief. All the passengers had got out of the train.

The wheels of the carriages were stained with blood. From the naves and spokes hung mangled pieces of flesh. Long red trails could be seen as far as the eye could reach on the white plain. The last of the Indians were disappearing in the south, in the direction of Republican River.

Mr Fogg, with folded arms, stood motionless, debating in his mind the grave decision he had to take. Aouda, beside him, looked at him without uttering a word, but he understood. If his servant was a prisoner, ought he not to run any risk to get him out of the Indians' hands? 'I shall find him, dead or alive,' he said quietly to Aouda.

'Ah, Mr — Mr Fogg!' cried she, grasping his hands, which she covered with tears.

'Alive,' added Mr Fogg, 'if we do not lose a moment.' By this resolve, Phileas Fogg was making a complete sacrifice of himself. He had just decreed his own ruin. The delay of a single day would make him miss the boat from New York. His wager was lost irrevocably. But face to face with this thought, 'It is my duty,' he did not hesitate.

The captain in command of Fort Kearney was there. About a hundred of his men had taken up a defensive position, in case the Sioux should attempt a direct attack upon the railway station.

'Sir,' said Mr Fogg, addressing the captain, 'three passengers are missing.' 'Are they dead?' asked the captain. 'Dead or prisoners,' replied Phileas Fogg. 'That is the very thing that should not be left in doubt. Is it your intention to pursue the Sioux?' 'That is a very serious matter,' replied the officer. 'These Indians may continue their flight beyond the Arkansas. I cannot leave the fort committed to my charge without protection.' 'The lives of three men are at stake,' rejoined Phileas Fogg. 'Certainly, but can I risk the lives of fifty to save three?' 'I do not know whether you can, sir, but it is your duty.' 'Sir,' replied the captain, 'it is nobody's place here to teach me my duty.' 'Very well,' said Phileas Fogg coldly; 'I will go alone.' 'You, sir,' cried Fix, coming up, 'go alone in pursuit of the Indians!' 'Do you want me to leave this poor man to his fate, to whom everyone here owes it that he is still alive? I shall go.' 'No, then, you shall not go alone!' exclaimed the captain, conquered by his emotion. 'No! you're a gallant fellow! I want thirty volunteers!' he added, turning to his men. The whole company came forward in a body. All the captain had to do was to choose among these brave fellows.

Thirty soldiers were selected, and an old sergeant placed at their head. 'Thank you, captain,' said Mr Fogg. 'Will you allow me to accompany you?' asked Fix. 'Sir, you will do as you please,' replied Phileas Fogg. 'But, if you care to oblige me, you will stay behind with the lady. Should anything happen to me — '

A sudden pallor spread over the detective's face. Was he to part from the man whom he had followed so persistently, step by step, and let him thus venture out in this desert! Fix gazed searchingly at Mr Fogg, and then, in spite of himself, notwithstanding his suspicions and the struggle that was going on within him, his eyes fell before that calm, frank look.

'I shall stay,' he said.

A few minutes later, Mr Fogg pressed the young woman's hand, committed his precious travelling-bag to her keeping, and went away with the sergeant and his little band. But before starting, he said to the soldiers, 'My friends, there's a thousand pounds for you, if we save the prisoners.'

It was then a few minutes after twelve. Aouda withdrew to a room in the station and there waited by herself, thinking of Phileas Fogg, of his simple and large-hearted generosity and his serene courage. Mr Fogg, after sacrificing his fortune, was now exposing his life, and all this out of duty — no hesitation, no words. In her eyes Mr Fogg was a hero.

Very different were Fix's thoughts, and his agitation was beyond control. He walked about the platform in a state of feverish excitement. He had allowed himself to be dominated by Fogg's personality for a moment, but was now his true self again, and now Fogg was gone, he fully realised what a blunder he had committed in letting him go. How could he consent to part from this man whom he had been following around the world! As his real nature prevailed again, he blamed and accused himself, and treated himself as though he had been the Chief of the Metropolitan Police reprimanding a police-officer guilty of a simpleton's blundering.

'I have behaved like a silly fool!' he thought. 'The other chap, of course, let him know who I was, and he has given me the slip! Where am I to lay hands on him again now? But how on earth could I be hoodwinked in this fashion — I, Fix, who have in my pocket an order for his arrest! Evidently, I am nothing but a fool!'

So argued the detective, while the hours passed all too slowly for him. He was at his wits' end. There were times when he felt inclined to tell Aouda everything; but he had a shrewd notion of the reception that awaited his revelations. Whatever should he do? He had a mind to set out in pursuit of Fogg over the great white plains. He thought it just possible he might overtake him. The footprints of the soldiers were still stamped upon the snow. But soon, under a fresh layer, every trace disappeared. Fix now grew thoroughly dejected, and felt an unconquerable temptation to give up the game. And lo, the opportunity of leaving Kearney station and continuing this journey, which had been so full of disappointments, now presented itself.

Towards two o'clock in the afternoon, during a heavy fall of snow, protracted whistling was heard from the east. A huge shadow, preceded by a lurid light, was approaching slowly, much magnified by the mist, which gave it a fantastic appearance.

No train was expected from the east at this hour; the help which had been telegraphed for could not arrive so soon, and the train from Omaha to San Francisco was not due before the morrow. The thing was soon explained.

This engine, which was approaching slowly, emitting loud and prolonged whistling, was that which had been detached from the train, and had pursued its course at such terrific speed, carrying off the stoker and the driver, both unconscious. It had run on for several miles, and then, the fire getting low for lack of fuel, the steam had lost its force, and, an hour later, the engine, slowing down gradually, had stopped at last, twenty miles beyond Kearney station.

Neither driver nor stoker was dead; after remaining insensible for some time, they had recovered consciousness. The engine was then standing still. When the engine-driver saw himself in the desert, with an engine that had no carriages behind it, he understood what had happened. He had no idea how the engine had got detached from the train, but he felt sure that the train which had remained behind was in distress. He at once decided what to do. Prudence counselled him to push on towards Omaha, for to return towards the train, which was still perhaps being pillaged by the Indians, was dangerous. Regardless of such peril, coal and wood were shovelled into the fire-box, the flames revived under the boiler, the steam-pressure rose anew, and about two o'clock in the afternoon, the engine returned, running backward, to Kearney station. The whistling in the mist came from this very engine.

The travellers were delighted to see the locomotive take its place at the head of the train. They would now be able to resume their journey, so unhappily interrupted.

When the engine came in, Aouda, leaving the station, went up to the guard and said, 'Are you going to start?' 'Immediately, madam.' 'But what about the prisoners — our unhappy fellow-travellers — ' 'I cannot stop the service,' replied the guard. 'We are three hours late as it is.'

'When will the next train pass here from San Francisco?' 'Tomorrow evening, madam.' 'Tomorrow evening! That will be too late! Really, you must wait — ' 'It is impossible,' replied the guard. 'If you wish to go, take your seat.' 'I shall not go,' was Aouda's answer.

Fix had heard this conversation. A few minutes before, when he saw no possible means of getting away, he was resolved on leaving Kearney, but now the train was standing there, ready to start, and all he had to do was to resume his seat in the carriage, a resistless force riveted him to the spot. To remain on the station platform was torture to him, yet he could not tear himself away. The struggle within him was starting all over again. The sense of failure maddened, stifled him. He wished to fight to the bitter end.

Meanwhile the passengers, a few of whom were wounded — Colonel Proctor's condition was serious — had taken their places in the train. The overheated boiler was buzzing away, and the steam escaping through the valves. The engine-driver whistled, and the train started, mingling its white smoke with the whirling masses of snow-flakes.

The detective had remained behind. Some hours passed. The weather was very rough, the cold intense. Fix, sitting on a bench in the station, never stirred. One might have thought he was asleep. In spite of the squall, Aouda kept coming out of the room which had been placed at her disposal; she walked to the end of the platform, peering through the blizzard, in her effort to see through the mist which narrowed the horizon around her, and to catch any sound that might be heard. But she saw nothing and heard nothing. Then she would come in again, chilled to the bone, to return a few moments after, and always in vain.

Evening came on, and the small detachment had not come back. Where were they at this moment? Had they been able to overtake the Indians? Had they fought, or were they lost and wandering about at random? The commander of Fort Kearney was very anxious, but tried to betray no sign of his fears. Night came, less snow fell, but the cold grew still more intense.

To look into this dark immensity would have appalled the most fearless. The plain was wrapped in perfect silence. Neither flight of bird nor tread of beast broke the infinite stillness.

Throughout the night Aouda, her mind full of dark forebodings, her heart athrob with anguish, wandered about on the edge of the prairie. Her imagination carried her far away and showed her dangers innumerable. What she suffered through the long hours of that night words cannot tell. Fix had not stirred, but he, too, was sleepless. Once a man approached and even spoke to him, but the detective shook his head in reply and sent him away.

The night passed in this manner. At dawn, the half-extinguished orb of the sun rose above a misty horizon; but it was now possible to see two miles away. Phileas Fogg and the detachment had gone south. In the south there was absolutely nothing to be seen, and it was now seven o'clock. The captain, who was extremely worried, could not make up his mind. Should he send a second detachment to the help of the first and sacrifice more men with so slight a chance of rescuing those who were already sacrificed? His hesitation was soon over. With one resolute gesture he called one of his lieutenants to him, and was in the act of ordering him to make a reconnaissance to the south, when gunshots rang out. Was it a signal? The soldiers rushed out of the fort, and saw half a mile off a small band of men returning in good order. Mr Fogg was marching at their head, and near him were Passepartout and the two other travellers, snatched from the hands of the Sioux.

There had been a fight ten miles south of Kearney. Just before the arrival of the detachment, Passepartout and his two companions were already at grips with their keepers, and the Frenchman had felled three with his fists, when his master and the soldiers rushed up to their assistance.

Rescuers and rescued were received with shouts of joy, and Phileas Fogg distributed the promised reward among the soldiers, while Passepartout was repeating to himself, with some show of reason, 'Upon my word, it cannot be denied that I cost my master a nice amount of money!'

Fix gazed at Mr Fogg without uttering a word; it would have been no easy matter to analyse the impressions that were warring within him. As for Aouda, she seized Mr Fogg's hand and pressed it between her own two hands, unable to speak a word.

Meanwhile Passepartout had no sooner arrived than he looked about for the train in the station. He expected to find it there, ready to proceed at full speed to Omaha, and he hoped it might yet make up the loss of time.

'The train! Where's the train?' he cried.

'Gone,' answered Fix. 'When will the next train come along?' asked Phileas Fogg. 'Not before this evening.' 'Is that so?' The impassive gentleman said nothing more.

31

In which Detective Fix becomes a strong supporter of Phileas Fogg

Phileas Fogg was now twenty hours behind time; and Passepartout, the involuntary cause of this delay, was desperate. He had actually ruined his master!

At this moment the detective approached Mr Fogg and, looking him straight in the face, he said, 'Seriously, sir, are you in a great hurry?' 'I am, quite seriously, in a great hurry,' replied Phileas Fogg. 'Pardon me,' continued Fix, 'is it a matter of great importance to you that you should be in New York on the 11th, before nine o'clock in the evening, the time at which the boat leaves for Liverpool?'

'It is a matter of the utmost importance.'

'And if your journey had not been interrupted by this attack of the Indians, you would have reached New York no later than the morning of the 11th?'

'Yes, twelve hours before the departure of the boat.'

'Right; so you are twenty hours late.

Between twenty and twelve, the difference is eight. You have eight hours to regain. Are you willing to try to do so?' 'On foot?' asked Mr Fogg. 'No; on a sledge,' replied Fix; 'on a sledge with sails. A man has suggested this means of conveyance to me.'

This was the man who had spoken to the detective in the night, and whose offer Fix had rejected. Phileas Fogg did not reply to Fix; but Fix having pointed out the man, who was walking about in front of the station, Mr Fogg went to him, and, an instant later, he and this American, whose name was Mudge, entered a hut standing below Fort Kearney.

There Mr Fogg inspected a somewhat strange vehicle. It was a kind of frame resting on two long beams, slightly curved upwards in front like the runners of a sledge, and on which five or six people could find room. At a third of the length of the frame, forward, rose a very high mast with rigging for a huge spanker. This mast, firmly secured by metallic shrouds, held out an iron stay for hoisting a very large jib. At the stern a sort of scull-like rudder served to steer the machine. As a matter of fact, it was simply a sledge rigged as a sloop. In winter, when the trains are stopped by the snow, these vehicles travel at very great speed over the frozen plains, from one station to another. They carry a prodigious spread of canvas, more than even a racing cutter can, as the latter is liable to capsize. With the wind behind them, they slip along on the surface of the prairies with a speed equal, if not superior, to that of express trains.

It took but a few minutes for Mr Fogg to come to terms with the skipper of this land-craft. The wind was favourable, blowing fresh from the west. The snow had hardened, and Mudge was quite confident of being able to convey Mr Fogg to Omaha station in a few hours. From that place there are frequent trains and numerous railroads to Chicago and New York. There was a possibility of making good the loss of time. There could be no hesitation about chancing it.

Not wishing to expose Aouda to the acute suffering of a journey in the open air, in such a cold atmosphere, which would be made still more intolerable by their speed, Mr Fogg proposed to her that she should remain at Kearney station in Passepartout's care. The trustworthy fellow would make it his duty to bring her to Europe by a better route and in more pleasant conditions.

Aouda refused to let Mr Fogg go without her, and Passepartout was only too delighted with this resolve, as nothing in the world would have induced him to leave his master in the company of the detective.

What Fix's thoughts were now, it would not be easy to say. Had Phileas Fogg's return shaken his conviction, or did he regard him as an exceedingly clever rascal, who, at the end of his journey round the world, would naturally think himself absolutely safe in England? Possibly Fix's opinion of Phileas Fogg was no longer the same; but he was none the less determined to do his duty, and was prepared to do his utmost to accelerate Fogg's return to England. No member of the party was now so impatient of delay as Fix.

At eight o'clock the sledge was ready to start. The travellers, one might almost say the passengers, took their places, and wrapped themselves up closely in their travelling-rugs. The two great sails were hoisted, and, impelled by the wind, the vehicle slid over the hardened snow at forty miles an hour.

The distance between Fort Kearney and Omaha, in a straight line, or, as the bee flies, to use the American expression, is at most two hundred miles. Should the wind hold, the distance could be traversed in five hours. If no accident occurred, the sledge would reach Omaha by one o'clock.

What a journey it was! The travellers, huddled together, could not even speak, for the cold, made more intense by the speed at which they were going, would have silenced them. The sledge glided over the surface of the plain as lightly as a boat on the surface of the water, and without waves to contend with. When the breeze came skimming along the ground, it felt as though the sledge were lifted up by its sails, as by wide-spreading wings. Mudge was at the helm, keeping a straight course, correcting by a shift of the stern-oar any sheering the machine showed signs of making. Every bit of canvas was taut, and the jib was now clear of the spanker. A topmast was swayed up, and another jib put out before the wind, adding its propelling force to that of the other sails. The speed at which the sledge was travelling could not be calculated mathematically, but it must have been quite forty miles an hour.

'If nothing snaps,' said Mudge, 'we shall get there in time!' It was Mudge's interest to get there within the time agreed on, for Mr Fogg, true to his method, had held out a handsome reward.

The prairie, which the sledge was traversing in a straight line, was flat as a sea. It looked like an immense frozen pond. The railway running through this district passed up from the south-west to the north-west, through Great Island, Columbus, an important town in Nebraska, Schuyler, Fremont and Omaha. Throughout its course it followed the right bank of the Platte River. The sledge shortened this route by following the arc of the chord described by the railroad. Mudge had no fear of being stopped by the slight curve of the Platte River before Fremont, for its waters were frozen. The way was therefore quite clear, and Phileas Fogg had but two things to fear: an accident causing damage to the machine, or a change or lull of the wind.

But the breeze, far from falling, was blowing hard enough to bend the mast, strongly held in position by the iron shrouds. These iron ropes sounded like the strings of an instrument made to vibrate by the contact of a violin bow. The sledge flew along, accompanied by plaintive music of very peculiar intensity.

'These chords give the fifth and the octave,' said Mr Fogg. They were the only words he uttered during the whole journey. Aouda, carefully wrapped up in furs and travelling-rugs, was, as far as possible, protected against the biting cold. As for Passepartout, his face was as red as the sun's disc setting in the mist, and he sniffed up the keen air with positive delight. By nature incorrigibly sanguine, he was beginning to hope again. Instead of getting to New York in the morning, they would be there in the evening, but it was still possible this would be in time to catch the Liverpool boat. Passepartout even felt a strong inclination to shake hands heartily with his ally Fix. He remembered that it was none other than the detective who had procured the sailing sledge, the sole possible means of reaching Omaha in time. But some presentiment or other made him keep his usual reserve. There was one thing which Passepartout would never forget — that was the sacrifice which Mr Fogg had readily made to snatch him out of the hands of the Sioux. In doing so, Mr Fogg had staked his fortune and his life. No; never would his servant forget that!

While the travellers were pursuing such different thoughts, the sledge was flying over the boundless carpet of snow. It passed over creeks, the tributaries direct or indirect of Little Blue River, but no one noticed it. Fields and streams disappeared under one white shroud. The plain was perfectly desolate. Stretching between the Union Pacific railroad and the branch line which connects Kearney with Saint Joseph, it formed a vast uninhabited island. There was not a village, not a station, not even a fort. From time to time they saw fleeting by like a flash some distorted tree, whose white skeleton writhed in the blast. Now and again flocks of wild birds took wing all together, or packs of gaunt, ferocious prairie wolves, lashed by hunger, tore after the sledge, and Passepartout, revolver in hand, held himself in readiness to fire at the nearest. If the sledge had been stopped by some accident, the travellers would have been at once attacked by these fierce flesh-eaters, and their position would have been most critical. But the sledge held on bravely, and soon left the howling brutes behind.

At noon Mudge was aware, from certain facts, that he was crossing the frozen course of the Platte River. He said nothing, but now felt sure that he would reach Omaha station, twenty miles farther on. And before one o'clock, the skilful pilot, leaving the rudder, sprang forward, seized the halyards and lowered the sails, while the sledge, carried on by its enormous impulse, travelled half a mile more with furled sails. It stopped at last, and Mudge, pointing to a collection of roofs white with snow, said, 'Here we are.'

And, indeed, there they were at that station which is in daily communication with the east of the United States by numerous trains.

Passepartout and Fix jumped out, shook their benumbed limbs, and assisted Mr Fogg and the young woman to get down. Phileas

Fogg paid Mudge liberally, and Passepartout gave him a friend's hand-grip. Then all hurried to Omaha station.

The Pacific Railway, properly so called, has its terminus at this important Nebraska city. The line connects the Mississippi basin with the great ocean. Omaha is connected with Chicago by the Chicago and Rock Island Railway, which runs due east and carries the traffic of fifty stations.

An express train was ready to start. Phileas Fogg and his party had only just time to get into a carriage. They had seen nothing of Omaha, but Passepartout confessed to himself that this was not a matter for regret, as they had a far more important object at heart than sightseeing.

The train passed at very high speed across the State of Iowa, through Conneil Bluffs, Des Moines, and Iowa City. In the night it crossed the Mississippi at Davenport, and entered Illinois by Rock Island. On the morrow, which was the 10th, at four o'clock in the evening, it arrived at Chicago, already risen from its ruins, and standing more proudly than ever on the shores of its beautiful Lake Michigan.

Nine hundred miles separate Chicago from New York. There were plenty of trains at Chicago, and Mr Fogg was not kept waiting a moment. The fiery engine of the Pittsburg, Fort Wayne and Chicago Railroad left at full speed, as if conscious of the fact that the honourable gentleman had no time to spare. It ran through Indiana, Ohio, Pennsylvania, and New Jersey like a flash, passing through towns with antique names, a few of which had streets and tramways, but were as yet without houses. At last the Hudson came into view, and, on the 11th of December, at a quarter-past eleven in the evening, the train stopped in the station, on the right bank of the river, in front of the very pier of the Cunard Line, also called 'The British and North American Royal Mail Steam Packet Company.'

The *China*, bound for Liverpool, had sailed forty-five minutes before!

32

*In which Phileas Fogg comes to grips
with mischance*

Phileas Fogg's last hope seemed to have gone
with the *China.*

The boats of the French Transatlantic
Company, of the White Star Line, of the
Inman Company, of the Hamburg Line, and
others plying between America and Europe,
were all useless as far as Mr Fogg's projects
were concerned.

The *Pereire,* of the French Transatlantic
Company, whose admirable ships are equal in
speed and superior in comfort to any of the
other lines, without exception, would not sail
before the 14th, that is two days later.
Moreover, like the ships of the Hamburg
Company, she did not go directly to
Liverpool or London, but to Havre, and the
extra passage from Havre to Southampton
would have involved a delay fatal to his last
efforts.

As for the Inman boats, one of which, the
City of Paris, would sail on the next day, they
were out of the question. Being specially used

for the transport of emigrants, their engines are of low power; they run under canvas as much as under steam, and their speed is not great. They took more time crossing from New York to England than Mr Fogg had in which to win his wager.

This was all perfectly clear to Mr Fogg, who, by consulting his *Bradshaw*, was well informed of the sailings of the transatlantic liners.

Passepartout was in a state of prostration. The fact that they had missed the boat by forty-five minutes crushed him. And it was his fault: far from helping his master, he had done nothing but put obstacles in his path! When he reviewed all the incidents of the journey, when he reckoned up all the sums spent without any return, and purely on his own account, when he reflected that the enormous stake, together with the heavy expenses of this now useless tour, would completely ruin Mr Fogg, he called himself everything that bitter self-reproach could suggest. From Mr Fogg he heard not a word of blame. As he left the pier, all Mr Fogg said was, 'We shall see tomorrow what is the best thing to be done. Come.'

Mr Fogg, Aouda, Fix and Passepartout crossed the Hudson in the Jersey City ferry-boat and drove to St Nicholas Hotel, in

Broadway. Rooms were given them, and the night passed, short for Phileas Fogg, who slept soundly, but very long for Aouda, Passepartout and Fix, who were too worried and excited to rest.

The next day was the 12th of December. From seven o'clock in the morning, of the 12th to a quarter to nine in the evening of the 21st there were left nine days, thirteen hours and forty-five minutes. If Phileas Fogg had left the day before in the *China*, one of the fastest boats of the Cunard Line, he would have reached Liverpool, and then London, within the required time.

Mr Fogg left the hotel alone, after giving his servant orders to wait for him, and to warn Aouda to be ready to start at any moment. He went to the banks of the Hudson, and, looking about among the vessels moored to the quay or anchored in the river, he took careful note of those about to put to sea. Several were flying the blue peter, and were making ready to sail out on the morning tide; for in this immense and admirable port of New York no day passes without a hundred ships leaving for every part of the world. But they were mostly sailing vessels and therefore unsuited to Phileas Fogg's purpose.

It looked as if he would fail in this, his last

effort, when he saw, anchored before the Battery, a cable length away at most, a screw-steamer. She was a trading vessel of fine lines, and her funnel, emitting puffs of smoke, showed that she was making ready to leave port.

Phileas Fogg hailed a boat, got into it, and a few strokes of the oar brought him to the gangway-ladder of the *Henrietta*, an iron-hulled craft whose upper works were all of wood.

Phileas Fogg went up on deck and asked to see the captain, who was on board and came forward at once.

He was a man of fifty, a sort of sea-dog with a growl, who seemed anything but easy to tackle. He had large, bulging eyes, an oxidised copper complexion, red hair and a bull-like neck, and nothing of the man of the world.

'I wish to see the captain,' said Mr Fogg. 'I am the captain.' 'I am Phileas Fogg, of London.' 'And I am Andrew Speedy, of Cardiff.' 'Are you about to sail?' 'In an hour.' 'What is your destination?' 'Bordeaux.' 'And what cargo are you carrying?' 'Stones — no freight — going on ballast.' 'Have you any passengers?' 'No passengers. Never take passengers. They're cumbersome, grumbling goods.' 'Is your ship a fast sailer?' 'Between eleven and twelve knots. The *Henrietta*'s well known.' 'Are you willing to take me and three other persons to Liverpool?' 'To Liverpool? Why not to China?' 'I said Liverpool.' 'No!' 'No?' 'No. I am about to sail for Bordeaux, and to Bordeaux I go.' 'No matter what money I offer?' 'No matter what money you offer.' The captain spoke in a tone which admitted of no reply. 'Possibly the owners of the *Henrietta* — ' continued Phileas Fogg. 'The owners — I am the owners,' answered the captain. 'The vessel belongs to me.' 'I will charter her.' 'No.' 'I will buy her.' 'No.' Phileas Fogg did not flinch, although the position was critical. New York was not Hong-Kong, nor was the captain of the *Henrietta* like the skipper of the *Tankadere*. Up till now money had overcome every difficulty. This time money failed. Yet it was absolutely necessary to find a way of crossing the Atlantic by boat — or by balloon, which would have been very venturesome, and, in any case, was not possible.

Phileas Fogg, however, seemed to think of something, for he said to the captain, 'Well, will you take me to Bordeaux?' 'No, not if you paid me two hundred dollars!' 'I offer you two thousand.' 'Per person?' 'Per person.' 'And there are four of you?' 'Four.' Captain Speedy began to scratch his forehead, as if he were trying to tear the skin off. Eight thousand dollars to be made without changing his route! It was worth his while to discard his strong objection to all passengers. And then passengers at two thousand dollars apiece are no longer passengers but valuable merchandise.

'I start at nine o'clock,' said Captain Speedy, simply; 'if you and your friends are ready to go on board — ' 'We shall be on board at nine,' replied Mr Fogg in the same manner.

It was then half-past eight. To go ashore from the *Henrietta*, jump into a cab, rush to St Nicholas Hotel, bring back Aouda, Passepartout, and even the inseparable Fix, to whom he graciously offered a passage, such was Mr Fogg's task, and he accomplished it with that serene self-possession of which no circumstance could ever deprive him.

They were all on board by the time the *Henrietta* was ready to weigh anchor. When Passepartout heard what the cost of this last voyage was going to be, he uttered a prolonged 'Oh!' that ran through the whole descending chromatic scale.

Detective Fix, for his part, came to the conclusion that the Bank of England would not come out of it without loss. For, as it was, in the event of their reaching England safely, and without Fogg throwing a few more handfuls of money into the sea, there would be a deficit of more than seven thousand pounds in the banknote bag.

33

*In which Phileas Fogg shows himself
equal to the occasion*

An hour after, the *Henrietta* passed the lightship which marks the entrance of the Hudson, turned the point of Sandy Hook, and ran for the open sea. During the day she skirted Long Island, passed at some distance from the beacon on Fire Island, and made her way rapidly eastward.

On the morrow, December 13, at noon, a man went up on the bridge to take the ship's bearings. Of course, this man could be no other but Captain Speedy. Well, it was not. It was Phileas Fogg, Esquire. As for Captain Speedy, he was simply locked up in his cabin, roaring with pardonable rage; he was frantic.

What had happened was simple enough. Phileas Fogg wanted to go to Liverpool, and the captain would not take him there. Whereupon Phileas Fogg had agreed to go to Bordeaux, but, during the thirty hours he had been on board, he had handled banknotes with such skill and effect, that the whole crew, sailors and stokers, a somewhat scratch lot who were on pretty bad terms with the captain, were devoted to him. Thus it was that Phileas Fogg was in command instead of Captain Speedy; that the captain was locked up in his cabin, and that the *Henrietta* was heading for Liverpool. One thing was clear, however, from the way Mr Fogg handled the ship, Mr Fogg had been a sailor.

What the end of the adventure would be, the future alone could show. Aouda said nothing, but was none the less anxious. Fix was at first dumbfounded, while Passepartout thought it a simply splendid piece of work. Captain Speedy had said 'between eleven and twelve knots,' and, so far, that was the average speed of the vessel. If then — for there were still many ifs — the sea did not become too rough, if the wind did not shift round to the east, if the ship suffered no damage, and everything went well with the machinery, the *Henrietta* might cross the three thousand miles from New York to Liverpool in the nine days from the 12th to the 21st of December. It is true that, at the end of the voyage, the *Henrietta* affair, coming on top of the Bank affair, might land Mr Fogg in a worse mess than he might care for.

All went well with the ship during the first days. The sea was not too unkind; the wind seemed settled in the north-east; the sails were set, and, under her try-sails, the *Henrietta* forged ahead like a real transatlantic liner.

Passepartout was delighted. His master's last achievement, to the possible consequences of which he was wilfully blind, filled him with enthusiasm. Never had the crew seen a more cheery and nimble fellow. He was on the friendliest of terms with the sailors and astounded them by his acrobatic performances. He was profuse of the kindliest compliments and lavish of the most attractive drinks. In his opinion the sailors sailed the ship like gentlemen, and the stokers stoked like heroes. His genial good-humour was infectious. Forgetting the past, with its troubles and perils, he thought of nothing but the goal, now so nearly attained, and at times he boiled over with impatience, as if heated by the furnaces of the *Henrietta*. Often, too, the worthy fellow kept close to Fix, looking at him with eyes full of meaning; but he did not speak to him, for their intimacy was quite at an end.

As a matter of fact, Fix was now completely baffled. The *Henrietta* taken by force, the crew bribed, this fellow Fogg handling the boat with faultless seamanship: all this stunned the man. He no longer knew what to think. Yet, after all, a person who began by stealing fifty-five thousand pounds might well end by stealing a ship. So Fix was naturally led to believe that the *Henrietta*, under Fogg's direction, was not going to Liverpool at all, but to some place where the robber, now become pirate, would quietly seek safety. This supposition, it must be confessed, was a most plausible one, and the detective began to feel exceedingly sorry he had embarked in the affair.

As for Captain Speedy, he went on bawling in his cabin, and Passepartout, who had to see to his meals, performed this duty with the greatest caution, in spite of his own great strength. As far as Mr Fogg was concerned, the fact that there was a captain on board seemed to have passed out of his mind completely.

On the 13th they passed the end of the banks of Newfoundland — a dangerous spot this, especially in winter, when fogs are frequent and squalls dreadfully violent.

The barometer, which had fallen sharply since the day before, announced an approaching change in the atmosphere; and during the night there was a change in the temperature, the cold became sharper, and at the same time the wind shifted to the south-east.

This was a misfortune. Mr Fogg had to furl his sails and use more steam-power, so as not to get out of his course. Yet the vessel's speed slackened, owing to the state of the sea, the long waves of which broke against her stem. She pitched violently, and this delayed her progress. The breeze was gradually turning to a gale, and it became necessary to face the fact that the *Henrietta* might no longer be able to keep her head to the seas. But, should they have to run before the storm, they would be facing the unknown with all its possibilities of mishap.

Passepartout's face darkened with the sky; for two days the good fellow was in a state of cruel anxiety. But Phileas Fogg was a bold seaman; he knew how to fight the waves, and held on under full steam.

When the *Henrietta* could not rise to the wave, she went right through, swamping her deck, but undamaged. Sometimes her screw rose, lashing the air wildly with its blades, a mountainous sea having lifted the stern out of the water, but the ship still pressed on.

The wind, however, did not attain the force that might have been feared. It was not one of those hurricanes that sweep by at a velocity of ninety miles an hour. It never went beyond a gale, but, unfortunately, it remained persistently in the south-east, making it impossible to put up canvas. And we shall soon see how invaluable any aid to the steampower would have been.

The 16th of December was the seventy-fifth day passed since the departure from London. After all, the *Henrietta* was not dangerously behind time. They were nearly half-way, and the worst parts of the sea were behind them. Had it been summer one could have answered for success. In winter there was always the weather to reckon with. Passepartout expressed no opinion, but was hopeful at heart. Should the wind fail them, he relied on the steam. Now on this very day the engineer came on deck, went up to Mr Fogg, and had an earnest talk with him. Without knowing why — it was doubtless some presentiment — Passepartout felt a vague uneasiness come over him. He would have given one of his ears to have been able to hear with the other the words that passed between them. He did catch something of what was said; he heard his master ask: 'Are you absolutely sure that what you state is correct?' 'Absolutely, sir,' replied the engineer. 'You must not forget that, since we started, we have been keeping all our furnaces going, and, while we had coal enough to go under easy steam from New York to Bordeaux, we have not enough to go with all steam from New York to Liverpool.'

'I will think it over,' replied Mr Fogg.

Passepartout understood, and was seized with mortal anxiety. The coal was running out! 'Ah, if my master can get over this,' thought he, 'he will indeed be a wonderful man!' Meeting Fix, he could not help telling him how matters stood.

'So,' replied the detective, with clenched teeth, 'you really believe that we are going to Liverpool!' 'Of course!' 'You fool!' returned the detective, shrugging his shoulders, as he drew off. Passepartout was on the point of showing sharp resentment of the epithet, though the real reason for Fix's offensive term necessarily escaped him; but he bethought himself how disappointed, how humiliated in his self-esteem the wretched detective must feel, after following a false scent so foolishly around the world, and he forgave him.

And now, what line of action was Phileas Fogg going to adopt? It was no easy matter even to imagine what he could do. Nevertheless he apparently did come to a decision in his own phlegmatic way, for, that very evening, he sent for the engineer and said to him, 'Go ahead with fully-stoked furnaces until your fuel is completely exhausted.'

A few moments later, the *Henrietta*'s funnel belched forth torrents of smoke.

The ship pressed on as before under full steam, but two days later, on the 18th, the engineer reported that the coal would run out during the day, as he had said it would.

'Do not let the fires down,' replied Mr Fogg. 'Far from that, let the valves be weighted for full pressure.'

About noon on that day, after ascertaining the ship's position, Phileas Fogg called Passepartout and ordered him to fetch Captain Speedy. The worthy fellow felt just as if he had been told to set loose a tiger, and he went down to the poop-deck muttering, 'He will be absolutely mad!' And in a few minutes, amid shouts and curses, a bomb tumbled on to the poop-deck. The bomb was Captain Speedy, and it was obvious that the bomb was going to explode. 'Where are we?' were the first words he uttered, choking with rage. Had the good man had the slightest tendency to apoplexy, he must have gone under. 'Where are we?' he repeated, purple in the face.

'Seven hundred and seventy miles from Liverpool,' answered Mr Fogg, absolutely unperturbed. 'You pirate!' cried Andrew Speedy. 'Sir, I sent for you — ' 'You sea-robber!' 'To ask you to sell me your ship.' 'No! By all the fiends in Hell. No!' 'The fact is, I shall be obliged to burn her.' 'To burn my

319

ship?' 'Yes, her upper works at least, for we are running short of fuel.' 'Burn my ship!' cried Captain Speedy, who was now reduced to spluttering. 'A ship worth fifty thousand dollars!' 'Here are sixty thousand,' replied Phileas Fogg, offering the captain a bundle of banknotes. The effect on Andrew Speedy was prodigious. No American can remain quite unmoved at the sight of sixty thousand dollars. In one instant the captain forgot his wrath, his confinement, in fact every grievance he had against his passenger. His ship was twenty years old. There might be a fortune in this. The bomb was already non-explosive. Mr Fogg had taken the fuse out.

'And am I to keep the iron hull?' he asked in a peculiarly softened tone of voice.

'The iron hull and the machinery. Is that settled?' 'Done,' said Andrew Speedy, seizing the bundle of banknotes which he counted and slipped into his pocket.

While this scene was enacted Passepartout went white in the face, and Fix nearly had a stroke. After an expenditure of nearly twenty thousand pounds, there was this fellow Fogg giving up the hull and machinery, that is, about the total value of the ship. True, the sum stolen from the Bank amounted to fifty-five thousand pounds.

When Andrew Speedy had pocketed the money, Mr Fogg said to him, 'All this will cause you no surprise when I tell you that I stand to lose twenty thousand pounds, if I am not in London by the 21st of December, at eight forty-five in the evening. Now I missed the boat at New York, and you refused to take me to Liverpool — ' 'And, by the fifty thousand fiends in Hell, I did the right thing,' exclaimed Andrew Speedy. 'I made at least forty thousand dollars by that.'

Then he added more quietly, 'You know, Captain — ' 'Fogg.' 'Captain Fogg, there's something of the Yankee in you.' After paying his passenger what he considered a compliment, he was moving away, when Phileas Fogg said to him, 'The vessel now belongs to me?' 'Certainly, from the keel to the truck of the masts; that is, all the wood of her, of course.'

'Right; then have all the inside fittings pulled down, and use the pieces for fuel.' One can imagine what a quantity of this dry wood had to be consumed to keep the steam up to sufficient pressure. That day the poop-deck, deck-houses, cabins, bunks and spar-deck were all sacrificed.

On the morrow, the 19th of December, the masts, rafts and spars were burned. The masts were brought down and chopped up.

The crew worked with amazing zeal, and Passepartout hewed, hacked and sawed away like ten men. There was a perfect frenzy of destruction.

On the 20th, the hammock-nettings, bulwarks, dead works and the greater part of the deck were given to the flames, and the *Henrietta* was now as flat as a hulk. But on that day they sighted the Irish coast and Fastnet Light.

At ten o'clock in the evening they were still only abreast of Queenstown, and Phileas Fogg had not more than twenty-four hours in which to reach London. It would take the *Henrietta* all that time to get to Liverpool, even under full steam; and our much-daring hero was at last on the point of having no steam left at all.

'Sir,' said Captain Speedy, who was now greatly interested in his project, 'I am truly sorry for you. Everything is against you. We are only off Queenstown.' 'Oh,' said Mr Fogg, 'are those the lights of Queenstown?' 'Yes.' 'Can we enter the harbour?' 'Not for three hours. Only at high tide.' 'We shall wait,' replied Phileas Fogg calmly; and his face showed not the slightest sign that a supreme inspiration was urging him to try and overcome once more the thwarting vagaries of fortune.

Queenstown is an Irish port at which the transatlantic liners from the United States drop their mail-bags. The letters are then carried off to Dublin by fast trains always in readiness. From Dublin they cross over to Liverpool in boats of great speed, thus gaining twelve hours on the fastest vessels.

Phileas Fogg meant to do like the American mail, and gain twelve hours also. Instead of arriving at Liverpool on the *Henrietta* in the evening of the next day, he would be there at noon, and so would have time to get to London before a quarter to nine in the evening.

The *Henrietta* entered Queenstown Harbour at high tide, about one o'clock in the morning, and Phileas Fogg left Captain Speedy on the levelled hulk of his ship, still worth half the money he had sold it for; the captain shaking him heartily by the hand at parting. The passengers landed at once. Fix, at that moment, was sorely tempted to arrest Fogg, but did not do so. Why? What conflict was going on within him? Had he changed his mind about Mr Fogg? Did he at last realise that he had made a mistake? Be that as it may, Fix did not leave Mr Fogg, but joining him, Aouda, and Passepartout, who was breathless with impatience, he got into the train at half-past one in the morning, arrived at Dublin at dawn, and embarked immediately on one of those steamers, regular spindle-shaped machines, all engine-power, which scorn to rise, and invariably go right through the surge.

On the 21st of December, at twenty minutes to twelve, Phileas Fogg at last landed on Liverpool Pier. He was now only six hours from London. At that very moment, Fix went up to him, laid his hand on his shoulder, and, showing him the warrant, said, 'There is no mistake, you are Phileas Fogg?'

'Yes, I am.'

'In the Queen's name, I arrest you!'

34

*Which gives Passepartout the opportunity
of making an atrocious, but
possibly new, pun*

Phileas Fogg was in prison. He had been
confined in the Custom House lock-up,
where he would spend the night; he would
then be transferred to London.

When his master was arrested, Passepartout would have fallen upon the detective had
he not been held back by policemen.

Aouda was horrified by the brutality of the
proceeding and was quite bewildered, for she
knew nothing of the circumstances. Passepartout enlightened her, telling her how the
honest and courageous gentleman to whom
she owed her life was arrested as a thief. The
young woman protested against this monstrous allegation; her heart was filled with
indignation, and, when she saw she could do
nothing, attempt nothing to save the man
who had saved her, she wept. As for Fix, he
had arrested the man, because it was his
imperative duty to do so, guilty or not guilty.
The law-court would settle the matter.

It then occurred to Passepartout, and a terrible thought it was, that he was the real cause of the whole trouble! Why had he concealed the motive of Fix's journey from Mr Fogg? When Fix had revealed to him his profession and his errand, why had he taken it upon himself to keep his master ignorant of the fact? Had Mr Fogg been forewarned, he would doubtless have given Fix proofs of his innocence, and convinced him of his mistake. At all events, he would not have conveyed at his heels, and at his own expense, this troublesome member of the police force, who had made it his first business to arrest him the moment he set foot on English soil. As he thought of his blunders and reckless conduct, the poor fellow was wrung by remorse; he wept piteously, and felt like dashing his head to pieces.

Aouda and he remained in the porch of the Custom House, in spite of the cold. Neither of them would leave the spot, so anxious were they to see Mr Fogg once more.

He was now a ruined man, and just as he was reaching the goal. This arrest was quite fatal. Having arrived at Liverpool at twenty minutes to twelve on the 21st of December, he had till a quarter to nine to put in an appearance at the Reform Club; in other words, he had nine hours and a quarter, and he only wanted six to reach London.

Anyone walking into the Custom House lock-up at this moment would have found Mr Fogg on a wooden bench, sitting perfectly still, without anger, impassive. Whether he was resigned or not, there was nothing to show, but this last blow had been powerless to produce any sign of emotion. Was there brewing within his breast one of those pent-up storms of wrath that are all the more terrible because they are repressed, and that burst at the very last moment with resistless force? None can say. But Phileas Fogg was there, calmly waiting — waiting for what? Had he still some hope left? Did he still believe success possible, with this prison door between him and liberty?

What is certain is that Mr Fogg had carefully placed his watch on a table, and was observing the progress of the hands. Not a word passed his lips, but his gaze was strangely set. In any case, the situation was a terrible one; for any but the man who could have read in Mr Fogg's conscience, there was but one alternative: Mr Fogg was honest but ruined, or a rogue and caught.

That the thought of flight occurred to him, if there was a possible means of exit from the lock-up, seems credible, for, at one moment, he examined the room all round. But the door was safely locked, and the window secured with iron bars. So he went back to his seat and took out his journal from his pocket-book. On the line bearing the words, 'December 21st, Saturday, Liverpool,' he added, '80th day, 11.40 a.m.,' and waited.

The Custom House clock struck one. Mr Fogg observed that his watch was two minutes fast by this clock.

Two o'clock! If, at that moment, he could get into an express train, he might still be in London, and at the Reform Club, before a quarter to nine that evening. A slight wrinkle creased his brow. At thirty-three minutes after two there was a sudden din outside, as doors were noisily thrown open. Passepartout's voice and Fix's voice were heard.

Phileas Fogg's eyes brightened for one moment. The door of the lock-up opened and he saw Aouda, Passepartout and Fix rushing towards him. Fix, his hair all dishevelled, and so out of breath that he could not speak, mumbled, 'Sir, sir — forgive me — a most regrettable resemblance — thief arrested three days ago — you — are free!'

Phileas Fogg was free! He stepped up to the detective, looked him straight in the face, and, with the only quick motion he had ever made or would ever make, he drew back his arms and, with automatic precision, landed both his fists on the wretched detective.

'Well hit!' cried Passepartout, and, indulging in an atrocious pun, quite worthy of a Frenchman, he added, 'By Jove! this deserves to be called *Une belle application de poings d'Angleterre*.'[1]

Fix lay on the floor without saying a word. He had received nothing but his due. Mr Fogg, Aouda and Passepartout left the Custom House, jumped into a cab, and a few minutes brought them to Liverpool Station. Phileas Fogg asked if there was an express train about to leave for London.

The time was then forty minutes past two, and the express had gone thirty-five minutes before.

Phileas Fogg then ordered a special train. There were several fast engines with steam up, but, owing to traffic arrangements, the special train could not leave before three o'clock.

At three o'clock Phileas Fogg, after saying a few words to the engine-driver about a certain reward to be obtained, ran at high speed for London, with the young woman and his faithful servant.

He intended to accomplish the distance between Liverpool and London in five hours

---

[1] *Point d'Angleterre* means English lace.

and a half, a perfectly possible achievement when the line is clear throughout. But forced delays occurred, and, when Mr Fogg reached the terminus, every clock in London informed him that it was ten minutes to nine.

After travelling all round the world, Mr Fogg was five minutes late. He had lost his wager.

35

In which Passepartout does not need to be told twice what his master orders him to do

On the morrow, the people in Savile Row would have been surprised had one assured them that Mr Fogg had returned home. Doors and windows were closed as usual. There was absolutely no change in the outward appearance of the house.

After leaving the station, Phileas Fogg directed Passepartout to buy some provisions, and went home.

He bore his trouble with his usual tranquillity. Here he was, ruined! And through the blundering of that detective! After treading that long road with a sure step, after overcoming a thousand obstacles, braving endless dangers, and finding time to do some good on the way, to be wrecked in harbour by an act of brute force, which he could not foresee and against which he was unarmed, was truly terrible! Of the large sum he had taken with him he had very little left. His fortune now consisted in the twenty thousand pounds deposited at Baring's, and these twenty thousand pounds were now due to his fellow-members of the Reform Club. The expenses had been so heavy that, had he won the bet, it would certainly not have enriched him; moreover, it is probable that he had not sought to enrich himself, for he was one of those who bet for honour's sake, but the loss of the wager spelt absolute ruin.

Howbeit, Mr Fogg's mind was made up; he knew what he had to do. A room in the house in Savile Row was set apart for Aouda, who was distracted with grief. Certain words of Mr Fogg had led her to conclude that he was revolving some fatal project or other.

Well aware that certain Englishmen, prone to monomania, sometimes resort to the most lamentable of rash acts under the stress of a fixed idea, Passepartout kept an eye on his master without appearing to do so.

But the first thing the good fellow did on arriving was to go up to his room and turn off the gas, which had been burning for eighty days. Having found a bill from the gas company in the letter-box, he thought it was high time to put an end to this expense, for which he was responsible.

Mr Fogg went to bed; whether he slept or not is a matter for conjecture. Aouda had not a moment's rest; Passepartout watched outside his master's door, like a dog. So the night passed. On the morrow Mr Fogg called him, and in a few peremptory words bade him see to Aouda's breakfast. He himself wanted nothing more than a cup of tea and a piece of toast.

He hoped Aouda would excuse his absence from breakfast and dinner, as all his time would be devoted to putting his affairs in order. He would not come down, but begged Aouda to be good enough to give him a few minutes in the evening, as he had something to say to her. Passepartout, having received his instructions for the day, could only do what he was told. He gazed at his master, who gave no sign of what he felt, and could not make up his mind to leave the room. His heart was heavy, his conscience racked with remorse, for he blamed himself more than ever for the irreparable disaster. If only he had warned Mr Fogg and disclosed to him Fix's intentions, he would certainly not have taken the detective with him to Liverpool, and then —

Passepartout could hold out no longer. 'My master! Mr Fogg!' he cried. 'Curse me, for it was all my doing that — ' 'I blame no one,' replied Phileas Fogg in the calmest manner. 'Go!' Passepartout left him and went to Aouda, whom he informed of his master's wishes. 'Madam,' he added, 'personally, I am quite powerless! I have not the faintest influence over my master's mind. You might — ' 'What influence could I possibly have?' replied Aouda. 'Mr Fogg is proof against every influence! Has he ever understood that my gratitude is full to overflowing? Has he ever read in my heart? You must not leave him for a moment, my friend. You say he has expressed the wish to speak to me this evening?' 'Yes, madam; no doubt Mr Fogg is anxious to make arrangements for your stay in England.' 'Well, we can only wait and see,' said the young woman wistfully.

During the whole of that Sunday the house in Savile Row might have been empty, and for the first time since he had lived there, Phileas Fogg did not set out for his club when Big Ben struck half-past eleven.

Why should he go to the Reform Club? He was no longer expected there. Having failed to appear in the drawing-room of the Reform Club at forty-five minutes past eight in the evening, the day before, that fateful date of Saturday, December 21, Phileas Fogg had lost his wager. He was not even under the necessity of going to the Bank for the twenty thousand pounds, for his adversaries held a cheque signed by him, and all they had to do was to fill it in, endorse it, and pass it through

Baring's, in order to have the amount placed to their credit.

There was therefore no reason why Mr Fogg should go out, and he stayed at home. He remained in his room and put his affairs in order.

Passepartout went up and down the stairs continually. Time stood still for the poor fellow, who kept listening at the door of his master's room without feeling in the least indiscreet. He even looked through the key-hole and thought himself perfectly justified, for he dreaded a catastrophe at any moment. Now and again he thought of Fix, but a complete change had come over his mind. He was no longer angry with the detective. Fix, like everybody else, had misjudged Phileas Fogg; in shadowing and arresting him he had only done his duty, whereas he, Passepartout — the thought crushed him; in his own eyes he was the lowest of low wretches. Whenever he could no longer bear his misery in solitude, he knocked at Aouda's door, went in, and sat down in a corner without saying one word, gazing at her sad, pensive face.

About half-past seven Mr Fogg sent word to Aouda asking whether she could see him, and a few moments later they were together alone in her room.

Phileas Fogg took a chair and sat down near the fire-place, opposite Aouda. His face expressed not the slightest emotion. Between the Fogg who had returned and the Fogg who had gone away there was not one tittle of difference. There was just the same impassive calm. He sat silent for five minutes, then, raising his eyes to Aouda, he said, 'Madam, can you forgive me for bringing you to England?' 'I, forgive you, Mr Fogg!' answered Aouda, trying to repress the throbbing of her heart. 'Please let me finish,' replied Mr Fogg. 'When I conceived the idea of taking you right away from that country which had become so full of danger for you, I was a rich man, and I intended to place part of my fortune at your disposal. Your life would have been one of happy freedom. Now I am ruined.' 'I know, Mr Fogg,' returned the young woman. 'I will ask you, in my turn, whether you can forgive me for following you, and — who knows — for having perhaps helped to ruin you by delaying your progress.'

'You could not remain in India; your safety could only be assured by removing you far enough to be out of reach of those fanatics.'

'So, Mr Fogg,' resumed Aouda, 'not content with snatching me from the jaws of a horrible death, you thought it your duty to secure my position abroad?' 'Yes, madam,' replied Mr Fogg, 'but I have been unfortunate. However, may I have your permission to dispose in your behalf of the little I still possess?' 'But, Mr Fogg, what is to become of you?' asked Aouda. 'Of me?' rejoined he coldly. 'I have need of nothing.' 'But how are you going to face the future that awaits you?' 'As it should be faced,' replied Mr Fogg. 'At all events,' continued Aouda, 'a man like you is beyond the reach of poverty, I suppose. Your friends — ' 'I have no friends.' 'Your relations, then — ' 'I have no relations left.' 'Then I am truly sorry for you, Mr Fogg, for loneliness is a sad thing. What! not one heart to share your troubles! Even poverty, they say, is bearable for two!' 'They say so, madam.' 'Mr Fogg,' said Aouda, standing up at this point of the conversation and stretching out her hand to him, 'would you have at once a relation and a friend? Will you have me for your wife?'

On hearing this, Mr Fogg stood up too. His eyes betrayed an unaccustomed light, his lips the semblance of a tremor. Aouda looked into his face. The sincerity, the candour, the firmness and sweetness of that glorious look of a noble woman, daring all to save the man to whom she owed all, first astonished and then thrilled him. He closed his eyes for a moment, as if to prevent this look from entering deeper still into his being. And when he opened them again, he said simply, 'I love you. Oh, yes, in the name of all that is most holy, I love you, and am yours heart and soul!' 'Oh!' cried Aouda, raising her hand to her heart.

Passepartout was summoned, and came forthwith, to see Mr Fogg still holding Aouda's hand in his. He understood, and his big, round face beamed like the tropical sun at its zenith.

Mr Fogg asked him whether it would not be too late to give due notice to the Reverend Samuel Wilson, of the parish of Marylebone.

Passepartout, with his best smile, replied, 'It's never too late for that.' It was then not more than five minutes past eight. 'You want it to take place tomorrow, Monday?' he added.

'Would tomorrow, Monday, do?' asked Mr Fogg, looking at Aouda.

'Yes, tomorrow, Monday,' she replied. And Passepartout hurried off as fast as he could go.

36

In which Phileas Fogg is again at a premium on 'Change

It is now time to say what a great change took place in English public opinion when it was known that the real thief, one James Strand, had been arrested on December 17 at Edinburgh.

Three days before, Phileas Fogg was a criminal whom the police were making the most energetic efforts to capture; now he was a most honest gentleman, mathematically performing his eccentric voyage around the world.

The papers were full of it, and great was the excitement. All those who had made bets for or against him, and had already forgotten the case, came forward again as if by magic. All the old transactions became valid again, all engagements binding, and it should be said that the people's revived keenness resulted in many a new bet. Phileas Fogg's name was again at a premium on 'Change. His five fellow-members of the Reform Club passed those three days in a state of anxious suspense. Phileas Fogg, whom they had forgotten, now suddenly loomed before them! Where was he at this moment? On the 17th of December, the day of James Strand's arrest, Phileas Fogg had been gone seventy-six days and absolutely nothing had been heard of him. Was he dead? Had he given up the contest, or was he pursuing his journey along the settled route? And would he appear on Saturday, the 21st of December, at a quarter to nine in the evening, on the threshold of the Reform Club drawing-room, as the very god of punctuality?

The anxiety in which English society existed during those three days is beyond description. Telegrams were dispatched to America and Asia for news of Phileas Fogg. The house in Savile Row was kept under observation morning and evening. — Nothing. Even the police could not say what had become of Fix, who had so unfortunately followed up a false scent. But betting again took place on a larger scale than ever. Phileas Fogg, like a racehorse, was nearing the last turn in the course. The odds against him were no longer quoted at a hundred, but at twenty, at ten, and five, and paralytic old Lord Albemarle bet even in his favour.

Thus it was that, on the Saturday evening, a great crowd was assembled in Pall Mall and the adjoining streets. It looked like a dense mass of brokers permanently established around the Reform Club. The traffic was more or less blocked. People discussed and disputed, and quotations of 'Phileas Fogg Stock' were shouted, as with Government scrip. The police had great difficulty in controlling the crowd, and, as the hour at which Phileas Fogg was due approached, the excitement became prodigious.

In the evening of that day, his five fellow-members had been together in the large drawing-room of the Reform Club for nine hours. The two bankers, John Sullivan and Samuel Fallentin, the engineer Andrew Stuart, Gauthier Ralph, the director of the Bank of England, and Thomas Flanagan, the brewer, were all waiting anxiously. At the very moment when the clock in the drawing-room indicated twenty minutes past eight, Andrew Stuart got up and said, 'Gentlemen, in twenty minutes the time agreed between Mr Phileas Fogg and us will have expired.'

'At what time did the last train from Liverpool arrive?' asked Thomas Flanagan. 'At twenty-three minutes past seven,' replied Gauthier Ralph, 'and the next train will not come in before ten minutes past twelve.' 'Well, gentlemen,' continued Andrew Stuart, 'if Phileas Fogg had arrived by the 7.23 train, he would be here now. We can therefore look upon the bet as won.'

'We must wait; we must not decide yet,' rejoined Samuel Fallentin. 'You know that our friend is a thoroughly eccentric fellow. His precision in all things is well known. He never arrives too soon or too late, and I should not be altogether surprised to see him turn up at the last minute.'

'And I,' said Andrew Stuart, who was in his usual nervous state of mind, 'if I saw him appear, I should not believe my eyes.'

'Naturally,' resumed Thomas Flanagan, 'for Phileas Fogg's project was insane. No matter what his punctuality might be, he could not prevent delays that were bound to occur, and a delay of two or three days only was enough to make his enterprise next to impossible.'

'You will observe, too,' added John Sullivan, 'that we have received no communication from him, although there are telegraphs all along the route.'

'He has lost, gentlemen,' continued Andrew Stuart; 'he has lost a hundred times over! As you know, the *China*, which was the only liner he could come by soon enough from New York to Liverpool, arrived yesterday; and here is the list of her passengers, published by the *Shipping Gazette*; Phileas Fogg's name is not there. On the most favourable supposition, he

342

has scarcely reached America! According to my reckoning, he will be twenty days late, and old Lord Albemarle will also be a loser, to the tune of five thousand pounds!' 'Of course,' replied Gauthier Ralph, 'and all we shall have to do tomorrow will be to present Mr Fogg's cheque at Baring's.'

At this moment the clock indicated 8.40. 'Five minutes more,' said Andrew Stuart. The five friends looked at each other.

One may surmise that their heart-beats were slightly accelerated, for, even for bold gamblers, the stake was a large one. But, wishing to appear perfectly calm, they took their places at a card-table, Samuel Fallentin having suggested a rubber.

'I would not give my four thousand pounds share of the wager, were I offered three thousand nine hundred and ninety-nine for it,' said Andrew Stuart as he sat down.

The hand at this moment pointed to 8.42.

The players took up their cards, but their eyes were constantly on the clock. One may safely say that, however secure they might feel, never had minutes seemed so long to them.

'8.43,' said Thomas Flanagan, as he cut the cards placed before him by Gauthier Ralph. There was a moment's pause, during which the spacious room was perfectly silent.

Outside, however, the hubbub of the crowd could be heard, dominated at times by sharp cries. The clock's pendulum beat every second with mathematical regularity, and each player could count every sixtieth of a minute as it struck his ear.

'8.44!' said John Sullivan, in a voice that betrayed his emotion.

Only one minute more and the wager would be won. Andrew Stuart and his friends left off playing. They forgot the cards to count the seconds!

At the fortieth second, nothing. At the fiftieth, still nothing! At the fifty-fifth they heard a thunderous burst of noise outside, applause, hurrahs, and even curses, spreading far and wide in a continuous roll.

The players stood up.

At the fifty-seventh second the door of the drawing-room opened, and before the pendulum beat the sixtieth second, Phileas Fogg appeared, followed by a delirious crowd that had forced their way into the club, and in his calm voice, said, 'Here I am, gentlemen.'

37

In which it is shown that Phileas Fogg gained nothing by travelling round the world, unless it were happiness

Yes, Phileas Fogg himself.

The reader will remember that at five minutes past eight in the evening — about five and twenty hours after the travellers arrived in London — Passepartout was sent by his master to arrange with the Reverend Samuel Wilson for a certain marriage ceremony which was to take place on the very next day.

Passepartout set out on his errand highly delighted. He lost no time in reaching the clergyman's house, but he had to wait, as the parson was out. He waited a good twenty minutes. When he left, it was thirty-five minutes past eight; and what a state he was in! dishevelled, hatless, he ran along furiously, as never was man seen running before, knocking down the passers-by, rushing over the pavements like a waterspout.

He was back in Savile Row in three minutes, and staggered, out of breath, into Mr Fogg's room.

He was unable to speak.

'What is the matter?' asked Mr Fogg.

'My master — ' stammered Passepartout, 'Marriage — impossible — '

'Impossible?' 'Impossible — for tomorrow.'

'Why?' 'Because tomorrow — is Sunday!'

'Monday,' replied Mr Fogg.

'No — today — Saturday.'

'Saturday? Impossible!'

'Yes, yes, yes, yes!' cried Passepartout. 'You made a mistake of a day! We arrived twenty-four hours before the time — but there are only ten minutes left!'

Passepartout had seized his master by the collar and was dragging him away with irresistible force.

Phileas Fogg, thus rushed without having time to think, left his room, then his house, jumped into a cab, promised the cab-man a hundred pounds, and, having run over two dogs and collided with five carriages, reached the Reform Club.

The clock indicated 8.45 when he appeared in the big drawing-room. Phileas Fogg had accomplished the journey round the world in eighty days!

Phileas Fogg had won his wager of twenty thousand pounds!

But how was it that a man, who was so precise and scrupulously careful, could possibly make this mistake of one day? How came he to think that the time at which he arrived in London was the evening of Saturday, December 21, whereas the real time was only Friday, December 20, not more than seventy-nine days after his departure?

His mistake is very easily explained. Without suspecting it, Phileas Fogg had gained one day on the journey, and for the sole reason that he had travelled ever eastward; he would, on the contrary, have lost a day had he travelled in the opposite direction, that is, westward. Going eastward, Phileas Fogg had advanced towards the sun, and, consequently, the days grew smaller for him by as many times four minutes as he crossed degrees of longitude in this direction. The earth's circumference contains three hundred and sixty degrees; these three hundred and sixty degrees, multiplied by four minutes, make exactly twenty-four hours — that is, the day he had gained without knowing it. In other words, as he advanced eastward, he saw the sun pass the meridian eighty times, whereas his friends of the Reform Club in London saw it pass seventy-nine times only. So it was that on that very day, which was Saturday, not Sunday, as Mr Fogg believed, they were waiting for him

347

in the drawing-room of the Reform Club.

And the fact would have been recorded by Passepartout's precious watch, which had always kept London time, had it marked the days as well as the hours and minutes!

So Phileas Fogg had won the twenty thousand pounds, but, as he had spent something like nineteen thousand on the way, the proceeds were small.

As we have said before, however, the eccentric gentleman's object was sport, not money. The thousand pounds that remained he divided between the worthy Passepartout and the luckless Fix, to whom he could not find it in his heart to bear any grudge. But, as a matter of principle, and for the sake of regularity, he deducted from his servant's share the cost of the nineteen hundred and twenty hours of gas consumed through his fault.

That evening, Mr Fogg, as calm and phlegmatic as ever, said to Aouda, 'Is it still your pleasure to marry me?' 'Mr Fogg,' she said in reply, 'it is for me to ask you this question. You were ruined, you are now a rich man — '

'Pardon me, madam, my fortune is really yours. If the thought of this marriage had not occurred to you, my servant would not have gone to the Reverend Samuel Wilson's, I should not have been informed of my mistake, and — '

'Dear Mr Fogg!' said the young woman.

'Dear Aouda!' replied Phileas Fogg.

Needless to say, the marriage took place forty-eight hours later, and Passepartout, resplendent, simply dazzling, gave the bride away.

Had he not saved her? was not this honour his due?

Next day, however, as soon as it was light, Passepartout banged at his master's door. The door opened and Mr Fogg, without the least excitement, asked, 'What is it, Passepartout?' 'Why, sir, I have only just this moment heard — ' 'What have you heard?' 'That we might have gone round the world in only seventy-eight days.'

'Of course,' replied Mr Fogg, 'by not going through India. But if I had not gone through India, I should not have saved Aouda, she would not have been my wife, and — '

And Mr Fogg quietly closed the door.

So Mr Fogg had won his wager. He had made his journey around the world in eighty days! To this end, he had made use of every means of conveyance — liners, railways, carriages, yachts, trading vessels, sledges, elephants. The eccentric gentleman had displayed in this venture his marvellous qualities of coolness and precision. But what then? What had he gained out of all this travelling? What had he brought home?

Nothing, say you? Granted; nothing but a charming woman, who, unlikely as it may appear, made him the happiest of men!

And forsooth, who would not go round the world for less?